The Murder Book

Also by Darrel Sparkman

Osage Dawn

Tyler's Road

The Apocalypse Chronicles

Shepherd's Fire

Blood Justice

Broken Arrow

Shepherd's Sword

Chrysalis

After the Fall

Coble Bray Series

Hallowed Ground

Hard Times

The Murder Book

A Coble Bray Western Mystery
Book 3

Darrel Sparkman

WOLFPACK
PUBLISHING
— EST 2013 —

The Murder Book
Paperback Edition
Copyright © 2024 by Darrel Sparkman

Wolfpack Publishing
1707 E. Diana Street
Tampa, FL 33610

www.wolfpackpublishing.com

Paperback ISBN 978-1-63977-340-4
Ebook ISBN 978-1-63977-339-8
LCCN 2024947009

The Murder Book

Chapter One

TOMLIN HARP PACED THE TEN-FOOT SQUARE CELL with nervous energy. His cell was at the very back of a long row in the city jail, which housed drunks, whores who couldn't pay their fees, and the occasional murderer. The front of the building was the domain of LC Hamilton, city marshal of Joplin, Missouri.

Most everyone in jail or prison was filled with hate. Harp had none, except for fleeting thoughts of what went wrong. That he'd been caught was inevitable. The man who'd controlled Harp's actions thought himself too intelligent to be caught, until a relentless lawman put an end to him. His mind dancing around the memory of Deputy Marshal Coble Bray, he smiled. They would meet again, and Harp would show the lawman the results of real power.

Instead of hatred, Harp had wants and very few needs. He wanted women, and his tastes ran to the young ones...unblemished and inexperienced. He wanted good food, not the swill served by the jailers.

He wanted power and was confident it would be brought to him.

But right now, Harp needed a bottle of laudanum more than he needed air to breathe. That he was hooked on opium was no secret. Up to a few days ago he'd been able to have it delivered to the jail for medicinal purposes. But not the last couple of days. For some reason his source had dried up.

His eyes burned and skin itched as he paced in his poorly lit cell. Even as he paced, he knew he'd beat this too. He was too strong to be beaten.

Harp didn't notice the man sitting in front of his cell door right away. The man had apparently brought in a stool to sit on and seemed to be enjoying the sight of Harp pacing back and forth. He was a nattily dressed man in a broadcloth suit and bowler hat. The silver knob on his walking stick glinted in the sparse light.

Flinching away from the door, Harp hissed, "Who are you? What do you want?"

The man reached into his pocket and pulled out a brown, opaque bottle of liquid. "I have something you need."

When Harp reached for it, the bottle was pulled back out of reach.

"My name is Mr. Adair." He motioned toward the back of the cell. "Pull your chair close so we can have a conversation."

When Harp complied, Adair continued. "Mr. Harp, you have some skills that would be useful to me. If we can come to an agreement, you will have a job in my organization. As I understand it, you had a handler once before who kept you supplied. With your particular talents, you need someone to stand between you and the law. I would be happy to fill that same role for you."

"I did have a handler." He did, but the question was if he needed one. Here was the power, being handed to him on a platter...although the man didn't know it yet.

Controlling his shaking with a visible effort, Harp said, "I'm in jail for murder. There are other charges as well, I think they're still making their list. What of them?"

Adair waved a dismissing hand. "Leave that to me. Those charges are just high points on your resume. I run a new organization in town, actually in several towns. We offer protection against the lawless element that preys on the gambling halls and whorehouses. The business is quite lucrative."

"What would be my job?" Harp felt he was fishing, letting out a little line, waiting for a bite before setting the hook.

Adair smiled and then gave a small shrug. "Why, your task would be making sure everyone pays. Even the city marshal pays, although he's quite cooperative as long as we let him carry out his own graft." He held the bottle up and swished the contents side-to-side. "An unlimited supply. Interested?"

And the need for laudanum faded, replaced by another need. Power. "When can you get me out of here?"

Adair handed the bottle through the bars. "That's entirely up to you, Mr. Harp. We'll consider it a test. When you're out of jail, come to the back door of the restaurant at the House of Lords. Knock twice. We'll let you in."

After taking a large swallow from the bottle, Harp asked, "Do I have to wear one of those hats?"

Nodding, Adair replied, "If you pass your test, it will be your privilege."

———

IT WAS past midnight when Harp watched from the shadows as old Amos Gentry moved toward the end of the cells. Even in the darkened hallway, the old man looked like ten miles of bad road. His aching joints kept him moving slowly, but his only job was to feed the inmates and clean the empty cells. He didn't need speed. Harp was sure the old jailer had been doing the same job for years.

The screeching noise of metal bending drew Gentry's attention to the last cell. Walking slowly toward the end of the row, his eyes widened to see the bars bent aside and the cell empty.

Turning to yell a warning toward the front of the jail, a massive hand grabbed him around the throat and throttled him against the wall. Gentry's eyes bulged and his feet kicked as he fought for air. Rough hands searched his pockets for keys.

Satisfied with finding the key ring, Harp snapped the jailer's neck and dropped him to the floor. Moving to the back door, he tried different keys until one fit. Leaving the door swinging on squeaky hinges, he paused a moment to take a deep breath of fresh air and moved into the night. He was confident now, knowing exactly what he must do.

He knew Coble Bray would come for him. This time, he'd be ready.

———

THE JAIL'S only other occupant was in the next cell watching with little interest. Men were an endless progression with her. She'd survived long enough to learn to read them well. At one glance she knew Harp was a killer, other people's lives meant nothing to him. Although she tried to avoid him, she once grew careless and had offered little resistance when the huge man pulled her against the dividing bars and had his way with her. When he was finished, he shoved her away. She pulled pieces of her torn dress around her and lay on her cot.

Maybe she'd get a favor from him later. Maybe he'd forget her, and she would live. Or he'd kill her when her madam paid her fine. Live or die, it didn't matter much to her anymore. Pulling the threadbare blanket over her, she went back to sleep. Most whores would rather be arrested and jailed than return to their brothels. The food wasn't bad in the jail. It was cleaner and safer behind bars. Usually.

Chapter Two

DIGGING A GRAVE IS BACK-BREAKING WORK. DOING it while your wife and her stillborn child lay wrapped in bloody sheets nearby is a punishment a mind and body should not endure.

The depth of prairie topsoil in eastern Kansas stops at a couple of feet down and then becomes hard clay. Digging coal with a pickaxe couldn't be any more difficult when dirt comes out in gray chips like splinters of rock.

Coble Bray took a long drink of water from a canvas-covered canteen stoppered with a chunk of wood whittled to shape. The October sun blistered his neck and arms, and on some guilty level, he was glad it wasn't July or August. Exhausted, unable to continue, he hoisted himself from the grave and stood, hands on the small of his back, trying to stretch away the hurt. A pity it wouldn't reach his soul and turn away the guilt.

The doubts had started. What if he'd given up the badge? What if he'd paid better attention to her?

Would she still be alive? Once the mind goes down that rabbit hole, there's no ending to it. It was an agonizing trip.

With curiosity hungry for distraction, he watched a dust trail edge closer. A month ago they'd have appeared as a mirage through the heat waves. Now it was a little cooler. Shading his eyes, he could see two people on horseback. He was reaching for his gun belt before recognition came. He strapped it on anyway. It was a dangerous world, and often things weren't as they seemed.

Within minutes, his friend August Schuler, forever dubbed Priest, the self-defrocked minister, and new wife Juana appeared. She'd nursed Priest back to health after a gunshot wound. Apparently Priest decided he needed ongoing care.

They stopped within feet of the grave, gazes bouncing between the wrapped bodies and Coble, eyes alive with questions. No words were spoken for a moment as Coble tried to catch his breath in the heat.

Always impatient, Priest broke the silence. "You're covered in blood and dirt, brother. What happened?"

Coble gestured toward the body wrapped in blood-stained sheets. "Maria."

"No." Crossing herself, Juana exclaimed, "Santo Dios."

"Oh my god, indeed." Priest gave him a long look. "Shot? Murdered? You didn't..." He paused a moment. "Sorry, I just remembered all the anger between you two."

It was a fair line of questions, given the history. Sighing, he waved them toward the house and the shade of the veranda. Stalling for time, he watered and tethered their horses before climbing the steps and finding his own chair.

"It was a miscarriage. She hadn't been feeling well for some time. Then she started cramping and bleeding. In less time than it takes to saddle a horse, she was gone."

———

HE'D FIRST ACQUIRED this small ranch a couple of years ago. Being west of Lamar, Missouri, and a few miles into the Kansas prairie, there wasn't much in the way of hills. When he brought Maria Santos home the first time, after they'd corralled and put away a degenerate preying on young girls, she thought the house needed shade. On a slightly elevated knoll behind the house, they'd planted a pin oak. The nurseryman in Kansas City assured them it was fast growing and would grow anywhere, so they hauled it home on a buckboard. The tree had grown some, and they'd carried buckets of water for it often, but it still offered little shade.

By the time they came home again from chasing murderers in the cities of Hard Times and Joplin, the tree was starting to grow. It wasn't a given that their marriage would grow with it. Their marriage vows had taken a body blow to the most important and unwritten canon—trust.

He'd thought the marriage would mend, he was willing…but it was slow going. Maria had a temper and a growing aversion to his job or any solutions he'd offer. Admittedly, it was a thankless job. His was a special appointment as a Deputy United States

Marshal. God, or the devil, depending on who you ask, gave him certain skills that led him into harm's way, chasing people with an affinity for evil. Maria objected to that calling.

Then, after a nightmare event, he found himself waist-deep in a freshly dug grave beside her stalwart oak tree. His arms and shirt front were covered in dirt and blood. Maria's blood. As often happens in life, he was unprepared when the emergency unfolded. She began bleeding.

Earlier in the day, she began not feeling well, and she'd laid down on the bed to rest. A few moments later he heard her scream in pain. Running to her side, she said it must be a miscarriage, that she'd be alright. Trying to reassure him, she'd said women do this all the time—give birth or miscarry.

He was stunned for a moment. He didn't know she carried a child. Her strength for reassuring him quickly faded as she became weak. The bleeding didn't stop. From the amount and copious flow, she may as well have had her throat cut.

All he had to work with was hot water and no midwifing skills. She'd gotten weaker, finally giving up putting pressure on her abdomen. He'd tried packing her with cloth, sheets, and towels, to no avail. He'd seen wounds aplenty, some his own, some he inflicted on others, so he knew to put pressure on a wound. It didn't work. Nothing worked.

When he looked at her pale face and sad eyes, she gave him a weak smile. She must have known the fight was over. When he looked again to try and give her assurance, to stay with him, she was staring into an existence you have to die to achieve.

The mantel clock had struck eight times just before she'd laid down that morning. Breakfast was long over, and they were enjoying coffee. The clock, if properly wound, gives a small chime on the quarter hour. She never made it that far. Fifteen minutes, start to finish.

———————

"I COULDN'T HELP HER." Coble paused a moment, fighting guilt, his haunted gaze staring at the wrapped body by the grave while wiping his face with a faded red bandanna. "Something must have broken loose inside her."

He raised his hands and looked at them. "I've never seen so much blood. I didn't know what to do."

Juana was kneeling beside him by then. "I'm so sorry, Coble. Losing your child, your wife. It is hard."

Meeting Priest's gaze, he shrugged and said, "Given her last few months, I doubt it was my child...and she was hardly my wife—there was an annulment she obtained under sketchy circumstances. We hadn't come back to the marriage bed. Although she was trying to talk it through, trying to find reason for what she did. I'll give her that. We both were trying to reach common ground."

"So it was Oxford Graham, the killer?" Priest was nodding. "She was last with him. What a convoluted mess."

"Unfortunately, correct on all counts. For all the time they were together, she claimed he preferred the company of boys, and their union was all a sham to serve a purpose. I'm thinking that was a lie meant to derail my anger."

Juana was slowly shaking her head, one hand gripping his forearm. "No. That can't be. She loved you. I know this to be true."

"Maybe." He shook his head slowly. "I'd like to think so. Love takes many forms. But her love was a crooked trail, winding to an uncertain end. Perhaps I just didn't know how to navigate it."

She gave a puzzled glance at Priest. He said, "I'll translate later."

"I'm sorry," she said. "English is not my first, or even second, language. I need small words, and short sentences, to understand your meaning."

Priest snorted. "That would render him mute."

He patted her hand that rested on his shoulder. She wasn't the first to say he talked in soliloquies and misdirected prose. "No apologies necessary. Often, I don't understand my own words. Especially in times like this."

At some unknown signal between them, Priest and Juana stood, moving to the steps of the porch.

"So," said Priest. "I'll finish the burying, if you'll allow. You look worn out."

Juana was looking at Coble and shaking her head. Message received. "That's alright, Priest. I know you're still recovering from your wound. I'll take care of it. It's my duty."

Coble gave his friend a small smile. "It will be your job to provide a prayer, something I can't seem to dredge up at the moment. Meanwhile, maybe you could rustle up a bite to eat with some coffee? I won't be long."

"As you wish," Priest replied. "But, my friend, wounds of the mind are much harder to treat than a gunshot or cut. Don't hold in your grief. Recognize it for what it is and let it out."

Juana shook her head and sighed. "This round-about talking is catching like a bad fever."

———

LOWERING the body into the graveCoble gave some thought to unwrapping her face to see her one more time, to say goodbye. But the pain would still be etched on her face even in death, and he didn't want to see that again. She did not go easy. It was a look mirrored by his own.

The dirt went back into the hole much easier than it left. A grave marker would be made, and he wondered if he'd be around to maintain it. Just like that, with little fanfare, he was a widower. Looking around the ranch grounds, colors didn't seem as bright, the horizon seemed vague and unclear. If nothing else, their turbulent relationship had brought color to his life. Now that was gone.

And he was alone with guilty thoughts. If God was in his heaven, he'd have to ask why? Why now? Why her? Why take the baby? And another unbidden thought. If the bloodline held true, would Oxford Graham have fostered another demented killer? He sighed. Another rabbit hole to get lost in—or break a leg in.

Standing before the grave, none of his thoughts came through as speech. Eloquent words wouldn't come so he simply said, "Goodbye, Maria. Godspeed."

It would have to do.

Chapter Three

BEFORE ENTERING THE HOUSE, HE MOVED TO A RAIN barrel and buried his head in the water. Taking off his shirt, he used it to clean his hands and arms—the tepid water did little to revive the dullness in his mood.

Once he stepped inside, Juana stared openly at him. "You are the only man I have seen who has more scars than August."

"I wasn't aware," he replied. "Priest would never show me his scars or admit to them."

After retrieving a shirt from the bedroom, he paused a moment at the bloody mattress and splotches on the wall and bloody linens on the floor. The memories etched into the walls with anguish and desperation seemed to have gaps. How did those get there? Vowing to never enter the room again, he moved into the kitchen and sat at the kitchen table made of heavy timbers worn smooth from years of use. It had taken two men to carry the long planks inside and then to fit them on the frame. Built for a future family, it was now a long encumbrance in a short room.

Finally, he thought Juana's comment on scars deserved a better answer. "It's hard to say if we're blessed or cursed for still being alive, Juana. At least Priest has come through his trials with a good woman and nurse. He's been blessed."

Juana had found some salt pork and bread for a late snack, and the coffee was black and strong. "Sorry," she said. "Your luck will change."

She continued, shrugging at the table. "There's not much here in the way of food."

He chuckled, caught himself and sighed. Was there a rule about humor at a burial? "Maria had many skills. Cooking wasn't one of them. She was used to the city and prepared meals. I often wondered how she allowed herself to be brought here. I'll admit I wasn't much help."

She gave a stifled laugh. "Most men are helpless that way, unless burning a rabbit over an open fire counts."

"She never forgets a thing," Priest said, rolling his eyes and then addressing her. "It was one time, Juana. And you distracted me. One time only."

Coble nearly asked what the distraction was but caught himself. After a moment, Priest tapped the table to get his attention, studiously not meeting his gaze. "In the interest of déjà vu, I have news."

"I don't know this word?" Juana gave them a puzzled glance.

"Don't worry," Coble said with a sigh, raising his gaze to meet Priest's eyes. "It means we've been here before, at this very table, and I probably won't like his news any better than the last time."

He watched his friend with detached curiosity, his mind still on a bloody morning filled with anguish and futility. Retired Pastor August Schuler, Lutheran minister. A man with a past before taking up the cross. Now, with no church, a decision brought on by the murder of a female friend and subsequent revenge killing of the wrong man. He wondered if Priest's need to serve the cross still burned within him. Did he have words for a congregation that hadn't been said a thousand times before? Or was he complacent in retirement?

Priest pulled a folded paper from his inside vest pocket, glancing at his wife before smoothing it out. "It's a telegram."

"I can see that." Coble watched him closely, noting how nervous he was. It was odd. Priest was a steady man, whether facing bullets or unbelieving parishioners. "The yellow paper with telegram written across the top was a pretty good hint."

"Someone sent a message from the depot in Joplin to Tom Speers in Kansas City." Priest glanced up at him. "You remember Tom, the city marshal of Kansas City?"

He managed a grin. "We've had occasion to meet, but I think calling him a friend is a stretch. Usually he's asking me when I'm going to leave his town and offering train fare. For some reason, he calls me a trouble magnet. Can you drag this out any more? Why would someone send a message to Tom?"

Coble could think of a lot of reasons lawmen might converse, but just an open telegram without naming the sender was odd. From one lawman to another, it would usually be a more private letter. Often it would be a wanted poster with notes on the back sent by post on a stagecoach or train. Telegrams are never private, and telegraphers never discreet.

"Yeah, well. It seems Tomlin Harp escaped jail recently. Someone decided to send word out in all directions to watch for him."

"I wonder why LC Hamilton, the Joplin marshal, didn't send that." Coble was puzzled.

"Who knows. Maybe he delegated."

Coble gave his friend a quizzical look. "And this big mystery prompted you to ride all the way out here with your lovely bride on a hot, dusty day? Who's this Harp?"

Priest slowly raised his gaze from the paper.

"Really?" He shook his head in wonder. "You never heard the name? Does the Pianoman ring a bell?"

Coble felt as if cold water had been poured down his back. First came fear, then came anger. The Pianoman was the term they'd given the man arrested for the long-distance killings around the small town of Hard Times months before. The killings had been at the direction of Oxford Graham. At least, that was their thinking. At the time, the Pianoman had refused to give his real name. They'd given him the moniker because he played piano so hard you could hear it streets away, even over the noise of the bawdy houses. Some wondered if there could be a criminal charge for beating a musical instrument to death.

He snatched the paper from Priest's hand. When he looked at the writing on the telegram, his hand trembled. Somehow he wished the handwriting by the telegrapher wasn't so clear, that maybe it was a mistake. How could this be? They knew how dangerous this man was. Surely extra precautions were taken? The man should have been in chains.

Coble gazed out the open door. The few trees he could see were showing color, in sharp contrast to the green of the prairie grass. Finally, he calmed his nerves. Everyone is afraid of something. They have lost and won, loved, experienced joy, anger, sadness, and every other emotion known to the human condition. Good person or bad, there is life in their eyes, a window into their soul.

When he'd looked into the eyes of the Pianoman, it scared the hell out of him. A man muscled like a prized bull, with a face dull as oatmeal that held dead, black, reptilian eyes tracking prey with no mercy. The man behind those eyes broke out of jail. He was loose. And he would be killing. It was his nature.

Coble sighed long and hard, the sigh of the afflicted and downtrodden. "I need to burn this table. Seems like bad news always drops on it."

Shaking his head, he held his silence for a moment. Then... "I still don't see it as my problem. There are capable lawmen all around here. LC must have twenty or more deputies on his force. If he escaped LC's jail, they'll be after him."

When he glanced at Priest and Juana, their silence stretched out as they returned his gaze. Were they waiting for him to come apart right in front of them? What expectation did they have?

He tried again, his resolve weakening. "Well, it's not my problem. Other men can pick up this cross. I don't want it." His voice sounded weak, even in his own ears. It was like he was arguing with himself.

Priest spoke softly. "If he returns to Hard Times, it will be a bloodbath. Who's going to catch him there? Tom Fallon? Fred Curry? Who? City marshals won't leave their towns to come and help. Most Deputy US Marshals are down in the Nation chasing their tails. County sheriffs are few and far between, and have problems of their own. You know the old saying. If not you, who then? If not now, when?"

He knew Tom Fallon was good enough for a peaceful town but lacked experience. He was capable and would try too hard. Fred Curry was the irascible old hostler at the stable. Together the two men tried to keep peace in their town and had done pretty well. But they expected men to have a conscience. They did not understand men who killed for the fun of it, didn't know the soulless evil that drives them. He was afraid neither man would understand the kind of men you gave no even break, no chance at all. They'd get too close expecting fair play, trying to make an arrest. With someone like the Pianoman, who killed without remorse or warning, too close was an invitation to death.

Most people, even most lawmen, expect some kind of conversation before guns are pulled. The truly dangerous people didn't need any motivation to kill, didn't need to work themselves up. There was no thought to it, just action, leaving dead men with surprised looks on their faces.

"Dammit, Priest. That's not fair." He suppressed a chuckle. "If Maria were alive, she'd skin you for even mentioning this."

Priest's voice was gentle. "I think you found out this morning that fair is an illusion. Good or bad, God's will or no, you have no ties here. Not now. And we are genuinely sorry about that. Our choice would be that she still lived to cause problems for you or for us."

He disagreed. "This is still my home, it was mine before she came, though Maria's ghost may be haunting its halls. I do have ties here. I have much to lose, Priest."

Coble gazed at Priest, trying to come up with a reply witty enough to shut him down, to prove him wrong. But he could never verbally joust with Priest. He called him "Priest" just to get under his skin. Having given up the church, the man was dressed similar to Coble, with two pistols in a fore and aft position, plus a skinning knife in a scabbard. Probably a little pepper-box derringer hid somewhere. Priest had always been his sounding board, someone he could talk with when troubled. Confession, therefore Priest. But that was when he wore the cloth. It was difficult now.

It was a sad thought. Maria had never taken over that chore of confidant. They could never discuss anything without anger coloring the conversation. Watching Priest and Juana interact together, he could tell Juana had assumed that role for Priest. She was like his second skin, always touching him, watching him, evaluating, anticipating, and quick to defend. There was love there, and Coble envied him.

He wasn't surprised when Juana spoke.

"No," she said. "August cannot go with you."

We both looked at her—him in alarm, me with

acceptance. I vowed never to play chess with this woman. Though she gave off an aura of being a simple woman or housewife, maybe even taking care to look a little too plain, he was sure she took delight in being underestimated. Everyone had their vision of a Mexican housekeeper or subservient wife. They'd be dead wrong in her case.

He raised his hand to stop any comment from Priest. "She's right, my friend. When I go, I'll go alone, and I'll need to move fast." Coble gave him a small smile. "And I may have to move in some circles a man of the collar would be uncomfortable in."

"How do you mean?" Priest tried to look affronted but failed. "I'm no innocent."

"There was no need to alert surrounding towns of his escape. I'm thinking Mr. Harp won't move far from Joplin. If I remember right, he is an addict. When I talked to him, he mentioned a need for opium. That's how Oxford Graham controlled him."

"He could still have fled the city." Priest shrugged. "It doesn't take much to carry along a bottle of laudanum. Opium is the main ingredient."

Nodding, Coble said. "A good point, but I wonder how many bottles it would take to slake his need. And as I understand it, the need grows."

Priest nodded, glanced at Juana, and then spoke. "Not to speak ill of the dead, but if her old lover controlled the Pianoman this way, do you think Maria...?"

"No, I don't." Coble shrugged and then reconsidered. "But then, I didn't think she'd do the things she did. So..."

"There is one more problem." Juana said as she stared out the open doorway.

Glancing at her, his reply was sarcastic. "Only one?"

She ignored his tone. "What about Maria's father?"

"Pete?" Coble's shoulders slumped, feeling guilty he hadn't thought of him sooner. "Dammit, I forgot about him. I need to go see him before I can do anything about the Pianoman. This'll break him. He dotes on that girl."

"Well," she said. "I don't think you'll have to wait."

Chapter Four

THERE WAS NO FINER MAN THAN PETE SANTOS. HE and Coble had met years before when Pete had been recommended to help trail a bail jumper. They'd rode many trails since then. A short, bow-legged man, born to a saddle, always hiding under a wide-brimmed hat and handlebar mustache, he was relentless in cutting for sign. Coble considered himself good at it, but never as good as Pete. Since then, they'd become a team of sorts and good friends. All long before he knew Pete had a daughter. He sometimes wished he'd never known.

The sad thing was that she'd lied to him too. While Pete thought she was attending a women's college back east, she was doing work for the Pinkerton Agency just for the adventure. Coble never got out of her what exactly she did, but he had a fertile imagination. Any agency like the Pinkertons were all about information. She would have been hard to resist, and the circumstances were probably better left unsaid to a father.

The last Coble had seen of Pete was when he was headed to his small spread in Oklahoma to recuperate from a bullet wound, an affliction that seemed to hit everyone of late. He was not sure if Pete had seen his daughter since he went home.

Oddly, the coming confrontation didn't make him feel nervous...just sad. He stood as Pete tied his horse to the rail and, like any westerner, paused a moment to check the brands on the other two horses, and then he moved up the steps, stomping his boots to rid them of dust. His quick smile turned to puzzlement as he took in their expressions.

"Pete." Coble quickly shook his hand. "You remember Priest, and this is his wife Juana."

"Folks." Pete nodded, giving everyone a wary eye. "Y'all look like you've seen a ghost."

Clearing his throat, Coble held on to the shake. "Pete, I got bad news."

Slowly taking his hand away, he glanced around the room before settling on Coble. "Well, Coble. We've known each other a long time. Spit it out."

He could think of no better way to do it. "Maria is dead."

It's odd to see a man who was burned brown by the sun turn pale and shrink in stature as you watched. "How...? When?"

"I'm sorry, Pete. It was early this morning. She had a miscarriage. Things went wrong. I'm still trying to get my head around it myself."

Pete was a tough man who'd been wounded, killed people himself, and had seen every misbegotten thing one human can do to another. They'd done a lot of it together. Men like this do not know how to cry. When they do, it's gut-wrenching.

Leaning against the table, staring at Coble, he gave a cry of pure anguish, pulled from his chest in one awful, ragged sob before he caught it and tried to hold the pain in. If Coble lived to be a hundred, he'd never witness anything as agonizing.

When Pete straightened, his gaze was white hot. "You were supposed to protect her. She was your wife." His emphasis on wife came out as a bellow.

It wasn't in Coble to lie, often to his own detriment. "Well..."

Priest interceded before Coble could say something stupid. "It wasn't his fault, Pete. No one can prevent something like this."

Pete whirled on Priest. "I don't need a used-to-be padre to tell me..."

Juana stepped into the fray, coming around the table and forcibly pulling the small man into a full-body hug, holding on until the man's anger relaxed. In other circumstances, it would have been laughable as he struggled against her for a moment. Pete would never hit a woman and simply didn't know what to do to extricate himself.

"Please, Mr. Pete," she said. "It is a sadness, but it happens. Don't let your grief harm those around you. It was God's will, not Coble's."

Coble hadn't seen it, but Pete's hand was on his pistol, and her hand was latched on his like a clawed talon. He realized his friend might have shot him out of pure unhinged anger and grief over losing his daughter. He'd seen it happen over the years—blind and deadly anger over some perceived affront between friends, saddle partners, or just drunks leaning against a bar rail. Death in an instant, regret for a lifetime. And it wasn't always guns. Knives, clubs, or anything close at hand played a part. He'd seen a man brained with a brass spittoon once.

Pete finally dropped his angry gaze from Coble's and moved his hand from under hers. "You Mexican women. I got one at home just like you. She's a treasure."

Juana patted him on the shoulder and pushed him into a chair. "I'm more Indio, but I'll take the compliment."

Pete took a monstrous breath, followed by a sigh before he looked at Coble. "Buried?"

Nodding, his voice was hoarse with pent-up relief. Deep down, he knew he wouldn't be able to defend himself. Not against Pete.

"Behind the house on the knoll, by the oak tree she planted...best I could do. I figured, in this heat, the trip to your place would be too long."

It was a small lie, but he thought it was appropriate to defuse the situation. It was true, just sadly an afterthought.

Pete nodded, staring into the distance a moment. "If you don't mind?" Standing, he moved toward the door. "I'd like some time alone."

He didn't wait for an answer, just moved out the doorway on bones that were a thousand years old.

When Coble looked an hour later, he was still kneeling by her grave on painful knees too old to be bending, too proud not to. He had the thought of someday putting a small bench by her grave. Hat in hand, Pete seemed small and frail, backlit by a fading sun.

Juana put together a meal of beef stew and fry bread with coffee strong enough to float a horseshoe. They sat around the table remembering the good times and some of the bad. Books could be written about some of their experiences, but no one would believe it. Most folks were more likely to read and believe the stories in Frank Starr's new pocket novels. He advertised twenty-five cent books for only ten cents. All it took was a dime and a suspension of belief. His heroes always won the day, always got the girl. Their six-guns were blazing fast and never ran out of bullets. It was a fantasy people wanted to believe.

Always worried for Coble's soul, Priest had asked him about closure for Maria, if he needed time to grieve, but he just shrugged it off. There is something about being there when someone dies, fighting for their life, meeting their gaze when you both know there is no use trying anymore. Your hands painted with blood up to your elbows, their gaze full of acceptance, watching them slip away. He couldn't think of more closure than that. It is final, and you've already said goodbye. You've tried your hardest, already gone through every emotion you're capable of giving. All that leaves is the feeling that you could have done more—should have done more. But there are no second chances.

He would move on from that. If there was anger felt from the uselessness of the situation, perhaps he could transfer that feeling toward Pianoman or something more useful.

"So, what now, Coble?" Pete's voice was soft. "Back

to the badge? There's nothing holding you back now. From what I've seen, the lawbreakers are winning. Even down in the Nation where there's a marshal behind every bush, I see them letting the little fish go so they can try and get the big ones. And I can't help you anymore. I'm too old for the trail and need the comforts of home."

Juana interjected. "Or the comfort of your woman at home? Yes?"

Pete nodded and shrugged.

"Well," Coble said. "Pianoman would be considered a big fish."

"More like a big cockroach, feeding on offal in the darkness." Priest looked up from his coffee when Juana slapped his arm. "Did I say that out loud?"

Coble must have been staring at the mantel where the source of most of his troubles lay. He'd hoped the object he stared at would gather dust and be ignored. He knew for certain Maria had hoped that. Moving to the fireplace and taking the badge from its place in ignominy, he polished it against his shirt. No matter how many times he put it away, the badge always won. Or he lost. Depends who you ask.

"Seems like I have a job to do down toward Joplin. There's a man who needs to be fetched. I guess I'll go see about it."

He didn't expect congratulations, slaps on the back, or well wishes. They were sending him off to do something they could not. It was a somber bunch, each knowing it might be the last thing Coble ever did.

Chapter Five

PETE DECIDED TO STAY AT THE RANCH AWHILE, along with Priest and Juana. He wasn't ready to leave his daughter. Coble rode out the next morning. They'd suggested he take the rail, it would be faster, but it would take him out of the way. The Kansas City-Fort Scott & Gulf railroad, commonly known as the KATY would take him out to Baxter Springs, Kansas. After that it would route him back into Webb City, a town just outside of Joplin. He'd done it before but was not thrilled to ride in an iron and wooden box pulled by a coal-fired steam engine belching black smoke at forty miles an hour. To be truthful, he didn't want to be in, or on, anything moving that fast.

Coble wanted a more direct route so he pointed the nose of his horse south. It was only thirty miles to Joplin, and assuming there was no high water to cross, it would be an easy two-day ride. Above all else, he needed the time alone. His friends accepted the lie that he was alright.

Priest had argued that the wasted time would give

the Pianoman an extra day to kill someone. But who knew what that number was since he escaped. And there would be more before he was found. One thing Coble knew about someone like the Pianoman, he wouldn't stop killing even when he knew someone was looking for him. It was his nature to kill, but not to flaunt it, and Coble didn't think he would be looking for trophies. A man like him had little regard for life, simply snuffing it out and then moving on with no thought about it. Deep down, he didn't think the Pianoman would come to him like others had. He'd have to dig him out or lure him out, and that was a risky proposition.

The ride south began innocently enough, the morning starting out cool. Within a few hours, a haze lay between the rolling hills as the sun baked moisture from the soil. It hadn't rained in a good long while so the creeks and gullies were mostly dry. Eastern Kansas is not flat, and he rode with caution.

According to the newspapers from back east, this land was at peace. Of course, the papers normally just chronicled what the government told them. There were close to a hundred deputy marshals working the Indian Nation alone and were there for a reason. Peace was subjective. The occasional robberies and killings along the trails didn't count, unless you were the recipient. There were many who skirted around the fringes of law and fair play that would not pass up an opportunity to cross the line if something were presented to them far from prying eyes. The definition of honesty is how you act when no one is watching. Sadly, many failed that test.

And there were people of every stripe and pedigree

trying to make a dollar without working for it. They would not consider themselves criminals, simply opportunists.

A year ago last September, Dull Knife led some of his people away from the reservation in Indian territory, making a break for their ancestral home in Nebraska.

Without doubt, the conditions on the reservation were atrocious. That was well documented. Coble couldn't blame them for breaking out. No man should have to endure that. But on the other hand, the seventeen settlers they killed in Decatur County were just trying to make a living themselves, oblivious to the deals and shenanigans between the government and the natives. The Indians were justified in their actions by having been treated terribly. But brutalizing settlers who had nothing to do with their plight was uncalled for. It was a matter of perception.

When Dull Knife left with his roughly eighty warriors and two hundred fifty women and children, he just wanted to lead his people home. But the journey of war rarely has a good ending, no matter what side you're on. Never has.

Coble's horse seemed grateful for the rest when he was reined in. Lost in thought, he'd pushed the animal too hard. Not a wise choice in ambush country. Ahead was a fair-sized stream, maybe the Spring River. It'd been a dry summer, so rivers were down to a trickle. Seems creeks and streams changed names as often as outlaws. If a man named Smith camped a few days on its banks, it would likely become Smith's River.

Smoke rose from a campfire ahead, and a trail of churned dust by shod-hooves led toward it. The trail was fresh, otherwise the relentless wind would have covered the tracks within a half hour.

It was nearing evening, so his first inclination was to avoid any company. It takes a lot of trust to bed down around a fire with strangers. He didn't have it in him to do that.

Starting to turn his horse away from the trail, a woman's scream carried to him on the breeze, followed by the echoing boom of a shotgun. Nothing else sounds like a shotgun, and it usually is a defensive weapon. He figured some angry woman just punched someone's ticket.

With a sigh and slow shake of his head, Coble turned his horse to follow the trail. His immediate thought was about a verse he'd read in a hymnal, something about seeing trouble all your days. After a couple of minutes at a fast walk, the horse carried him around a small rise to reveal a setting that could have been a painting on the cover of a dime novel.

A wagon sat by the creek, nestled among the trees for shade and protection from dew at night. Standing behind a well-setup campfire stood a woman holding a shotgun pointed at two men. Another man lay on the ground. Even from a distance Coble could tell the man wouldn't be getting up, not with the amount of blood showing. A shotgun will do that to you.

He'd approached quietly, and they hadn't heard him. The sound of a shotgun at close quarters will put a ringing in your ears like a crack of lightning. You don't hear many subtleties in sound after that.

"Lady, you had no call to do that." The man who spoke was tall, wearing a short coat and beat-up gray Stetson with a notch in the top. "We weren't going to hurt you if you'd just give us what we want. A little fun and cooperation never hurt nobody. Now you've spoiled it."

"Well, you ain't getting what you want." The woman's voice was calm. "I'm not that kind of woman, and even if I was, a couple of no-account, dirty-faced, would-be highwaymen wouldn't be getting it from me. So you move on down the trail and leave us be." She gestured toward the body with her chin. "Take that piece of trash with you."

The other man laughed. He was short and broad, wearing a plaid shirt with his shirt tail hanging out. He had something like a miner's skullcap on his head and wore his belligerence like a Halloween mask. "Lady, you only got one shot left. So I'm thinking it'll be worth it for whichever of us don't get shot. You are a spunky woman, and I like that."

The man paused a moment and then hooked his thumb toward the other man. "I'd shoot him. He's the one most likely to hurt you with what's coming. He's got a mean streak a mile wide. I'm gentler with my women."

The men started separating, moving around opposite sides of the fire.

She looked determined to shoot again, and it was almost worth it to see which man she would choose. But not quite. Coble's voice carried across the clearing. "Stop."

The men were good at following orders. The man with the miner's cap actually paused with one foot in the air.

"You men turn around," he continued. "Although

I'm curious to see how long you can stand on one foot."

Both men turned, and the man in the coat spoke. "Mister, you got no say in this. Shooting you would just be a warm-up for taking this woman."

Chuckling, Coble shook his head. "You won't be getting any kind of warm-up today. What's your name?"

The man straightened and stuck his chin forward. "I'm Will Tunny."

It was hard not to laugh. Apparently his name was supposed to mean something. "Sorry. Your name doesn't ring a bell, so I'll save my knee-shaking for later."

"How about you?" Coble shifted my gaze to the other man. "You got a name?"

"What the hell is it to you, mister? You need to get on down the trail and leave us be."

When I didn't say anything, he relented. "Frank Boyd."

Coble shook his head again, pretending to search his memory. "Nope. Still nothing."

Raising his voice, Coble spoke to the woman. "Ma'am, I know that Greener is getting heavy. You can lower it now. Besides, I'm kind of in the line of fire."

She was blonde with light-colored eyes and slat-thin in her shapeless calico dress. Her voice didn't match her look. It came out strong, not an ounce of fear. "I can manage the weight, mister. Far as I can tell, my choice of who to shoot just went from two to three. It'd be helpful if y'all would bunch up some."

Movement behind her caught his attention when two little blonde heads peeked over the top of the sideboards on the wagon. They looked like twin girls and miniatures of their mother.

Both men had their hands on the butts of their pistols and didn't look inclined to reason.

"Alright. Here's how this is going to go. My name is Coble Bray." He moved his vest to the side with his left thumb to show the badge hanging on his shirt pocket. "I know my name isn't near as scary as yours, but I'm a Deputy US Marshal. I want you men to take out your weapons real easy like, and lay them on the ground. And ma'am? I need you to move to the side and tell your kids to duck back down in the wagon. I'm shooting a forty-four caliber, and it will go through these men like a hot knife through butter. If things get frisky, you're in the way."

"Coble Bray?" Boyd glanced at his partner and then grinned. "You know there's a bounty on your head? One hundred dollars in gold coins. All we have to do is bring in your badge. Or, if we bring in your ears, I bet we could get a new bowler hat."

He was surprised at that. "Only a hundred? I'm insulted. Now just who would you take my ears to?" When they didn't answer, he continued. "Look, it's a fool's errand. You can't collect if you're dead. Give me a name, and I might let you go."

The men were not impressed with the threat. Like a choreographed play, both reached for their pistols. Very few men had perfected any kind of a fast draw. Pistol barrels were too long and holsters too deep, coattails and vest bottoms got in the way, and it took practice most wouldn't commit to. It was obvious they had not. What commitment they had must have been to stealing from helpless women and shooting at beer bottles.

Coble's pistol was already in his hand, hidden from sight by the pommel of the saddle. The woman stepped to her right to get out of the line of fire, and the kids dropped like prairie dogs into a hole. His first shot notched Will Tunny at the top button of his shirt, his second coincided with the boom of a shotgun, and Frank Boyd, hit front and back, went down like a sack of potatoes, confused on which way to fall.

Ears ringing, Coble settled his horse while watching the men through the gun smoke slowly clearing on the slight breeze. He heard the shotgun break and saw the woman pull out the empty shell casings, reach into her dress pocket, and feed fresh shells into the breech. Snapping the action together, she turned to face him. Cool under fire was an understatement. She may as well have been quail hunting.

Coble's left arm was stinging, and he glanced to see a spot of blood on his upper arm. Another scar.

"Mattie Hurst."

Distracted from feeding two shells into his pistol, he blinked at her. "What?"

"Seems like you were taking names, Marshal. I gave you mine."

Dismounting, he left the horse ground-reined. Glancing around he could tell it was a typical camp but well maintained. The cookfire was surrounded by rocks to contain it, any leaves or debris around it brushed away to minimize the danger of embers landing on something dry. Fire was a traveler's greatest fear, holdup artists notwithstanding. A metal tripod was positioned over the fire with an iron pot hanging over the coals. Camp chairs, low three-legged stools, were sitting close. They were built to stack, one on top of the other, to conserve room in a wagon. He could see two draft horses hobbled and staked next to a patch of grass. They'd been here a while, because the grass was short in their circle.

Giggling came from the wagon. Weren't these people scared of anything? His knees were knocking in the aftermath of the shooting. "How about the two munchkins? Do they have names?"

"Riley and Rita. They're twelve years old. A little bigger than munchkins." She glanced toward the wagon. "Although they don't act it sometimes."

It was a surreal setting. Here he was holding a normal conversation with the woman while two children played around the area, not seeming to be bothered by three dead bodies lying in disarray just beyond their campfire. It was fortunate the breeze took the smell of blood away.

Shaking his head, he matched the kids' gazes a moment. Finally, one giggled again and broke the spell. "Riley and Rita? Why didn't you just give them the same name? It would save a lot of trouble because I don't think anyone can tell them apart."

Mattie gave a short laugh. "You could be right. Riley is the oldest, though. She's the bossy one."

"By what, a minute?"

The corner of her mouth quirked into a smile. "Actually about ten minutes, but I wasn't counting too well at the time."

His gaze must have been obvious while looking over her thin frame.

"I know, I'm skinny." One hand drifted down her

body, smoothing the front of her dress. "They sucked the life right out of me."

Not all of it. The lady still looked quite capable, especially with her attempt at humor. "Sorry, no disrespect intended. I didn't mean to stare. What happened here?"

"About what you'd expect. Those three men rode up and saw I was alone." She gestured toward the kids. "Or pretty much. They decided to dispense with the courting and go right to the honeymoon. Apparently my opinion on the subject wasn't needed."

He laughed at her direct approach, although it didn't seem appropriate for him to do it. She rewarded him with a small smile and shrug.

"Can I ask what you're doing out here alone?" The girls were starting to wander toward the dead outlaws, and he stepped between them and the bodies. He was sure they didn't need a close-up look at that, especially the one who'd taken a double dose of buckshot and pistol ball.

"Girls, come back to the wagon." She sighed, leaning her shotgun against the wagon wheel. "We haven't been. Alone, I mean. We buried my husband yesterday, out behind the trees."

"I'm sorry for your loss. How did he die?" His first thought was that these men killed him, but the timing was off a day.

"He caught a fever. It came on him suddenly, and he passed quickly. The last town we were in was Carthage, not too far over the Missouri line. Maybe he caught something there since we were in town a few days. I'd picked up some work there, had our wagon parked on the square, and was making a little money. I thought we'd stay awhile. But all of a sudden he decided to move on."

She paused, watching the girls picking up sticks for the fire. "If you're worried, I'm sure we don't have anything you can catch. The kind of sickness he had generally spreads quickly from one person to the next, so if he were contagious, we'd already have it. We do not."

Her shoulders slumped a moment, and then she straightened. "We've been camped here a little over a week. Like I said, we buried him yesterday."

A cold chill stiffened his spine. "I buried my wife yesterday."

Her gaze met his, eyebrows raised. "Well, that's just..."

"Strange." He nodded, watching her closely. "I know."

She broke the awkward silence that followed. "You're bleeding."

"Yeah. Seems like I caught some buckshot recently." He gave her a pointed look while rubbing his arm.

"That's the bad part about a shotgun," she said. "It takes saints and sinners alike. Well, come here by the fire. Since I seem to have shot you, I'll get that patched up. When I'm through, maybe you can do something with those boys. They'll be drawing flies before long."

Chapter Six

MATTIE RETURNED FROM THE WAGON WITH A BLACK leather satchel and a roll of cotton cloth, motioning for Coble to sit on one of the camp chairs close to the fire.

He nodded at the bag. "Seems a strange bag of tricks for a homesteader. You're well equipped."

"You'll need to take off that shirt, unless you want me to rip the sleeve off." She waited expectantly.

"I'll take it off." His hands moved immediately. "I don't have that many shirts."

Shrugging, she began helping him take off the vest and then shirt. "To answer your implied question, I'm a trained nurse. I can usually find work anywhere. That's what I was doing in Carthage."

She hesitated a moment. "Well, I can find work any place that doesn't think women have only one use. We passed through several of those towns. All the women are either home having babies and cleaning house or holding court at the nearest whorehouse." Prodding his shoulder a moment, she continued. "That old wound is barely healed. Looks like you're trying to wear out your body with gunshots."

"The good news," he said. "Is that people keep missing my heart. Mostly I'm just losing a lot of skin."

"You cheated." Her attention was on his wound so her comment surprised him.

"I'm sorry?" He cocked his head like he didn't hear.

She snorted, wiping at fresh bleeding she'd caused by poking and prodding. "Your pistol was already drawn. You had the advantage."

"Of course I had the advantage. I try not to be stupid." He gave her a steady gaze. "It's a matter of opinion if that's cheating. You're thinking that's not fair? There's not a lot of fair in this world. They were warned and given a choice, and they made it. Besides, there's only one rule in a gunfight."

She paused a moment. "Which is?"

"Live to tell about it."

"There's another rule. Avoid it." She shook her head. "Although in both our cases, that didn't seem to be an option."

Coble winced as she poured a good amount of whiskey on his wound. "Sounds like there's a story here. I can't see someone with your nursing skills packing up and heading west. What did your husband do for a living?"

After digging out a double-ought pellet from his arm and tossing it into the fire, she took a small piece of cloth and cleaned out the wound. Finally satisfied, she irrigated the wound with whiskey again.

He flinched and groaned, trying to stifle the noise. The giggles of the towheads sitting by the wagon were clearly heard. He was the evening's entertainment.

"So, how did your wife die?" Her voice was soft, ignoring his question. "If you don't mind my asking?"

"Miscarriage." He was getting used to saying it. Maybe if he said it enough, the pain would go away. "Something went wrong, and she bled to death. I couldn't stop the bleeding."

Sitting by the comfortable fire, he was again lost in thought. Tired, but keyed up at the same time. Sleep would not come easy this night.

She gently said, "Sometimes it's easier to unload to a stranger, someone who doesn't judge like friends."

He didn't know why, but he gave her the whole story about Maria and the hunt for the killers, her involvement with the master manipulator. She listened without interruption until he finished.

"Sounds like a sad tale. Seems like there's always someone around to lead a good woman astray. Mistakes are made." Her voice was noncommittal, like they were discussing the chance of rain. "You don't think the baby was yours?"

"I do not." He'd done the math and explored possibilities. "We'd not been back to the marriage bed."

"I'm surprised. That's usually the first thing on a man's mind, or hers if she's trying to make amends." She stared into the fire, stirring the coals with a blackened stick. "She was healthy?"

"Strong as a horse." He watched her closely, wondering where this was going.

"Well, I didn't know her, and I don't know you. But maybe she did make a mistake, just not the one you're thinking of." She shrugged. "This is just speculation, which I don't usually do. But true or not, it might give you something to ease the guilt."

When he didn't speak she continued. "There's a plant that grows around here. Pennyroyal, or some call it mosquito plant. There are other plants that do the same job, but it's the most used. The women in bawdy houses use it to get rid of unwanted pregnancies. The madams are very good at making potions. They grind it up and make it into tea. It's actually kind of a mint and smells good, but if used too strong? It's deadly."

"Why would she...?"

"Dunno." She glanced at him. "Again, I didn't know her. But from what you've said, guilt maybe? Guilt can make us do awful things. Think about it. If she loved you, and it's not your child? If you were trying to work things out, she may have thought someone's bastard child would stand between you. Being strong as you say, I doubt she thought dying was a possibility. She probably figured on being sick for a little while...worth the risk. We're all bulletproof, you know. Until we aren't."

She continued. "And you are not, with the scars to prove it."

"I learned that lesson long ago." He nodded. "Your theory kind of makes sense. She did like her tea."

Dammit Maria, what did you do? He was lost in thought for a few moments, and Mattie seemed to be doing the same.

While wrapping his wound with the cotton cloth, she commented, "To answer your question...my husband was a carpenter, made a good living at it. Then he caught some kind of ailment that convinced him he was a farmer, and the only thing we could do was head to Kansas for the free land they're giving away under the Homestead Act. I honestly think he lost his mind. There's just no other answer that makes any sense."

"A pretty common tale," he said. "Ill-conceived for the most part. It takes a lot of planning, including a season's worth of food in your wagon. Most home-steaders I've seen starve out in the first year. Moisture for crops isn't guaranteed here on the prairie, that's why you see mostly cattle and horses. In the dry season, the grass cures on the stem, and it's like hay, so there's always something for them to eat. The best farming is done east of here."

Watching her a moment as she stared into the fire, he knew there was more. It was his turn to pry. "So what happened? I feel your husband didn't just die of a fever."

Glancing up, she gave a low laugh. "Oh, he died of a fever. But you're right, that was just the end of the story. The start of it was when he lost all our money in a card game in Carthage, money we needed for the food and supplies you mentioned. Some men brought him staggering back to the wagon and said he still owed them money, and if I didn't have it, out of the goodness of their hearts, they would take the remainder out in trade with me. They even implied my husband suggested it."

"You know something?" Her smile was bitter. "I can see why so many women turn to being whores. Every man you meet wants something."

She shook her head like trying to clear a memory. "Anyway they left when I cut one of them. Seems they had no stomach for dealing with someone who wasn't helpless and lost whatever ardor they had."

"Men are not all like that." He shook his head,

smiling. "That's twice that men have tried to have their way with you that I know of. People have called me a magnet for trouble, but I'm thinking you have me beat. You haven't been fortunate in the men you meet."

"And look at me. I'm certainly no prize. I'm just a skinny woman with two kids that I don't want to watch starve. Men must be desperate."

Putting his shirt and vest on, he stared at her a moment. "So to be clear, you killed two men tonight. It's obvious to me you would have clubbed the other to death if I hadn't shot him first. You also seem to be proficient with a blade. In self-defense, of course."

He gave her the best smile he could muster. "As a bonafide federal marshal, should I be interested in your past? Seems medicine isn't all you're trained in."

Her sigh was long and breathy. "I can't help what interests you, Mr. Marshal, and I can't help it when trouble finds me. The fact is, I come from a shooting family in Tennessee. You can't farm on the side of a hill, so we hunted to feed ourselves. If we couldn't shoot it, skin it, and cook it, we didn't eat. We planted corn just to lure in coons for their meat and fur. If we couldn't protect ourselves, we didn't live. It was my father's great disappointment that all he could raise were girls."

It was a common story with hill folk. They lived off the land, just as their ancestors had. "And your name before marriage, if I might ask? Just curious."

She gave him a long look before replying. "McKinney."

Mattie McKinney. Lawmen talk and read posters. Some of them also read newspapers to keep up with world events. It was a name he'd heard. Some folks in Tennessee lived by the feud. Well, most did. Rumor had it she'd quit all that and joined a traveling carnival for a while as a trick shooter. Contests were often held, with prizes given, for the best shooters. Some men didn't take losing to a woman with grace. Sometime after that she'd disappeared. But it was all supposition, far away and none of his business. But still... interesting.

He gave his best imitation of thinking hard. "Nope. Can't say your name rings a bell. You're in the clear with me."

"Well, thank the good Lord for that. I'm tired of shooting people today." Her gaze was direct. "I've heard your name too, Coble Bray. There were folks in the hills with both your names."

"Good things, I hope?"

"Not a damned bit, but consistent with the day we've had."

———

AFTER MATTIE and her children were bedded down in the wagon, Coble sat by the dying fire. He'd gone through the dead men's pockets for any identification, letters and such, and used his horse to drag the men to a gully he'd seen riding in. The horse was not happy about that.

He decided their guns and pistol belts, boots, plus the small amount of money they had, would go to Mattie. The three horses the miscreants rode would also go to her. Digging out some paper and pencil from his saddlebag, he wrote out a statement of ownership in case she needed it. The horses were branded, but he doubted these men were the original owners. If nothing else, she and her little family were no longer penniless.

He was surprised as Mattie returned to the fire, wrapped in a threadbare blanket and carrying a coffee tin. As she sat on a camp chair with a sigh, she pulled a little brown cigarillo from the tin and lit it up with a burning twig.

"Couldn't sleep." Her voice was low and throaty. She waved the cigarillo. "Nasty habit."

He relaxed, sitting across the small fire. With a smile, he jabbed at her. "You hail from Tennessee. Figured you'd chew tobacco."

She snorted. "Tried it, but I don't like brown teeth."

"Me neither." He stared into the fire, a bad habit under normal circumstances. Staring into a fire loses your ability to see into the darkness, at least for a moment. Sometimes a moment is all it takes. Seems he had too many thoughts running around to sleep too.

"Tell me something more," she said. "Tell me about your wife and this scalawag you're chasing now."

"Why?"

"There's a darkness about you, Coble Bray. It's like watching a mountain lion on a narrow trail. You can't pick a direction to jump until the cat picks one. I'm afraid you're blaming yourself for things happening around you that are out of your control and will do something stupid."

It was a mystery. He should have been talking to Priest or maybe Juana. But he told her more detail than he had before, while she stared into the dying coals—from the missing girls at Big Springs to the demented killers leaving notes and clues in Hard Times and Joplin. It took a while, he'd never learned the gift of fast talking. The fire was nearly gone to ashes when he added a few sticks of kindling.

"You've picked a god-awful trail to follow. But it's done. You need to let it go," Mattie finally said. "It's not your fault, Coble. Especially with your wife. Maria didn't deserve to die. The baby didn't deserve to die. It was just bad luck, the kind you see in life every day. She drew a bad hand."

She was close enough to lay her hand on his arm. "Think about it. A horse steps into a hole and rolls over on a good rider just because his boot gets caught in the stirrup. Someone serves you some bad food. You catch a fever. There's a dead carcass in the water upstream from where you're drinking, and you get the trots until you die. Hell, I treated a gunshot wound on a man a full block away from a saloon fight. He was just standing there talking with his wife, without a care in the world, and took a gunshot to the neck from a spent bullet. Didn't even go through."

"You're depressing the hell out of me, even though what you're saying is probably true. Did he make it? The man?"

She sighed. "No. His wife was just like you. She couldn't stop the bleeding. I couldn't either. Just bad luck that left a widow with children to care for."

The Pianoman was on his mind. Coble needed to figure out where to look for the man. "What can you tell me about addiction?"

Smiling, she picked up the tin and shook it.

"Not that." He smiled back at her. "I mean heroin, opium...the bad stuff."

She put her tin of cigarillos down and looked at him with interest. "The man you're looking for is an addict?"

"So he told me."

Giving him a long look, she continued. "The man is a criminal and a killer. You actually believe what he tells you?"

That set him back a bit. Of course she was right. But it was all he had to go on.

"It's the only lead I have, so I guess I'll find out."

Mattie took his hand, pulling him to his feet. Nearly his same height, her gaze into his eyes was intense. Finally she pulled him into a long embrace where he learned she wasn't as slat-thin as he thought and was uncommonly strong.

Moving back toward her wagon, she spoke over her shoulder. "Next time you keep me up all night, you'd damn well better take me out for a nice dinner...someplace fancy with tablecloths...maybe candles."

Surprised, he glanced to the east and noted a rosy glow on the horizon. She was right, they'd talked the night away.

Shaking his head, he stirred the coals of the cook-fire. He had some more bacon in his saddlebags. Those girls were going to be hungry.

For a few moments, he thought of Tomlin Harp, the Pianoman. Where would he be? Like any animal, humans have their traits, their trails, and habits. Once he figured out his quarry's habits, it was a simple matter—not getting killed in the process was the problem. Apparently the Pianoman expected him to come looking and had already put out a bounty. He was sure his continued health was not a consideration and dead would be preferred. From now on he would have to be careful around everyone. Of course, Mattie's comment about expecting truth from criminals could apply to the men they'd just killed. Was the truth in them? Was there really a bounty on his head?

Coble sighed, eyes caught in a distant gaze. He had to confess, after talking with Mattie, the Pianoman wasn't foremost on his mind. He tossed the remainder of his coffee into the fire. Maybe it was fatigue, but he felt little enthusiasm for the job ahead.

With an early start, they'd pull into Hard Times about noon. Once he got Mattie settled, the hunt would begin.

Chapter Seven

THE SMELL OF BACON AND COFFEE IN THE MORNING can cause a near-sensory overload. The only other smell in the world as enticing as those, is a woman in passion. Coble settled for the first two, the last a distant memory steeped in confusion and regret.

No words were spoken as he added to the fare by emptying his bag of hardtack biscuits into the bacon grease. The girls watched with anticipation as the dough soaked up the grease, softening the biscuits in the process. He'd heard a rumor that when David ran out of rocks slaying Goliath, he used hardtack biscuits. Unsubstantiated, of course, not knowing if they had that kind of flour back then.

He didn't eat but did take coffee. It had been boiled over a few times but still had some kick. Mattie didn't eat either, and it was a good bet she and her children were close to being out of food. It was easy to see her priority. Her twins were rambunctious and well fed, while she was rail thin and gaunt. After breakfast, he helped clean up the camp and hitch their two horses to the wagon.

Apparently, none were morning people. Without speaking, she took the two girls in hand and walked down toward the creek. He gave them some time and then followed. They stood by a freshly dug grave, with two sticks tied together for a cross. Most flowers had dried up on the prairie, but the twins had picked some Queen Anne's Lace on the way and laid it on the grave. It was a somber moment, and he didn't want to intrude.

He knew little of Mattie Hurst, but wondered if the husband had died of the fever or lead poisoning. To be stranded on the prairie is a death sentence for the uninitiated unless they were lucky. And a woman with two children? He hadn't seen her mad yet, even when confronted by the three men, and had no desire to test those waters. He would guess she was not happy with her circumstance.

Standing with hat in hand, he broke the morning silence. "Ma'am. If I may suggest."

Her hug in the early morning hours had been all about consolation, like hugging someone at a funeral. In a sense it was, since they'd both laid their troubles to rest the previous day. Now she seemed more formal and reserved. She glanced at him as her eyes leaked tears, giving a frustrated gesture toward her wagon.

"I'm all ears, Mr. Bray. I'm open for suggestions... well, on most things anyway. I'm running out of options here."

"There's a little town south of here called Hard Times—"

"Heard of it. People in Carthage called it a bawdy town. It's no place to raise children."

"—that's the new part. The older, original part of town has some good folks and decent business from the farms and ranches around the area. Although they're a bit standoffish, there's even a German farming settlement close by."

He went on to describe the town and what he knew of the people. "I know a few of the folks, and I know for a fact they could use a good nurse, probably set you up with a place to live and work. When I was wounded, they had to get a doctor from Joplin to come over. Don't know much about pay, probably wouldn't be much, but you wouldn't starve and might get ahead some. You know," he played on her words. "To have better options."

Shuffling his feet, staring at the ground, he continued. "And about that. You're not penniless anymore. Those misguided souls who accosted you had a few things, and no relatives were indicated from their papers and such. You can sell their artillery that I pulled off them, although you might keep some for yourself. Their horses and tack will sell. The saddles are a bit worn, but serviceable. It'll give you some startup money, should you want it."

Mouth open, she seemed startled. She pinned him with her gaze for a long moment, and he felt he was being evaluated, taken apart piece by piece and put back together. He thought of giving her his tally book and stub of a pencil so she could take notes.

"That's kind of you, Mr. Bray. Actually, very kind." She glanced at her girls. "I don't like being beholden to anyone. I was taught to make my own way. But they do say when you have children you are hostage to fortune, that you make decisions you don't ordinarily make, do things differently. I didn't understand it when I heard that said, shrugged it off as nonsensical. Now it makes sense."

Her glance was direct. "We'll go to Hard Times if you think it's best." She hesitated a moment and then nodded. "With you."

He wasn't sure what she meant. Was she putting her trust on him to do the right thing, to help them? Or something else. He had to admit a spark had passed between them during their early morning embrace, he'd felt it. But it could have just been indigestion. The last thing he needed was an entanglement, especially with his sort of wife one day buried. He'd be willing to bet Mattie felt the same. But then again, there was something about her. And he'd given up trying to understand a woman's thinking a long time ago.

Chapter Eight

HARD TIMES HADN'T CHANGED MUCH IN appearance. Coming in from the north, the old part of town was straight before them. It was laid out like a ruler, with buildings on both sides of the street. A few small buildings were set back on the west side, behind businesses. Most folks lived where they worked, it was simpler that way.

The windmill in the center of the street appeared to have been repaired, so there was water from the well flowing into a trough. There were still bullet holes in the blades, and he wondered if it would whistle in a high wind. You could fill the basin on one side to water horses or use the spigot on the other side for drinking water. Handy. There was a rumor about some drunken cow pusher being shot for letting their horse foul the water in the trough. Knowing the irascible old hostler from the stable, he didn't doubt the story.

Perpendicular to the one-street town, the newer part pointed straight toward Joplin ten miles to the east. The new street was mostly saloons and houses of chance, the chance being if you carnally visited the women, there was a good chance of catching something you'd have trouble getting rid of. He wondered if the madams had a potion for that too. Not that he'd ever find out. There was just no way of delicately asking that question.

Leading the small parade of a springboard wagon filled with chattering females and pulling three saddle horses, he stopped in front of Fred Curry's stable. Tying his horse to a corral post, he stepped inside and didn't see anyone.

"Tell you what." He reached into his jeans and pulled out a gold piece he'd taken from the newly departed highwaymen. "Why don't you take the girls over to Jenny's Café and order up a meal? I'll water the horses and join you in a few minutes."

The twins were already across the narrow street before Mattie could say thank you. Shaking her head, she just followed along.

Loosening the cinch on his paint's saddle, he led him to the trough in front of Fred's. The other horses were unsaddled, so he untied them and did the same, finally leaving all four horses tied to the rail.

Stepping inside the café, he saw Fred Curry and Tom Fallon sitting in a corner conversing over ham and beans, sopping it up with bread. As he walked toward them, a little voice called from the other side. "We're over here."

Detouring, he went to their table. "Did you order lunch?"

Mattie nodded. "Had a choice of beef and beans or ham and beans, side order of cornbread. I ordered four plates with coffee and water. That work for you?"

"It does. Sorry, there never was much variety here. Look, I need to talk to those men in the corner for a moment. Do you mind?"

Mattie snorted. "It's not like we're on a date, Mr. Bray. Talk away. One warning though. If you don't get back in time, we'll finish your plate too."

"Yeah," the twins said.

———

MOVING to the table where Fred Curry and Tom Fallon were finishing up their meal, he took an empty chair. "Looks like you two have survived my absence so far."

Shaking hands all around, Coble continued. "Things are peaceful?"

"Was until you showed up." Fred looked disgusted. "Now Tom will have to quit his job."

Tom was shaking his head. "Now Fred, that ain't so." He turned to Coble. "Got married to Marcie right after you left."

"Like we didn't see that coming. Congratulations." He nodded. "Fine girl."

"Yeah, well. She likes things kept smooth, kinda like that lane to the German settlement west of town. Things like me being shot at tend to upset her. I've discovered she has a temper."

Coble laughed. These were friends, and he was glad to see them again. "I'm afraid a temper is part and parcel to the female species. That should not have surprised you."

Glancing outside, he continued. "I didn't come to cause trouble, although there might be some." He hated to ruin their day, but couldn't see a way around it. "I'm just stopping a while before going into Joplin. Got news the Pianoman escaped. I feel like I need to round him up."

Tom looked startled. "That may not be so easy."

Fred was watching the girls at the other table going through their food like coyotes after a rabbit. "Who are your friends? Speaking of tempers, I'm thinking that wife of yours wouldn't want to see you dragging all these women around."

"Maria died, Fred. Had a miscarriage, and things went wrong. She bled out." He wondered if every time he told the story it would get shorter. The memory was a lot longer than the telling of it.

The table was silent for a moment before Tom spoke. "Right, sorry to hear that, Coble. It must be hard. You sure you should be chasing after a killer when you've got that on your mind?"

That seemed to be the question on everyone's mind. Nodding, he shrugged. "Yeah, it's complicated. I see your point, but I'll be alright. Keeps my mind out of a dark hole."

"So?" Fred inclined his head toward Mattie and the girls. "What's their story?"

It took a few moments to bring them up to date. Digging his tally book from his vest pocket, he showed them the names of the men. "Ever hear of them?"

Tom shook his head. "What language did you write that in? Your handwriting is worse than mine."

"Never heard of them," said Fred. "Although the one you list as unknown rings a bell. I've seen a lot of unknowns come through here. Mostly headed up the street for a hot bunk and the gambling houses."

"Smartass. Well, I'm not surprised you don't know them. Probably not their real monikers anyway. Nothing in their pockets or saddlebags had names on them—which was kind of odd."

"Which brings me to something else. I brought in their hardware and horses. If you could help find buyers for them, the money should go to Mattie and her girls. They are flat broke and on the edge right now. She lost her husband, and they were just sitting there by the creek running out of food."

He grinned at Tom. "I brought them here because I know how kind Fred is and that he would help them through their troubles."

"Now, wait a minute." Fred started to protest.

"We'll be over to your place when we're done eating. They'll also need a place to stay."

Fred shook his head. "Of course they will."

"And maybe a job?"

Rolling his eyes, Fred rose from the table and stomped out the door.

THE FOOD WAS WELL ATTENDED, and as he watched, Mattie was taking food from her plate and adding to her girls' plates. Shaking his head, Coble walked over. When he sat down, he took his full plate and traded it with Mattie's.

"What are you doing?"

"You need to eat. There's plenty of money for food. You don't have to skimp and starve yourself to feed your children. Not now."

"Just all of a sudden?" She sighed. "I'm not sure I could eat a whole meal at once. I'm not used to it."

He leaned back in his chair. "Take your time and try. We got all day."

After their bellies were full and the coffee gone, the group drifted back to the stable. Fred was looking over the horses.

"What do you think, Fred?" Coble asked.

Taking off his hat and rubbing his bald head, Fred made a show of thinking a moment. Finally...he said, "Well, you got three horses with saddles. I can give you about a hundred fifty for those."

Mattie glanced at Coble before answering. "I'm thinking good saddle stock will sell for close to two hundred apiece. That's without saddles and bridles, blankets, ground sheets, and saddlebags."

Startled, Fred frowned at Coble. "You brought me a ringer, didn't you?"

He held up both hands, fighting back laughter. "Well, she's not wrong."

"I ain't sure I can come up with that kind of money to pay you, and if we wait for buyers it may take a while. Maybe we can make a deal."

"I'm all ears," Mattie said.

Changing the subject, Fred asked. "Can you cook?"

They watched him for a moment, wondering what was bouncing around in his head.

"I reckon I can," she finally said. "If I have the right tools and supplies. But I won't be a chuck wagon cook for anyone. I don't want to travel with the girls. We've had enough of that."

"I wouldn't expect you to. Here's the deal." Fred stood with a foot up on a corral pole. "I own Jenny's

Café over there. I'm sure you noticed the menu didn't take a lot of imagination. The lady who runs it met some biscuit shooter from over the Joplin way and decided to work in his eatery. She's leaving as soon as I can get her replaced. There's a good-sized living quarters in the back, with a well. The privy isn't too far out the back door, and it's pretty clean."

"How far apart are the well and the privy?" Mattie asked.

Fred gave her a startled look. "Fifty feet or so. Why?"

She spoke softly. "So the water should be boiled. You're crapping in your own water supply."

Fred's jaw dropped. Before he could reply, Coble commented. "Isn't there a spring coming from that limestone outcropping behind the building?"

"Yeah, it's a little farther away."

"Problem solved. If I remember right that water is so cold it'll freeze the..." He glanced at Mattie. "Well, it's a cold spring, so the water comes from way down deep. It's not runoff water. It should be pure."

"So, Fred." Getting the conversation back on track, he said, "You get everything you want plus three horses? That ain't much of a deal."

Mattie cut him off. "I can't afford..."

Fred held up his hands. "Not asking you to buy it. Think of it as a grubstake. If you throw your wagon and draft horses into the deal, you've got a job and a place to live. I'll foot the bill for supplies until you can make it pay."

"Without my wagon and horses, I won't have any way to leave, should I want to."

Fred grinned at her. "Unintended consequences."

After a moment's thought, Mattie said. "I don't know how to repay..."

"I got a hankering for doughnuts. Can you do something like that?"

Mattie looked at Fred, eyebrows raised, and then smiled. "They'll melt in your mouth."

"Then it's a done deal. That lady over there, bless her heart, couldn't make a doughnut if her life depended on it. When she tried, they looked like something stepped on a cow pile."

Mattie glanced at him. "What do you think, Coble?"

"Not for me to say, although I do think this old thief should pay for the horses." He was watching the two girls chase a small brown dog around the outside of the corral. They always seemed happy. "It might give you something to keep the girls busy with, washing dishes and busing tables. If it doesn't work out, you can always tell Fred to make his own damned doughnuts."

He turned to her and met her gaze for a moment. "It'll let you settle down and get your feet on the ground. Then you can decide what to do. Remember? Options? You've also got your nursing to fall back on."

"Wait. What did you say?" Fred whirled and looked at her. "You're a nurse? Any good at that?"

Mattie nodded. "Trained at Kentucky Baptist college. Even have a certificate."

"Well, I'll be damned. That's worth a hell of a lot more than—" Fred interrupted himself and looked at Tom Fallon who was nodding.

"See that little building attached to the café?" Fred

continued. "I'm envisioning a sign that says Infirmary on that."

"I don't like sick people so close to where we serve food, but I suppose if there's no connecting door inside it would be alright."

Continuing, she asked. "Does it have windows and doors in the back? Fresh air is important for healing."

She paused a moment, looking at Coble with a hint of moisture in her eyes. "One minute I'm destitute, a widow with two children to care for and little food. The next I've a chance at two businesses and a home. Just because one man rode by my campsite. And now I seem to have friends. It's a lot to take in."

After staring at Coble for a moment, she turned to Fred and stuck out her hand. "I'll do it, Mr. Curry. I'll need some help getting started and moved in."

"How long before you can make doughnuts?"

"Extra sugar?"

"Damned right."

She smiled. "I'll have to check the oven first, but I might have something by nightfall."

Fred was already stomping across the street toward her wagon. "Let's get moving."

"I never knew a chance at eating a doughnut could cause so much excitement." She was shaking her head with a smile.

"I've heard of ranch hands riding all day for doughnuts, or some call them bear sign." Coble said. "That alone will make your business thrive and bring suitors to your door every day."

"Suitors I do not need or want." Mattie lightly touched his arm. "You can be my first patient."

Amazed at the whirlwind of events happening

around him, he simply tipped his hat. "The arm is fine, Miss Mattie. I've some business to attend to. You'll be in good hands while I'm gone."

Another amazing thing was what he said next. "Don't get married off before I get back. Courtships are sudden in this country."

She didn't reply as he turned and walked toward his horse. He knew her gaze was boring holes in his back, and hopefully she wasn't reaching for a gun.

Chapter Nine

RIDING INTO JOPLIN FROM THE WEST, ALL COBLE could see was the smoke from the smelters that left most of the foliage along the narrow road covered with gray dust. It was a wonder anything would grow, having to wait for a flushing rain to clean the leaves. And it hadn't rained in a while.

Crossing a slow-running creek with water the color of old blood and smelling like rotten eggs, it wasn't hard to keep the paint's head up so he wouldn't drink. A good rule of thumb is don't drink water a horse won't drink. His horse didn't want to walk through this creek, much less drink it.

Surrounding most of the smelters and mine entrances were makeshift homes abounding in squalor. People lived in old wagons, tents, boxes, and all manner in between. Women were hanging freshly washed clothes on ropes strung between trees and hoops of the wagons. Children who should have been in school were rushing between tents, rolling barrel hoops and chasing dogs, surviving their situation as only children can do. They wouldn't know they were poor unless someone told them. But he was sure they knew hunger.

Between the hard labor and bad air of the mines, plus disease from contaminated water, most of their fathers would be dead by forty years old. Their mothers might last a bit longer. The children wouldn't fare much better. It was a hard life.

Unexpectedly, he thought of the twins and wanted their life to be better. Did Hard Times have a school? He'd have to ask.

The road weaved between dug mines and tall mounds of loose rock, a byproduct of the quest for lead ore. But the lead mines weren't the main focus for the mining companies. A byproduct of smelting lead gave them zinc, or jack as it was called, and it was being used in everything from making paint last longer to lining metal buckets so they don't rust. He hoped the innovation was worth the cost because it seemed they were ruining a large amount of land to achieve it.

He moved through all this mining splendor, eyes wide as a youngster seeing a circus the first time. Bustling people were like an erupting ant hill. How could he possibly find one man among all this? He'd been here not too long ago, but progress was moving everything forward at breakneck speed. Hardly anything looked familiar.

Tying his horse in front of the city marshal's office, he unlimbered his rifle from its scabbard. With this many people around, he didn't want the rifle stolen. Looking around, he was going to be really surprised if his horse was still there when he returned.

Trust was a luxury he'd lost a long time ago. Most

people were rushing from one point to another, going to or leaving work, and were much too busy to worry about him or borrowing his horse. But there were others who you learned to watch for. They were watching him, or any other target of opportunity. They stood out like a rock in a stream, with water rushing around them. One man stood out immediately, because he wore a black bowler hat on his abnormally large head. He looked like a clown in a broadcloth suit.

————

LC HAMILTON, the marshal of Joplin, Missouri was sitting at a wide, stained-pine desk fine enough to grace the office of the banker next door who made money off your money. He was caught mid drip, pouring a drink from a half-empty bottle of whiskey. The label was worn off, and from what Coble knew of him, he must refill bottles by the dozen. Like most desk-bound politicians, he was spreading out around the middle. His mustache sported more hair than his head, and his unwelcome glare bore no welcome.

"How's the shakedown business, LC?" Coble grinned at him. "Still stiffing the gamblers and whores for licenses and fees?"

"So, you're back again." LC gave him a baleful stare and then glanced around the room. None of the half dozen deputies standing around the room seemed to be listening. "You know how it is. If I throw all the whores and gamblers out of town, the miners will quit, and the city fathers would grease my skids and send me packing. That's providing they don't just hang me, of course. Everything serves a purpose."

Pausing a moment, he continued. "And I don't need you stomping around here rocking the boat and telling me my business."

He probably didn't know what a colloquialism was, so Coble didn't comment on them. If they were taken out of western lingo, they'd be back to grunts and pointing.

"Well then, I reckon you know why I'm here?" He took off his hat and wiped the headband while watching the marshal closely. "I'm sure you have the man located by now so we can pick him up."

"Yeah, I know why you're here. Don't know how you found out, but you're wasting your time. Tomlin Harp is long gone." LC was shaking his head.

"How would you know, unless he missed his fee?"

LC's gaze snapped up and then dropped to the desktop. "Now, that's just hurtful."

"Sorry," Coble said. He needed this man's help, not animosity. "I'm in a peckish mood today. The weather's still hot, and the air is foul. How did he get away?"

Moving from the front office to the back of the jail through a heavy door, he noticed the cells were made of iron bars with no cross pieces. Iron isn't as strong as you might think, which is why many jails were putting in flat-iron, riveted into squares about head size.

"See what that monster did?" They'd reached the end cell where the bars were bent to the side enough to allow someone the size of Tomlin Harp, or two of Coble, to pass through. "He ruined my whole cell."

"And that wasn't all," LC continued. "He picked up my jailer by the throat and snapped his neck like a twig."

"You knew the man was strong." His admonishment didn't help LC's mood. They should have guarded him better, but that horse was long gone, and the barn doors were swinging in the wind.

"Doesn't help much," LC said. "We ain't man killers like you. We try to keep the peace by being a little gentler on the reins than you would. If we're too stringent, it just runs off business."

"How's that working out for you?" He shook his head. It was all about business and money. "So no leads from around town? Anyone see him actually do it, other inmates?"

"We had a whore named Sally in the next cell. She didn't see anything."

"I'd like to talk to her, but aren't they all named Sally? I can't go around asking for Sally."

"Pretty much. Sally or Sadie." LC shrugged. "Nobody's talking. Like I said, he's long gone. He has no reason to stay here in the city. Kind of like you."

He gazed at the marshal for a moment. Seemed like the man was awfully anxious for him to leave. "So, do you have a murder warrant filed for killing your jailer?"

LC shook his head. "I do not. It wouldn't do any good. My jurisdiction ends with the city boundaries, and like I said, he's long gone."

Coble disagreed but didn't push the matter. If Tomlin Harp had a need, he'd stay close to his supply. If he'd kicked that need, there was no telling where he would go. At that point, all he could do was pull in his horns and wait—or just forget it. One of the banes of his existence, he was not good at forgetting.

Leaving his rifle with LC, he crossed the street to

the House of Lords. The three-story building told the story of Joplin just by being there. It was subterfuge at its finest. Sometimes called Jack's Palace, you'd think the name would refer to a man named Jack, but it did not. Jack was the nickname for zinc, a byproduct from smelting lead. It was often said that Joplin was the town that Jack built.

The first floor was a fancy restaurant, complete with potted plants, fancy tablecloths, and chandeliers. Anyone from bankers and mine owners to lowly cowhands and miners could be seen eating there...as long as they cleaned up and had the money. They even boasted a chef in the kitchen, and no spitting or smoking was allowed in the restaurant to compete with the fine aroma of the cuisine. Often a three-piece band of stringed instruments would add to the evening entertainment. No trumpets allowed.

A wide staircase led to the second story, a large room full of gambling tables and a bar running the length of the building. From the finest whiskey down to homemade rotgut, there was enough liquid courage flowing to make sure there was little chance in the games offered.

The third floor housed soiled doves intent on fleecing whatever money was left over from the gambling hall below. From what Coble had been told, nothing was off the table once you went to the third floor. As long as their fees were paid, often by gamblers on the second floor, little thought was given to age. The youngest brought the most money, followed by Asian people and Black people.

Crossing immediately to the staircase, he moved up to the gambling hall. There was little chance he'd find the man he looked for in this place, but he needed to start somewhere. Moving among the tables, side-stepping around people watching the roulette wheel and blackjack tables, he heard a piano playing softly.

Walking toward the sound, he knew it wasn't the Pianoman. This player was small, hands moving over the keys in a distracted manner, eyes glazed with unknown memories. Tomlin Harp, the Pianoman, would caress the keys as if they were made of bricks and his hands were hammers.

The crowd thinned around the gaming tables. Poker players hold a dim view of anyone peeking over their shoulders to see what cards they held. It was too easy to transmit the card faces to another player, signaling with an innocent three fingers against their vest, coughing into hands with one finger held aloft— the signals were only restricted by the imagination of the players involved.

Ladies of the evening flitted around the gaming floor and congregated at one end of the long bar. Their once-fine dresses were stained dull from constant smoke and dirt from the floor...those who wore dresses.

A dapper man sporting a bowler hat and garters to hold up his ruffled sleeves stepped in front of Coble and blocked his way. The man wore a pearl-handled storekeeper's pistol, called so because of the short barrel, in a conspicuous shoulder holster. The rig was one favored by gamblers for easy access while sitting at a table.

After looking Coble up and down, he said, "You can't be here."

Now that was odd. Maybe it was because of his

range clothes, or his less-than-pretty setup of pistols on his worn leather belt, or perhaps the skinning knife nestled in a scabbard at the small of his back. Coble gave him the benefit of the doubt.

Moving his vest to the side to show the marshal's badge, he shrugged. "I'm thinking you're wrong, friend."

The man's hand inched toward his shoulder holster, an awkward move while standing. "We have an agreement with LC. No law dogs on the second or third floor. You'll have to leave."

"Really?" Coble glanced around at the people watching their little play. "And if I don't? What? You'll run and tell on me like a snitch in grade school? You'll reach for that pistol?"

The man's hand grasped the pearl-handled pistol. "You'll leave or..."

Coble laid his pistol barrel alongside the man's ear, and the bowler hat followed the man crumpling to his knees. As he fell, Coble snatched his pretty pistol and laid it on a nearby table. Looking around, people quickly lost interest. Shaking his head, he headed for the doorway. He'd seen all he wanted anyway.

Returning to the ground floor, he stepped outside and looked up and down the street. He had a House of Lords appetite, maybe a large steak with some fancy sauce, but a beef and beans budget. Spying a café sign down the street and across the way, he dodged ore wagons, horses, pull carts, and people walking and running to move toward the eatery. Two ore wagons were plugging up the street while the drivers engaged in a screaming match complete with bullwhips popping at each other. In the surrounding crowd, money was changing hands as people bet on the outcome. Entertainment at its finest.

Finding an empty table was easy at this time of day. He'd just settled in when a familiar voice sounded behind him.

"Well, as I live and breathe, if it isn't Coble Bray."

He smiled and purposefully looked her up and down, part and parcel to the flirting they'd done the last time he saw her. White-blonde hair framed corn-flower blue eyes, a testament to her German heritage, with maybe a Swede in the woodpile, she was a little thinner than he remembered. Although her chest would still enter a room well ahead of the rest of her.

"Mary Neumann, it's always nice to see you." He pointed to a chair. "Would you join me?"

Glancing over her shoulder toward the kitchen, she held up a menu. "I can for just a moment, but I'll need to take your order." She hesitated a moment. "Or should I order for you?"

He handed the menu back to her. "Surprise me."

Walking to the kitchen to place the order, she glanced back at him, laughing as he watched her. She knew he would be. Having helped nurse him back to health after a gunshot wound, she probably knew as much about his anatomy as his late wife. And that thought dampened his spirits. Maria was barely in her grave. His recovery from that ordeal seemed to have highs and lows.

"Lost in thought?"

Startled, he flinched. Mary had returned to sit in front of him. Better her than someone intent on doing him harm. He wouldn't have seen them either. Age and circumstance seemed to be dulling his senses at an alarming rate. He needed to be sharp as a tack.

"It's a habit lately. How have you been?"

Shrugging, she glanced toward the kitchen again. "Just fair. This was the only job I could find, other than a standing invitation to work the third floor of that monstrosity down the street. I can't see myself doing that."

"Good. I'd hate to see you go down that road. There's no good ending to it. No matter where you are, if you need help, just send word to me. I'll do what I can. Surely you know that."

Sitting, she favored her left side, and he noticed a faint bruise on her cheek. Furtive glances were stolen toward the kitchen door. "What's going on, Mary? Are you hurt?"

"I don't want to burden you with my trouble."

And, of course, she did.

She studied him a moment before continuing. "I didn't realize the farm we had was so far in debt, so when it sold I didn't get much out of it. There wasn't anything going on in Hard Times, so I tried my luck here in Joplin." She snorted, looking around. "So far it's all been bad. I've never seen so many people working for so little."

"And the bruises? I see you're favoring your side?" Even as he said it, a swarthy man with slicked-back hair stuck his head out the kitchen.

"Mary," the man shouted. "Clean up those tables."

She sighed, making no move to get up. "You know, the madam over at that fancy hotel offered me my own room, a maid to clean up after gentleman callers, pretty dresses, clean sheets, and all the hot water baths I could stand in a day." Her glance took in the kitchen door. "Sometimes that doesn't sound so bad."

Just the sight of the cook and, he presumed, manager of the place, put Coble on a slow boil. Without much thought, he commented. "There is another choice."

She batted her eyes at him. "You going to take me out of here? Save the damsel in distress? I'd go in a heartbeat, you know."

"After what I know you've been through and knowing just how strong you are, I doubt you need much saving. Maybe just a hand up." He watched her a moment. "There might be a solution, but it would be back in Hard Times."

She raised her eyebrows, still watching that door. "I'm listening."

He told her about Mattie Hurst and her twins taking over the café. "Since she's also a trained nurse, she's going to open up a little infirmary next door. Both places are owned by Fred Curry, so it kinda works out. I have a feeling she could use some help."

"I'm curious." Her gaze met his, her flirting banter thrown away. "Are you part of this solution?"

Well, that was direct. But then, she always was. "I don't know, Mary. Things have changed."

He'd just finished telling her about Maria's death when the cook banged through the kitchen door heading their way.

She was leaning on her elbows with her chin on her hands, looking at him with tears in her eyes. "I'm so sorry, Coble. I feel like an idiot now."

The man went to grab her arm when Coble booted

him in his right knee. With a yelp, the cook stepped back. "What the hell, mister? You got no call..."

"Shut up." Coble's voice was sharper than intended. He didn't get up, though his hand was on his pistol. "Mary, what does this man owe you for wages?"

"He owes me for two weeks, so I'd say about ten dollars." She gave him an amused look, ignoring the cook. "Did I just quit?"

"You did." He gave the man his full attention. "Mister, my name is Coble Bray. I'm a Deputy US Marshal and a very good friend to this lady. While I'm sure that doesn't mean much to you, it will if I go see LC Hamilton and tell him you're poisoning people with bad beef. I can't imagine what the fines and fees would be for that. He'd probably have to hire someone just to write them all up."

"Or." He shrugged. "You can reach in your pocket and give this lady a shiny new twenty-dollar gold piece for services rendered. If you don't do that, I can't imagine how bad the remainder of your day is going to be."

Since the cook was a weak-chinned and greasy sort of man, Coble wasn't surprised when he reached in his pocket, paid Mary, and stalked off. He was wishing the man had made an issue of it.

Keeping a weather eye on that kitchen door, he spoke to Mary. "Do you have a way to get to Hard Times?"

"I suppose I can rent a buckboard and horse, then leave it at Fred's. When that happens, someone usually throws some freight in the back for delivery. That's how I got here. Will you be coming with me?"

Shaking his head, Coble finally took his attention

away from the man lurking in the kitchen. Since he was the only customer at the moment, he guessed the man didn't have much to do. "Sorry. Much as I'd like to, I'm looking for a man here in Joplin, so it's best if you go alone. It's a well-traveled road, so I think you'll be safe enough. I'll wait here until you're ready to leave."

"Thank you. I got here all by myself, I reckon I can make it back. It may be first thing in the morning. But I'll do it." Her gaze was still watery. "Will I see you there?"

He shrugged. "Man's gotta eat."

"Yeah, and you'll probably need doctoring soon. You have a knack for that."

Chapter Ten

THERE WAS A STABLE JUST DOWN THE STREET FROM the café, so he headed there to put up his horse. His rifle was left under the watchful eye of LC Hamilton. Hopefully he wouldn't fine it for loitering and then sell it to pay the fine.

The hostler was a dour-looking man with a handlebar mustache and brown stains on his pants. His shirt sleeves were torn off showing arms with bulging muscles from swinging a hammer all day beating iron into submission. Thinking of Fred Curry in Hard Times, Coble wondered if the profession turned out men of sour disposition. Or maybe it was losing battles with kicking mules while trying to shoe them.

The main street was a kaleidoscope of poor planning. The stable was rife with all the smells of housing and feeding animals. The men cleaning out the stalls of straw and manure would shovel it out the back door or front door, whichever was closest. The chef at the restaurant a few doors down was trying to keep bad smells at bay to entice people to come in and try his fare. There was a bakery across the street adding the smell of fresh bread to the mix.

Coble longed for the prairie where the only bad smells were the horse he rode and his unwashed clothes. A conundrum with no clear solution.

Working on a hunch, he turned and made his way down Fourth Street into a different world. Where Main Street looked substantial with buildings of brick and mortar, this part of town was all ramshackle buildings seeming on the verge of collapse. Gray, weather-beaten wood seemed to be the material of choice. The dirt of the street was hard packed by crowds moving between the buildings with all the tightness of herds of cattle moving through a narrow pass.

And someone followed him. It was easy to pick up, even on crowded streets. His shadow was a well-setup man, dressed neater than most around him. He stopped when Coble stopped, moved when he moved, always taking great care to appear not to watch him. The most striking thing was he wore no hat. Everyone had some kind of covering on their head from miner's hats to trail-worn Stetsons.

The street was lined with whorehouses, washhouses, opium houses, and eateries so dirty he wouldn't take a dog inside, all packed with customers clamoring for their services. This was a twenty-four-hour town, with the mines running around the clock. Flop houses would rent beds by the shift, one man vacating in time for another to come in and sleep. Once again, he had to wonder why he needed to frequent these places hunting a man local law had little interest in.

On impulse, he turned into a shack fronted by a sign lettered in Chinese. He couldn't read it of course, but the acrid smell coming out of it was advertisement enough. Low benches lined the walls where people sat in stupor, pulling smoke from long pipes, and then laying back to visit worlds unknown or more likely, no world at all. There were days when that might seem attractive.

Trying to see into the dark corners, he asked. "Anyone speak English in here?"

"I speak it very well." The speaker was a shirtless and barefoot Chinaman stepping from a shadowy doorway, wearing trousers and a suit coat. "I am Jung. May I help you, Marshal?"

Well that was polite, though he may have started to feel giddy from the smoke filling the room. "How do you know I'm a marshal?"

The man smiled, and somehow it made him look less friendly. "You look like a marshal. Perhaps you work for LC? It is early to collect fees. I've already paid this month and have no wish to pay again."

"I don't have any connection to LC. I'm looking for a man." Coble went on to describe Tomlin Harp and how dangerous he was. "He's been known to use opium, maybe have an addiction. Have you seen anyone like this?"

"I have not." The man showed no interest, his voice disinterested and flat.

Not turning his back on the man, he scanned the room once more. A Black man and woman were huddled around a pipe in a corner, and I hoped their quest for free land didn't end here. The rest looked like miners still wearing their hats with the candle and reflector. He couldn't begin to catalog all the different nationalities sitting around. The town was a true melting pot of people. Knowing the existence they endured, he could hardly blame them for this divergence.

Before turning for the door, he asked. "Would you tell me if you had seen this man?"

Jung shrugged with the same smile that never met his eyes. "I would not."

"Well, at least you're honest. Thanks, I think."

"You should know our clientele prefer that no one knows where they are or what they're doing. It's a simple courtesy."

"Why?" I cocked my head at him. "It's not illegal."

The eloquent shrug again. "But still..."

He was right. It was frowned upon. With a sigh, Coble headed toward the door. The hard heels of his boots must have beat a cadence on the wooden floor because when he stopped at the threshold of the door, a club swished through the air at what would have been his next step. He had stopped to look at a poster tacked to the wall. Seems there was a fair coming to town with trick shooters, shell games, and miraculous feats on horseback.

He stepped on through the doorway with his gun drawn while the off-balance club-wielder was looking for somewhere else to be. The surprise attack foiled, he had little stomach to continue face-to-face.

"Looking to collect the reward?" Coble's voice was hard. "Why don't you tell Harp to come see me himself?"

The hatless man dropped his club, raised his

hands, and backed away. When Coble started after him he felt a gun barrel poke him in the back.

"Not here." Jung said. "Bad for business."

The attacker faded into the crowd, but Coble had seen something in his eyes just before he backed away. There was fear showing there, but he was looking at the Chinaman. He holstered his pistol and turned. Jung held an old LeMat Horse Pistol in both hands, index finger on the trigger.

Coble had used one of those pistols himself and knew the trigger was a might squirrelly—meaning it might jam solid and not fire at all, or it might fire the pistol if a cool breeze crossed it. There was a shotgun shell in one barrel, a pistol ball in the other. Sometimes they both went off at once, which would be a painful and abrupt way to end all his troubles.

"A word of advice, Marshal?"

Looking at the man, and then glancing at the gun pointing at his belly, he wondered if he could trust anything Jung said. "Never hurts to listen."

"This man Harp you are looking for is not the one you should worry about. He is a mere puppet. There is a much harder taskmaster in town. I have seen it in my own country. It is like an evil plant that grows unnoticed. It has roots everywhere and once established, cannot be stopped."

Well, there was a riddle if I'd ever heard one. Tipping his hat to Jung, he walked away. One thing he knew for certain. He'd not find the Pianoman by knocking on doors. The man likely only came out at night with the other cockroaches. But the word would be out. He'd know Coble was looking. And a puppet?

That rang true...he was a puppet before. Who pulled his strings now?

Chapter Eleven

SEVERAL DAYS WERE SPENT MOVING THROUGH THE streets, walking into little three-table bars that served homemade whiskey and dubious food. It was dark in these places, and Coble never trusted food or drink he couldn't see. Oftentimes, he imagined the back door slamming when he entered the front. He'd have to be extremely lucky to catch anyone this way, much less the Pianoman. On the bright side, there was another shadow watching his every move, but that was the plan.

Eventually Coble found himself in the city marshal's office. Being a man who enjoyed wide-open spaces, he was more tired of the city than he thought possible or cared to admit. There was simply too much humanity, everyone pushing and shoving for their little piece of real estate. He was told there were nearly eight-thousand people in the city, and he had to amend his opinion of the marshal and his deputies.

How can you protect and serve that many people from all the grifters, cardsharps, and thieves? All you could do was put bandages on wounds that were days old, while staying firmly out of touch with any other mayhem troubling the city. Proprietors and managers must take care of their own problems.

"Marshal Bray. I'm glad you stopped by." LC's pompous voice brought him out of his reverie while waving a paper at him. "I have a notice from the city council that asks politely for you to leave town. I agree with their assessment and want you gone. We don't need your kind of trouble in Joplin."

His kind of trouble? How many kinds of trouble are there? Being a curious sort, he said "I've started no trouble. All I've done is react to people trying to do me harm, half of them probably work for you."

"You've been bothering businesses all week." LC shook his head, ignoring the barb. "You were abusive to a restaurant owner."

Coble couldn't believe the man had complained. Maybe he wanted a refund of his licenses and fees. "He was withholding wages and abusing his waitress. I merely told him to pay up and stop."

"That's your side of the story." LC consulted a notebook in front of him. "You also disrupted a Chinese businessman down on Fifth Street. He was very distressed."

"I believe it was Fourth Street. Jung didn't look like a man who'd be distressed by anything, especially since he pulled a gun on me. Go down there and breathe the air, it will calm your temper, LC. Besides, I just asked questions that your deputies should have already asked."

The city marshal continued with his litany of

complaints. "You also assaulted an innocent gambler in the House of Lords."

"Really." Coble shook his head at this. "The man reached for a gun. He's lucky I didn't shoot him."

"Nevertheless, all things considered, there is no reason for you to be here. You are a disruption."

LC scowled and slammed another paper on the desktop. "I hate to do this. It pains me."

"Then my advice is don't do it." Coble interrupted.

Figuring the man took acting lessons, LC's gaze was filled with glee while his voice seemed regretful. "Here is an order from Judge Wampler, the federal judge over in Carthage. That's our county seat if you don't know. Your appointment as Deputy US Marshal has been revoked."

Lifting the paper from the tabletop, Coble looked at the signature. The name was familiar, and he had seen the signature on warrants. For a moment he was speechless. "I'll have a talk with Judge Wampler next time I'm over that way. In the meantime, I'll consider this a forgery."

LC glanced at his deputies and then at Coble. "I'll need to collect your badge."

"You will not." At Coble's level gaze, LC pushed away from his desk to get some distance between them.

"You have no authority to confront anyone. No arrest powers."

Coble shrugged, keeping his temper in check. "Sometimes authority is something taken, not given. I'll consult with the judge, not you."

"Keep the damned badge then. It's not going to make any difference, and it's illegal now for you to use it. The fact of the matter is the man you want is not in town. He broke out of jail and left. There's no warrant for him, and no reason for you to pursue him. I want you gone by morning."

Coble retrieved his rifle before he answered. "Tomlin Harp killed your jailer. You admitted that, and yet there is no warrant? Are you being paid to look the other way?"

The insult was deliberate and a shot in the dark. Most men would have been mad, but LC was a politician and simply stared back at him. Asked and answered. Berating him was a useless endeavor. There was something at play here that he knew nothing about, and one more reason he hated being in town. Out on the prairie things were simpler, even if often more dangerous.

This was LC's town. He and the town council were supposedly the voice of the people and could run it as they wanted. The men stared at each other for a long moment, and then Coble capitulated. He brought his heels together with a click and gave a slight, mocking bow. Time would tell.

It took a moment to realize he could no longer legally carry the badge. But surprisingly, the regret was minimal. The times he'd put it away for various reasons were too many to count. When he thought about it, leaving town wasn't bad advice. Leaving the Marshal's Service might be even better news.

Maybe it was angst, or just a bad temper, but LC's deputies still blocked the door. He didn't ask them to move, not with the smirks evident on their faces. The Winchester is a heavy weapon. He sunk the barrel halfway into the first man's gut, bending him over into a retching bow. That was going to be a mess to clean up.

The second deputy was bringing up a pistol when the butt of that rifle connected with his jaw. Coble could have shot him, but he was a deputy, so he caught a break.

Chapter Twelve

IT WAS A DAY OF SURPRISES. STEPPING AROUND THE mess on the floor and onto the boardwalk fronting the town marshal's office, a hatless man stood before him. The last time he'd seen this man he'd tried to take Coble's head off with a club.

The hatless man held up his left hand, palm out. The right hand rested on the plain, smooth walnut handle of his holstered pistol. "Please. No trouble. Mr. Adair has invited you to lunch at the dining room over at the House of Lords."

Coble asked. "Would you care to explain to me why you tried to whack me with a club the other day?"

After a moment's hesitation, the man said. "Can't really come up with an answer that won't get me shot."

Coble chuckled. "Well, at least that's an honest answer."

Holding his rifle on the man, Coble asked. "Who is Adair, and why would he extend that invitation?"

The young man smiled. "It would be advantageous for you, sir."

He thought for a moment. There was no reason to meet with anyone, especially since he'd been temporarily defrocked. "And who might this Mr. Adair be?"

The man's eyes got round in surprise. Apparently no one had asked him that question before. "He's a businessman."

"And your name?" Silence stretched a moment. "You do have a name, don't you?"

"Samuelson."

Samuelson was a discordant note, a sense Coble always paid attention to, and was seemingly unperturbed at being held at gunpoint. The man carried a sidearm positioned for a cross draw, or a belly gun as some called it. Unlike an amateur, his hand didn't stray to the pistol, and his gaze was dispassionate. Most men often touch their pistol, maybe for reassurance. This man was calm, even though he'd missed his try to spread Coble's brains all over the boardwalk. He didn't seem nonplussed about it.

"I'm curious. Why did you run away from me at the Chinaman's place?"

Emotion flicked across his face a moment, a slight twitch of his lips, and then he shrugged. "The advantage was lost."

"Well, Samuelson. Whatever line of work you are in, get out of it. You can't win by running away."

Calmly meeting Coble's gaze, the man finally smiled. "Your reputation precedes you. I'm still alive because I withdrew from the field. So in a sense, I won the engagement."

It seemed to be a day for unimpressing people.

Maybe he'd at least get a steak out of it, if nothing else. "Alright, let's go see what this Mr. Adair wants."

————

THEY APPROACHED a table in the back corner of the restaurant, passing the fake plants and tables with fine linen and cutlery laid out. The plates gathering dust looked to be china with pink roses etched into the porcelain, highlighted by a candelabra on each table.

The table they came to appeared to be a working space, and there wasn't anything fancy about it, unlike the man holding court behind it. Coble wasn't about to stand in front of him, hat in hand, like an itinerant looking for a job. He immediately took a seat across from the man he assumed was Mr. Adair.

Samuelson cleared his throat, appearing agitated a moment. Maybe sitting wasn't allowed, but he'd already made his assessment of the situation and the man before him.

Samuelson finally spoke. "Mr. Adair, this is Coble Bray."

Adair gave a small smile. "Thank you, Jonas. Well done. You may wait with the men."

A curious thing. Several men lounged next to the outside wall and a back door, leaning back in chairs on two legs, or sitting with their arms across the back of their chair—posed nonchalance. All wore the little black bowler hats he'd seen on the gambler. The jauntiness, or set of the hat, would be a study in itself.

"Why doesn't Jonas have a hat?"

The reply was instant. "Because he hasn't earned it yet."

Coble contemplated that a moment. "If he'd caved my head in outside the Chinaman's place, would he get a hat?"

"He would, indeed. So far, he's not done well on his assignments."

Adair sat, staring at Coble.

Coble was content to let the silence stretch out. He knew the technique and had used it many times when questioning someone. Most people can't stand the silence of unspoken words and try to fill that void. All you have to do is listen.

Finally, Adair tired of the game and broke the impasse. "I wonder if you might be interested in a job, Mr. Bray. It seems you've been dismissed from your duties as a Deputy US Marshal. I can always use a man with your particular talents."

Coble hoped curiosity wouldn't get him killed, like the proverbial cat, but what he needed was information. "I have a wonder of my own. I wonder how you knew that, given I was just informed by LC."

Adair's smile was condescending. "Mr. Bray, we already own most of the judges around here, and our town marshal is very cooperative. He sees the advantage of someone running things. Wide-open towns like Joplin need control. There is much money to be made by controlling the whorehouses and gambling halls. We provide this service."

Well, there it was. I'd heard of such in the big cities. There were crime bosses in New York, Chicago, and many other cities, Kansas City included. They were not a benevolent society. "You used the word control twice in the same statement. I assume that's what this is all about?"

"Of course. Very astute of you." Adair flicked ash from his cigar.

Coble assumed it was an affectation, since he'd never seen the man draw on it. Pushing for information, he continued. "You keep saying we, but you don't look like royalty. Just who are you referring to?"

"We"—he emphasized the word—"are an organization. We specialize in protection from lawless elements for a small percentage of a business's profits. You can call us the Bowlers. It's as good a name as any." With that, he motioned someone forward.

Coble wasn't surprised when Tomlin Harp came to stand beside Adair, although it made the hair on his arms stand up. It was a sickening feeling knowing the Pianoman had been standing close. He didn't know there was a puzzle to be solved, but the pieces were coming together. If Harp killed the jailer and then disappeared into the underbelly of Joplin, he had help. And he'd already earned his bowler hat.

The two men traded stares a moment before Adair broke in.

"I am intrigued. I'll confess, I thought you'd be more upset, Mr. Bray. This is the man you've been looking for, after all. He's now my right-hand man and is very useful. I take a dim view of my employees being harmed."

"Oh, I'm sure he's very adept at your kind of skullduggery." Coble shrugged, gaze never leaving Harp. "It makes sense. For a man to escape jail, kill the jailer whom I understand was an old and feeble man by the way, and then to have the city marshal shrug it off? I figured dirty fingers must be stirring the pot. Seems I've found the source of the spoiled soup."

Adair smiled. "Very good. I like that analogy. So, what do you say? Let bygones be bygones? I am prepared to pay you very well."

Coble resisted the urge to look, wondering who else was standing behind him. It wouldn't make sense for them to try something in a public restaurant, but criminals weren't always known for their brightness of thought. "Sorry. I could not work for you, no matter the amount of money. And I prefer my dirt to be of the honest kind, fruits of my own labor...so to speak. Your fruit always has a stink to it, no matter how bright and shiny it looks."

Harp couldn't wait. When he spoke, it was with all the emotion of grinding your heel on a bug. "I'm going to enjoy killing you. You don't have the protection of being a marshal anymore."

"That's funny." Coble gave him his best smile. "To the average citizen, I'm transparent, like I'm never there. That's the way it should be. And to folks like you? I don't think the badge being around is much of a deterrent. You're going to do whatever you want. Sooner or later, you'll pay the piper. Whether it's from me or someone else doesn't matter."

Coble's hand rested lightly on the butt of his pistol. "The removal of my badge, if it sticks, doesn't change what you've done, what you are. And you may kill me, but you'll have lead poisoning before you get it done. I will end you."

Raising his hand, Adair said. "Not now, Harp. Let it go. We'll discuss Mr. Bray later."

Adair paused a moment. "I'd hoped for a better outcome with you, Mr. Bray. I assume you can leave town on your own, or shall I have someone assist you?"

The man's smile never made it to his cold eyes.

There was a time when he wouldn't have let that insult pass, and bullets would have been flying. He was older now, so he'd call it self-preservation. Turning his head, Coble caught Samuelson's glance, realizing the irony. Samuelson had run from him earlier. Now Coble was doing it. To himself, he'd call his own withdrawal a tactical retreat not running, but the results were the same. He shrugged at the man. Samuelson was right. You take victories when you can, defeat when it's handed to you, and if you're lucky, live to fight another day. The main thing is to avoid being the fly under a swatter. He was alive. He'd take the win.

"Oh, I'm leaving. As for working for you? I don't feel compelled to set myself on fire just to light your path. And as you say, I no longer have authority. You appear to own the town, Adair. I can acknowledge that. If you have the city fathers and law enforcement convinced that this is the way to go, then that's their prerogative, and they deserve what they get. And I never buck a stacked deck. I'll just wait until I can deal the cards in a new game. We'll see how it goes."

"A very sensible view, Mr. Bray."

It was sensible but a bitter pill. Standing, he glanced at Adair's men, who'd wandered closer to the table. All held shotguns. His own rifle was nonchalantly pointing at Tomlin Harp's belly. If someone started shooting, it would be like a ten-man knife fight in a two-hole outhouse.

He met Harp's gaze. "And just from a westerner's viewpoint? That little hat looks ridiculous."

With that, he backed toward the door and took a big breath of what passed for fresh air outside. Even

laced with smoke from the nearby smelters, the
stables, and raw sewage running in the street, it was
better than the air inside. And he still didn't get that
steak.

Chapter Thirteen

ADAIR GAZED TOWARD THE FRONT OF THE restaurant, watching everything, seeing nothing, his mind wandering a moment. Most of the buffoons in these boom towns were all about power and strength and, lately, a fast gun stylized by stories in the newspapers and dime novels. He knew they were far from accurate.

The top dog was always the strongest, at least until now. Things were changing all over the country. Now things were done, and money made, by who you know and what influence they could bring to bear. Politicians could be bought and public officials influenced to bring about policy for the best advantage to those skirting the law. The average citizen couldn't care less as long as they weren't involved. No one cares if you tax a whore and gamblers. Businesses pay to be left alone, and then part of that money goes to councilmen and bankers who allow the contracts they are told to, and then other businesses pay for the privilege of getting that contract. Money in and money out. The organized crime bosses would have their fingers in all of it.

He knew this problem would be coming up. Most men would have been involved in a shoot-out with the marshal. That was old school. Adair simply let it be known what his wishes were. A message to a friendly judge in Carthage, friendly as long as the money kept coming his way, and the marshal's teeth were pulled. A message to the town marshal, and LC gave the good marshal Bray his walking papers. Problem solved. Now, if Coble Bray died, it was just another body added to those being hauled off by the cart load every morning. Nobody would care.

But Coble Bray had surprised him. He'd been told the man was a shoot first, explain later type of marshal. Quick to anger and take chances. He'd prepared for that.

This would work out better than any confrontation with the marshal. Once Adair gave the word, someone would simply step out of an alley some night and end his life with as little fanfare as possible, simply a chess piece removed from the board.

Once the ex-marshal left the building, Adair motioned to Harp. "Mr. Harp, I'll retire to my home for the evening. How about you grab a bottle of the bar's finest, go upstairs, and pick out a couple of ladies to entertain us? They need to be fresh and clean and as young as possible. Think you can take care of that?"

Harp looked at his boss for a moment. "As you wish. I'll be along shortly."

———

AFTER ADAIR LEFT, Harp turned to three men standing by the back wall. "You." He pointed to the man on the right. "I want to know every place Coble Bray goes. Follow him until I say something different."

The man sneered at Harp. "You ain't our boss."

Harp grabbed the man around the neck and lifted him from the floor, pinning him against the wall. Within seconds, the man was dead, neck snapped, feet twitching as he slid down the wall.

"You." He pointed at the next man. "Same job."

"Got it, boss," the man said, and left through the back door.

The third man was gone, as were all the other men. Harp stood alone, contemplating the turn of events. Although he wanted Coble Bray dead just on general principle, it wasn't a burning desire. There were other games to be played now. Adair was weak and would soon be under Harp's thumb or dead.

With that thought, he moved up the stairs to the third floor. He'd heard some new girls had been brought in, and they were young. Provided they signed their agreement to pay fees, their age didn't matter. Most were starving on the street or had run away from home. It didn't take much incentive to get them to sign papers. The promise of food and shelter was usually enough, along with a blade gently caressing their backs as they signed.

LC and Adair liked to put on a front of legality. Tomlin Harp smiled to himself. That would end soon enough.

IT HAD BEEN a week since Sally walked from the town jail Tomlin Harp had escaped from. Returning to work on the upper floor of the House of Lords was a mistake. Harp had found her and used her on two more occasions, each time with more force. She'd taken to wearing high collar dresses and long sleeves to hide the bruises.

She felt sick when Harp walked into the small parlor of the third floor, motioning her over to the door.

"What do you want, Harp?" Her voice was a rusty rumble of damaged vocal cords.

He reached out and pulled her to him. "You know where Adair lives?"

"I do."

Looking around, his gaze settled on a young girl. "Clean up that young piece and bring her there right away. Couple bottles of whiskey wouldn't hurt."

"No laudanum?"

He gave her a hard look. "Don't need that anymore."

She tried to pull away. "Why me, Harp? I ain't all that pretty. There's plenty of willing women on this floor."

"Yeah, that's so. But you can take it. I don't have to be careful with you."

With that he released her and stalked away, amazingly light on his feet for such a big man. She'd once marveled at his size, actually taken pleasure in it, but that didn't last. He was brutal.

He'd kill her, she knew that. Maybe not this time, but soon. It was getting worse each time. She looked around the parlor, at what her life had become. No money. No way out. Be used hard and then die.

She wouldn't do what she was told this time, nor tell the young girl to go to Adair's. She had a special dress, one she was saving for a dance or maybe church if she could dodge the lightning bolts. Some whores even got married to lonely miners or cattlemen, but she knew that would never happen with her. The scars were too deep.

Dressed in her finest, she left the building by the back stairs, dodging the refuse, rats, and feral dogs. It was only a few minutes before she came to the Chinaman's door. She had just enough money.

Standing slump-shouldered before him, she hadn't said a word before, with a knowing look, he led her into a back room. "What is it you wish?"

She finally met his gaze. "I'm tired. Used up. Tomlin Harp will kill me sooner or later. I want it to end." Shrugging, tears came to her eyes. "I just want to drink a potion, drift away, and never come back. No pain. No regrets. I'm ready to go home."

"I've heard this is a service you supply." Taking a wad of cash from her pocket, she shoved it toward him. "Please. I can't take it anymore."

The Chinaman took the money. When she sat on the cot, he finally spoke. "What is your name?"

"Sally. Not that it matters. I don't have money for you to put that on a tombstone."

"Sally." He shrugged. "I think half the whores on Fourth Street are named Sally. Do you mind if I use you first? You're still a beautiful woman. If you don't care if you live or die, why not give someone the pleasure of your body for a while?"

"You misunderstand. I do care." She finally shrugged, her gaze dull. "You'll have to ignore all the bruises. There's something wrong with my left arm, he may have broken it. So, potion first. Then do what you want. Just no pain."

He gazed at her a moment, finally nodding. "What if I could offer you a life with no pain, no danger or intimidation? Something close to normal?"

It was her turn to look into his eyes, finally giving a skeptical shrug. "Do you know how many promises men make whores?"

"I can imagine. With me, you wouldn't be a whore. And you may not realize this, but some men keep their promises."

"What makes you think Harp won't kill you? The man is an animal."

The Chinaman smiled. "I have met your Mr. Harp and also Mr. Adair. I believe their days are numbered."

She perked up for a moment. "All our days are numbered. Why do you think theirs are?"

"I met the man who will kill them."

Sally gazed around the dull room, and then back at the Chinaman. "I'd like to live long enough to see that happen."

"As you wish."

———

TOMLIN HARP MOVED up the steps of the two-story home, one of the finest in Joplin. The wraparound veranda was solid with no loose boards, and he could smell fresh paint. He wondered if the original owner, probably a mine owner or banker, was buried out back. More likely, they'd been invited to disappear.

A large man stepped from the shadows, placing his hand on Harp's chest. "You got business here?"

In a move abnormally quick, Harp took hold of the man's arm, bending it downward and off his chest, until he heard the crack of a bone. His other hand crushed the man's neck before he could cry out. Within a minute, the guard was limp and tossed over the porch rail into a flower bed.

Straightening his coat, Harp opened the door and stepped into the house.

"Did you see my new guard outside? He's the only man I've seen who's as large as you." Adair was sitting in the parlor on a padded and ornate love seat just to the left of the main entry with a glass of whiskey and a cigar. "Took you long enough to get here, and I don't see girls or whiskey. It's early in your employment to be failing me. Perhaps you'd like to leave and try again?"

Harp looked around at the ornate opulence of the room. He doubted he could ever get used to it. His own tastes ran to seedier places. Bringing his attention back to Adair, he said, "They should be along shortly. First, we have important things to discuss. Are we alone?"

The crime boss laughed. "Of course, except for the guard I mentioned. I gave the boys the night off. Otherwise, they'd want to share the women. I don't like to share."

"Neither do I." Harp moved toward the man, holding a long-bladed knife against his pant leg. "Please tell me where you keep all your records. You know the ones I want. Who owes you money, and how much? I especially need to know which businesses are paying you. Judges? Bankers?"

"I'm afraid that's information you can't have, and you don't need. What you need to do is leave." Adair sat up straight and then reached for a pistol sitting on a side table. The knife pinned his hand as he shrieked in pain.

"So, tell me," Harp said in a calm voice devoid of inflection. He may as well have been talking about the weather. "All of it."

Adair tried to pull his hand free, but the pain was too much. "I won't tell you anything. My men will kill you for this."

"Oh, you'll tell me. People always tell me what I want." Harp smiled. "And you don't have men anymore."

Hours later, he pulled Adair through the house by his hair. Leaving him in the street, the body would be picked up by the cart that passed by every day, picking up refuse. Until then it served as a warning. There was new leadership in town. By the time Adair's bosses in KC knew what was going on, Harp would be too powerful for them to do anything about it.

The next question was where was the whore Sally? She was supposed to bring whiskey and a young girl. That was something he shared with Adair. Thinking of it, he knew his addiction for young girls was a substitute for the laudanum. But it didn't matter, there were plenty of both, and he could afford it now.

Chapter Fourteen

COBLE HAD SEEN BETTER DAYS, BUT LEAVING THE foul air of the mining town was a soothing balm for the spanking he'd taken. He paused to take a deep, clean breath and was pretty sure his horse did too. He'd learned long ago that you don't always win every encounter. Every lawman has a list in his head of the people, or circumstances, which got away. LC, Adair, and Harp. An unholy trinity. He could go against them, guns blazing, and likely end the same way. There was a cost versus benefit aspect to it. The situation rankled, but there wasn't much he could do about it, at least for now. It'd been a few days since he'd been to Hard Times, and he was looking forward to visiting friends, getting a decent meal, and good night's sleep. It was time to regroup and reassess.

All things considered, he did keep an eye on his back trail, not forgetting Tomlin Harp. He seemed a man with a grudge, and Coble knew the man would not just let things go. If Adair thought he could keep Harp in line, he was sadly mistaken.

Lost in thought, not a good place to be for a man traveling alone, he nearly missed the deep-set gouge in the trail. It looked as if a heavy wagon had abruptly turned and the wheels dug into the ground. Glancing in the direction the tracks indicated, there was a small grove of trees a few hundred yards distant. The trail was as fresh as his curiosity.

From a distance he could see a heavy wagon, much like the one Mattie Hurst had used. It had once been pulled by a brace of oxen, but a closer inspection saw them lying on the ground. One still kicked sporadically. Wary of an ambush, he circled the small grove to make sure no one waited for him. All he found was a trail of two horses leading to the south. By the depth and distance apart of their hoof prints, those horses were stepping out like they were trying to grab some distance in a hurry.

Riding to the wagon, it was worse than he expected. He was expecting mayhem, not murder. Oxen are hard to kill. It looked as if the shooters must have reloaded a couple of times to account for all the bullet holes in the animals' hides. Why their animosity was taken out on dumb animals was a mystery. Ammunition wasn't cheap.

A man sat leaning against a tree, presiding over the bodies of a woman and small boy. Dressed in what we called Sunday-go-to-meeting clothes of a ruffled white shirt and black coat, he looked to have been torn from a far gentler life. Tears coursed down his mahogany face as he stared at Coble with an anguished expression.

Coble sat on his horse a moment, studying the camp—reading the story. By their bullet wounds, it was obvious the woman and child were dead. The woman's clothes were gone, except for one laced up shoe and stocking. She was a beautiful woman, even in death. He wondered why the man hadn't covered her body. He did not want to wonder what had gone on here but couldn't stop his mind from doing it.

Staring into the distance a moment, Coble sighed. It was a sadness seen all too often. Nothing could stop evil men from doing what came natural to them. There were no constraints. Men trying to enforce the law, or any kind of rules-for-the-road, couldn't be standing behind the nearest tree when you need them. Often they are miles away. Men of the cloth can preach against evil, telling people in great detail about how to recognize it, but cannot stop it.

There was nothing to be done against people trying to do harm, except defending your own. Sometimes that was impossible. You either win or lose that encounter, but a man had to try. Or, thinking of Mattie, a woman. Most times, all a lawman could do was arrive late and clean up the mess. But there was another calling, one Coble believed in. An often-quoted saying spoke of evil needing to watch the fire it starts and that good men need to ensure evil burns in that fire. Lately that seemed a losing battle. He was sure Priest would have a quote about Satan's minions that would apply here.

It didn't take much to figure it out. Two men, and he assumed they were men, must have accosted the wagon on the trail and made the driver turn off, probably at gunpoint. By not fighting back, that was the point the battle was lost. People always assume nothing bad will happen to them if they do as they are told. That is rarely the case.

Once under cover of the trees, and away from prying eyes, they'd raped the woman and then killed her. Why the small boy was shot was anyone's guess. But the larger mystery was the man leaning against the tree and holding a Dragoon Colt in both hands. It was a heavy pistol requiring strong hands, and the barrel rested on the ground gathering dirt.

The man hadn't moved the whole time Coble sat there on his horse. Finally, he stepped down. There was clothing and bedding scattered around the wagon. He found a threadbare blanket and spread it over the woman's naked body. The blanket was large enough to cover the boy next to her. Fetching his canteen, he held it out to the man while squatting beside him.

"Sir. Can you tell me what happened here?" he asked quietly.

After taking a long pull from the canteen, the man waved a limp hand toward the bodies. "They were killed. I've been praying for them."

Coble brought out his tally book. Lately, he'd begun to think of it as a death book where he recorded the names of souls departing life in unfortunate circumstances. "May I have your name?"

Mouth working, trying to conjure up speech, the man replied in a strained voice. "I'm Reverend Benjamin Comer." He waved his hand vaguely in the direction of the bodies. "That's Ben Junior and my wife Alice."

"The men who killed them, can you tell me anything about them, maybe what they look like? Did you hear names?"

Death is never easy. The smell, the shock of seeing a loved one violated, possibly watching their abuse, remembering your last touch...all at the front of your mind as you stare at the remains. It's hard.

The reverend started talking in a nonsensical direction before he caught himself. "They took her gold locket. She cherished that."

He shrugged and continued, still in a stupor. "One was a white man wearing a cowhide vest, it was black and white, like from a Holstein cow, and a big, fancy black hat. Kind of like one of those Mexican hats. The other man looked Indian. He had long hair and a low-crowned, gray hat with a feather stuck in it. He had beads around his neck."

"That's a pretty good description." Obviously the man in the cowhide vest made the biggest impression. Most people don't notice much detail in times like this. Three people describing the same incident would have three different descriptions, which often happened at robberies.

"I watched them." The reverend's voice was soft.

It took a moment to formulate an answer. "You what?"

His haunted eyes looked at Coble, seeming to appeal for understanding. "I told them to stop, pleaded with them to let my wife go. I begged them. They just laughed at me."

"You seem to be unharmed, at least physically." Coble took a long, deep breath, searching for his own understanding. "You have a gun. Why didn't you use it?"

The reverend lifted the pistol and looked at it. "This? I could not. It's for varmints and such. We've had trouble with coyotes. I'm a man of God. I couldn't break the commandment and take their lives. It goes against everything we believe. Thou shalt not kill. It's a covenant that cannot be broken."

It was actually thou shalt not murder, but now wasn't the time to argue the finer aspects of that. His voice spilled out in anger, without thinking. "You couldn't...? You could have shot them in the ass while they were distracted with your wife? Hell, you should have been pissing on their graves by now."

Coble took a deep, calming breath. This was no time for anger.

"God forgive me, I tried. I just couldn't pull the trigger. Not against another human being. What if I killed one of them by mistake?" He paused a moment. "We live by God's teaching. I am a gentle man. My wife and son were gentle people. We never harmed a soul. I don't understand why this happened. We did nothing wrong."

Shaking his head, Coble finally gave up on restraint. "I believe the original Greek translation of the Bible says 'Thou shall not murder.' There's a whole world of difference between a premeditated killing and protecting your family."

"A false justification."

He looked at the two mounds, covered by the thin blanket. "A fact. Listen. These weren't human beings. They were animals, varmints by any description."

"God's children, though misguided."

Coble had a hard time keeping disgust from his voice. And it was unwarranted. He didn't know this man, but first impressions are lasting and generally correct. In a way, he had some respect for him. It is easy to stand behind a pulpit and preach love and gentility. It's not so easy to put it into practice.

"A couple of reasons this happened. The first is evil men exist and do evil things. You should know that. That's a rule as old as time. You have to watch for people like that, avoid them if possible, or deal with them if needed. The second is...you let it happen. It was your duty to protect your family."

"I could not." He was shaking his head. "I wish they'd killed me too."

"That does not absolve you of the responsibility." Finally admitting defeat to himself, Coble continued. "Why did they shoot the boy?"

"He tried to help, struck one of them with a stick. I don't think they meant to hurt him, but he started the violence."

"Didn't mean to hurt him? How can you say that? They shot and killed him."

The reverend's anguish was real. Coble didn't believe for a moment that the man was a coward. But his response was flaccid at best. Why didn't he fight back? Why didn't he help his son? What did he do when his wife called out to him, as she surely must have?

It took a moment to get his thoughts together. The only thing that made sense was that this wasn't the real Reverend Benjamin Comer. The man before him was broken, a shell, speaking words from a mind holding no coherent reason.

There was a grumble of thunder off to the southwest, a smell of rain in the air, but the storm was moving away. "Will you be alright here? I'm going to fetch these men while the trail is fresh."

"I would ask you not to. Enough lives have been taken."

Coble gave it some thought, finally shaking his head. "These men must answer for what they've done."

"They will answer to God."

"Their souls will. I'll see to it." The man stayed silent so Coble continued. "Will you be able to bury your family?"

When he still didn't answer, Coble's shoulders slumped. "You can feed off your dead oxen until the meat spoils. That will last you a few days. Joplin is behind us about five miles, Hard Times ahead of you about the same distance. You can walk it easy."

"We were going to Nicodemus. It's an all-Black community..."

Coble interrupted. "I know what it is, and it's in central Kansas, north of here. You've wound up way south of where you should have been. Now it's a couple hundred miles away. You realize how far that is, how long it will take you?"

"I do." The man's voice was soft, listless. "We came all the way from Illinois."

"You're not a freed slave then?"

"I am not. All of our race were not slaves."

"Nor mine, though many are still indentured."

Coble mounted and turned the horse away. There was nothing left to do here except the burying. He had a choice to either help with that or get after the killers. He knew from experience anyone who could kill a woman and child would keep doing it until stopped. The burying? Let the reverend do it as penance.

He stopped a moment before riding away. "A word

of advice? I know things look bad now. Awful, in fact. You can get through it. Find a place to work, to live. I think you'll find most people are very accepting around here. Politicians love to make waves about race, be it black or brown, red or white. But look around you. There are people from all over the world here, all colors and nationalities. You'll find, once you leave the city, people are judged by their character and work ethic, and nothing else. The only time your skin color is brought up is when there is some advantage to be had. Usually money."

Coble gazed at the unresponsive man. Did he think this man would heed his advice? No. People all travel a trail they think is right, a trail laid out by whatever occurrences in life have shaped them. Differing opinions hold little sway and are but a distraction. Everyone is a slave to something. Some minor, some horrendous.

Booting his horse into a fast walk, he was a half mile down the trail toward the Indian Nation of Oklahoma when he heard the gunshot behind him. A gentle tug on the reins stopped the paint. Sitting a moment, he gave a small sigh and prayer.

"Dammit, I should have stayed." The paint shivered to rid itself of biting flies and gave him a side look. "Yeah, I know. Hindsight."

He coaxed the paint into motion again. The thing about riding alone is it gives you too much time to think. Was he too hard on the reverend? Possibly. He let his own anger and disgust form his replies to the man. A bigger question, born of morbid curiosity, was how the preacher found the courage to take his own life, but couldn't find it to protect his family. Courage is a strange animal. He'd seen men stand up against daunting odds and, on another day, run from the hint of a threat.

Is it courage, or faithfulness, to let someone you love die because of your belief? He could never get behind that thought, or brand of religion. This was Old Testament land. When there was a policeman on every street corner, maybe the New Testament would work for the faithful. People enjoying a life of gentility were always protected by others who were willing to sacrifice.

Coble didn't look back. It was possible the reverend shot a varmint, four-legged or two-legged was the question. Sighing, he shook his head. He was making a lot of assumptions. Maybe all these rambling thoughts were leaking from a confused mind. Maybe.

Chapter Fifteen

THE TRAIL HE FOLLOWED WAS EASY TO SEE, AND THE men he sought were making good time. These were men who gave little thought to right or wrong. They simply existed like a dung beetle, rolling their little ball of manure until something stepped on them.

The land he traveled was dotted with small homesteads and slip-shod ranches, each running a few cattle and horses, goats and sheep. It was a surprise to him he hadn't run into any Deputy US Marshals. Mostly working out of Fort Smith, Arkansas, he knew that more than a hundred worked Indian territory at any given time.

People running from the confines of the law gravitated to Indian territory. Not that it was lawless, but there were so many different factions and tribes trying to control their own tract of land they generally didn't have time for someone seeming to mind their own business.

It was a haven of sorts, with some small ranches having more riders than cattle and little means of explaining their income. But for today, that was someone else's problem. Stealing was a lesser crime compared to murder.

———

IT WAS two days before Coble crested a small knoll to see a small, ramshackle building nestled among the scrub brush of a small valley below. It was a common sight in the Nation, where an enterprising dealer would set up to trade for animal pelts and sell what merchandise they had to the surrounding people. Mostly it was whiskey and ammunition.

Smoke rose lazily from a precariously slanted tin-pipe chimney, and two horses were tied to a skinny tree in front of the building. Leaves were eaten off the limbs as high as a horse could reach. Out back, a corral of brush and cut saplings intertwined together held a couple more horses. Saddles and blankets were left out in the weather, and a good bet would be that the bloodstains on the blankets would match the sores on the horse's backs. He already disliked the owners.

Tying his horse next to the ones under the tree, he patted the other horses on the flank. Still wet, so they hadn't been there long. Moving the leather loops from over the hammers of his pistols, he pushed through the blanket used for a door into the gloomy interior, where fetid air competed with the slight breeze that seeped through the clapboard walls.

A countertop consisted of two warped boards laid across the top of whiskey barrels. There were oil lanterns suspended at each end of the boards casting a yellow glow that hardly penetrated the corners of the room. The only other lighting came from cracks in the roof and spaces between the boards on the sidewalls. Empty wooden crates stacked sideways on top of each other made storage behind the counter. The shelves were haphazardly stocked with whiskey bottles and dubious looking beef jerky hanging in strips. The strips appeared to move as flies consumed them. If he were a betting man, he'd say this place wouldn't last through the next windstorm.

A low table graced a corner to his left where two women sat smoking, both dressed in soiled bloomers and little else. Probably just trying to stay cool in the stuffy room on a slow business day. He didn't see another room and wondered where they plied their trade. But he guessed anyone desperate enough to plow those fields wouldn't be really concerned with privacy.

The description of the two men who'd raped and killed the woman and child was accurate. They didn't glance his way as he walked behind them, and what they were bartering put nails in their coffin. The argument with the trader was getting loud as Coble moved next to them.

"C'mon, Nate. This here locket is pure gold. It's worth more than a few cans of beans and beef jerky. We're needing supplies."

The man behind the counter, assuming he was Nate, was holding up his hands. "I don't want any part of this. I know you stole it, no woman would give up that locket voluntarily."

"So what? That's never bothered you before. And she ain't going to need it anymore."

Nate shrugged and shook his head. "A gold locket

like that comes from substantial people. Folks like that ain't too forgiving. I don't want to be caught holding that jewelry."

Hearing enough, Coble gave a harsh command. "You two at the counter, turn around."

Both men flinched like they'd been poked with a stick. The two complied slowly, the man with the cowhide vest with a sneer and the Indian with a wary look to him. "What do you want, mister?"

"I've trailed you knuckleheads for two days. You raped and killed a woman and killed her young son."

"We did nothing of the sort," Cowhide spoke up. "We've been on a hunting trip to Texas. Just got back."

Coble shook his head. "Nice try. That gold locket belonged to the woman you killed. It's time to pay up."

"I see a badge on your shirt. You got a warrant? A witness?"

"It doesn't matter, but yes. You should have killed the husband. He gave me your descriptions."

Old habits die hard, and he'd forgotten to put away the badge. It was a gray area for the moment, but one he was not willing to cross into. He gave a quick glance at the soiled doves. The last thing he needed was to get blindsided by one of them. But wise in the ways of the world, both women had their hands on the table. With his left hand, he lifted the badge holder from his shirt pocket, flipped it closed, and stuck it in his back pocket.

The trader behind the counter raised his hands and walked around the end of the barrels to sit with the two women. Coble shook his head. "Y'all go on outside. When bullets fly, they'll take saints and sinners alike."

The man gave a grateful nod and ushered the women out the hanging blanket that passed for a door.

Cowhide vest tried to bluster. "Mister, you can't just come in here threatening us. Besides, we're two to your one. You're outnumbered."

"Doubtful."

The man in the vest cast his gaze around the room, looking for help that wouldn't come. "She was just some Black woman. Nobody cares about that."

"She was a good woman who didn't deserve anything she got. Neither did her son."

The man tried again. "Look, we was drunk. I don't remember anything about this."

"I'll take that as your confession. You're not drunk now, and you remembered enough to try and sell the woman's locket."

Coble could see the men working themselves up to make some kind of move, and his pistol was coming out of his belly holster when a voice came from outside the building.

"Marshal, you better come out here."

Chapter Sixteen

COBLE'S PISTOL COMING OUT FAST CAUGHT BOTH men flat-footed and unprepared. "You men drop your weapons and come with me." He really didn't want to disarm the men, but the bartender's voice had a real nervous sound. As he slowly backed out of the room, the two men followed with hands raised.

Once outside he pushed the men against the wall of the shack and then backed away, turning to see what had the trader's attention.

At first glance, Coble estimated twenty men on horseback riding toward them. For a brief moment, he thought of forting up inside the building but was afraid the flimsy hut would just fall down around them.

One man in particular was looking at the trail Coble had followed. Glancing left and right, he noted more riders were coming through the scrub brush and low hills. If this were a military patrol, he'd think all the flankers and scouts were coming in, although it looked as if some were hanging back as perimeter guards. This was not a group of friends out for a ride.

An uneasy sweat trickled down Coble's spine. Two days ride into Indian territory, no help would be coming if things went wrong. In this land, the only law was what you could enforce by yourself.

The men stopped and sat on their horses staring at him while the scout came riding up, speaking to an older man sitting slightly ahead of the group.

He pointed at the two horses. "Those belong to the two men we follow."

The scout then pointed at Coble. "This one came later."

Dressed like normal cowhands you'd see on the range, except most wore knee-length leather moccasins, these men were far from being cowhands. One difference was the brass tacks pounded into rifle stocks. It was a tradition started in the late conflict between the states. In earlier years, it might have been a scalp or other trophy, sometimes ears threaded on a lance. Now it was one tack for one man killed.

While deputy marshals crawled all over Indian territory serving warrants for murder, robbery, and other general mayhem, there were some groups they knew to leave strictly alone.

These were not young men out for some adventure. Most were older. The rifle stock of the man facing him was covered in brass tacks on both sides. Coble took a deep, slow breath. Around fourteen years ago, at a place not too much farther south, an old mixed-race Cherokee had surrendered the last confederate forces close by Fort Dawson, at a place called

Doaksville on the Red River. That old man was Brigadier-General Strand Watie.

Coble hoped his voice sounded steady. "What can I do for you fellas today?"

The two men against the wall started moving to the side but were stopped by men on horseback.

The older man finally spoke. "My name is Jason. We are Cherokee." He looked around. "Well, most of us."

Nodding, Coble said, "Coble Bray. What brings you boys out and about this fine day?"

"You're the marshal?"

The men on horseback had made a semi-circle around the shack. One of the whores was crying while the other comforted her. The fear in their eyes was palpable.

"Used to be. I seem to have been fired at the moment." Coble gestured toward the trader and his women. "These people should go inside. They've done you no harm."

"And how would you know that?"

Coble chuckled. "Dunno, just can't see it. Unless they gave one of your boys the clap or something."

That brought laughter from some of the men surrounding them. Jason pointed with his rifle toward the shack, and the people scurried inside.

"We came upon a family of Black people a couple of days ago. They were dead. These men you have captured did this?"

Coble was surprised they knew of that, but wasn't about to argue with Cherokee scouts. There would be none better. "Best I can tell, they did."

"We have a prior claim, and we've been waiting for

these men to leave Joplin. Give them to us, and you can go."

A younger man edged up close to Jason. "We cannot, Grandfather. There can be no witnesses. Soldiers will come. Put them all in the building. Let their evil ways burn in fire."

"Why do you need these men?" Coble interrupted.

Hard eyes contemplated Coble for a moment. "They raped a young girl. When they were chased away by the girl's mother, they fled to the city. We've been waiting for them to return."

"Sounds about right." Coble nodded. "Seems to be their way of doing things."

"You can't do that!" the man in the cowhide vest yelled. "We give up, Marshal. You have to protect us."

"Well, he does have a point," Coble responded mildly and then glanced at Jason. "Although I keep saying I'm not a marshal anymore."

Jason smiled. "Or you can die with them. The thought of no witnesses has a certain appeal."

Coble had to remind himself that most of these men, especially the Cherokee, had a better education than a good amount of Whites. The government insisted there be schools on the reservation and that the Indians attend, presumably to acclimate them to society. It didn't work, but they did have decent schools.

Hearing the casual conversation about their deaths, the long-haired outlaw made his move, favoring the Arkansas toothpick kept behind his shirt collar. Coble was startled, not having found the knife. And he'd expected more bluster, more talking. The man was fast with it, nearly letting it fly before Coble's first shot took him in the throat. His second shot put another buttonhole in the cowhide vest of the man's partner, right above his heart.

Powder smoke drifted away with the breeze. Spinning on his heel, Coble stood ready with his pistol pointed at the man who wanted no witnesses.

"Your choice, Jason. Live or die."

The men surrounding Coble seemed surprised at the speed that he brought his pistol into play. Jason lifted his rifle, setting the butt on his thigh, barrel pointed at the sky. In a precision move, the others did the same.

"We had hoped for some time with these men," Jason said in a mild voice, not seeming to be upset at the way things played out.

Coble shrugged. "Better this way. I'll add their names to my book and report it to the nearest sheriff or marshal. They tried to resist arrest and paid for it. Case closed. Your names won't be mentioned."

Jason nodded and then gave a small smile. "The man in the cowhide vest wasn't armed."

"I felt threatened."

Again, soft laughter erupted from the men surrounding him.

"You said you're not a marshal anymore?"

"It's a gray area. Joplin is controlled by some bad men right now. They had a federal judge rescind my commission as marshal." He gestured toward the two dead men. "Besides, it's better this way. No blame can come your way since you are only witnesses. Justice was served."

Jason nudged his horse forward, leaned over and

shook Coble's hand. "Justice was served, indeed. Maybe we'll meet again."

"Maybe so. Got a last name, Jason?"

"Boudinot. Jason Boudinot. Strandhope Uwatie was an uncle."

Coble watched as the Indians filed slowly by the two dead men. At the last, Jason rode next to a slight figure who hadn't been obvious before. That it was a girl was obvious, once he saw her. She stopped a moment and looked back at Coble, nodded to him, and then spit on the two men. Booting her horse in the flanks, she followed the small brigade to the south.

Jason Boudinot gave a two-fingered salute and followed.

———

AFTER THE CHEROKEE HAD LEFT, Coble took a deep breath and walked into the building. He tipped his hat to the ladies and spoke to the trader. "The gold locket. Go ahead and keep it. Those misfortunate souls resting outside will need burying."

The trader was skeptical, until Coble tore a sheet of paper from his book and signed a statement of ownership for the locket. He was surprised the man showed so much integrity, or it could be he was over-protective of getting his neck stretched for stolen property. It wouldn't pay to be too skeptical.

The trader was looking at the paper. "Shouldn't you take the locket back to the owner, maybe there's a recovery fee?"

"They're all dead." He told him the story about the rape and killings. "They broke a good man. I think he was guilty over not protecting his family, no matter how much he leaned on his interpretation of his Bible. In the end, I think he committed suicide as an act of contrition. By his beliefs, it would send him to hell with no chance of uniting with his loved ones."

"That's awful," one of the women said. "I've never heard of such a thing."

"Well, that's not surprising," the other woman said. "It ain't like we get out in the world much."

The trader spoke up. "So you killed these peckerwoods out of revenge?"

He'd thought about it over the last two days. If you don't have your mind settled before you go into battle, indecision will kill you. Hesitation, once your course is set, is deadly. So he'd thought it out. "No, I didn't. It was respect for that little boy who tried to protect his momma and got killed for it. He might have grown into the kind of man we need in this country, that's the shame of it."

"Besides." Coble hesitated a moment, gazing out the door. "It's not like they gave me much choice."

Taking a three-legged stool and sitting next to the rickety counter, he pulled his book out. There were fresh entries for the three men who'd died at Mattie's wagon and three entries for the reverend and his family.

Finding space below those, he asked the trader. "Did you know those men outside?"

He and the women exchanged glances. "Never seen them before."

Coble wrote down entries for two killers deceased while resisting arrest. One in a cowhide vest, the other of possible Indian descent. No names available. He sighed and put his stub of pencil and book away. His death book held too many names to think about.

Riding away from that trading post, he realized he'd come to a decision. He was done. Five men dead in just a few days, though one was killed by Mattie. The first two men were happenstance. He was just in the right place when needed. Mattie might have handled both men with only one shot left in her gun, though it was doubtful. But there was no doubt in his mind she'd have gone down fighting and left two orphan girls.

The last two killings were premeditated, and he felt some remorse about it, not that he would have changed anything. Those men needed killing. That it was premeditated broke one of the shalt nots. He had no intention of taking them in for trial. Men like that would prey on others until stopped. No amount of jail time would change them. And that little boy shouldn't have died.

But it takes a toll on your body and mind, and he was taking too many chances. It was time to step back. He'd check in with his friends at Hard Times and then what? The ranch? He was undecided about that.

Before anything else he had to go back and bury Benjamin Comer and his family, if someone hadn't already done it. When judgment day came, he hoped the Lord would take pity on the reverend's soul for what he'd done. Another case of irony...ignoring his own list of shalt nots broken.

Chapter Seventeen

WHEN SOME SCAVENGER COMES ALONG AND STEALS everything a man owns, especially in a campsite with dead bodies, you'd think they'd at least bury the people. When Coble arrived at the killing site of the reverend and his family, all that was left were two dead oxen with hind quarters missing. Someone had stripped the harnesses and yokes, and then made the wagon and everything else of value disappear.

The camp was clean as bleached bones in the desert. Nature's cleanup crew came in for an oxen feast. Buzzards were waddling around flapping their wings and making gawking sounds, too heavy to fly after gorging on the animals. He saw signs of coyotes and foxes in the dust surrounding the dead animals.

Benjamin Comer had fallen to the side from where he'd leaned against the tree, close to his wife and son. His pockets had been turned out and his suit coat and suspenders were gone, as were his shoes, along with the old Dragoon Colt. Mercifully, at least for Coble's job, nothing had gotten to the bodies except the ants.

Unpacking his short-handled camp shovel, Coble commenced to dig. Three hours later he stood over a communal grave and said a few words. Not many. He was exhausted and walked jelly-legged to his horse. It was only about five miles to Hard Times. Hopefully he'd stay awake long enough to get there.

The sun was casting long shadows, and nearby cedars were full of a twittering cacophony of roosting sparrows when he rode up to the sheriff's office. No one was around, so he stepped inside. One thing had changed. In place of the back room he'd stayed in before, they'd added a cell. Without lighting a candle or lantern, he walked into the cell, dropped his saddlebags and possibles bag, leaned his rifle in a corner, and stretched out on the bed. The last few days had taken their toll. He was tired to the bone.

———

BANSHEE WAILS, clattering metal, and footfalls stomping toward him woke him from a deep sleep. Determined not to sell his life cheap, he scrambled to get off the bed, tangled in a thin blanket, hands slapping against empty holsters. Two high-pitched giggles stopped him. What the hell?

"We took your guns." Their wide grins lit up the dim interior of the jail. "We thought you were dead."

"You shouldn't..."

"Momma told us to," one of the twins said.

He didn't know which one spoke, probably never would. Getting a word in edgewise with these two would be impossible. His head nearly exploded when they demonstrated rattling their tin mugs down the line of iron bars again.

"Please stop."

"Momma said you're to come to breakfast right away." The girls waited expectantly.

"Tell your momma..." He went through as many responses as his muddled mind would allow on short notice that he could give twelve-year-old girls. "Tell her I'll be there shortly."

"But she said..."

"I'm going to the outhouse. Do you mind?"

The girls left him in relative peace. After visiting the bumble bee and spider-infested facility behind the jail, he walked out onto the front porch.

The first thing he noticed was his horse was gone. Hopefully someone had taken the poor beast to the stable. Otherwise, he'd run off with his saddle and oversized canteen. Knowing his horse, the second option was the most likely. Last night had been one of the few times he'd been so exhausted that he didn't properly care for his horse.

A few doors down the street to the south was the new eatery. It was easy to spot because of the men, and a few women, lined up along the boardwalk waiting to get in. The sun was barely peeking over the buildings, so he figured this was the breakfast crowd. That there was a crowd at all surprised him. It hadn't taken Mattie long to build up her trade.

Moving across the street, he was intercepted by Fred. "Glad to see you up and about. The twins said you were dead."

"I did feel like Lazarus. Have you seen my horse?"

Fred shrugged. "I did find a horse wandering about. Sold it."

"Did you find a saddle and canteen on this poor wandering horse?"

"Might have."

"Good."

Taking him by the elbow, Fred guided him down the side of the building. "We'll go to the back door. Won't have to buck the crowd."

The long building was bordered by trees in the back, making a shady area for a table and ladder-back chairs. As they started to seat themselves, Mattie burst from the back door, making a beeline for Coble. As soon as she was close enough, her slap nearly spun his head off his shoulders.

"Two weeks! Nearly two weeks you've been gone with no word. Your friends had no idea what happened to you."

His ringing ears made his voice sound hollow. "I've been working...had to trail a couple of damned killers down in the Nation."

Realizing he sounded plaintive, he stopped. And then watched open-mouthed as she marched back toward the building. Turning back to Fred, he said. "I've known that woman all of two days."

"You certainly do have a way with women."

"Yeah." He rubbed his face, watching her walk away. "They all want me dead."

Fred grinned at him. "I don't read it that way, but you never know."

Sitting at the table and relaxing a moment in the cool morning air, he asked, "So, what's for..."

A large tin plate that looked as if some miner used it to pan gold full of eggs, bacon, biscuits, and gravy was dropped in front of him. "If you want potatoes with this, they're extra." Mattie's voice was sugar sweet.

He gave her a wary glance. "No, this will do just fine. Thank you."

Fred interrupted him watching her walk away again. "You got more friends in town."

He turned back to the hostler. "Who?"

"That fella Priest is here, along with your ex-pap-in-law. Know Pete. He's a good man. He's headed back to his ranch tomorrow. Dunno what Priest is wanting."

Coble had nearly finished his plate. "He's wanting something I can't give him right now."

His plate was whisked away by one of the twins, and Mary Neumann set another plate in front of him, along with a mug and pot of coffee.

Fred helped himself to coffee. "You find any more damsels in distress, send them our way. Mattie is pure-dee gold, and Mary is a godsend around here."

"Hello, Mary." Coble smiled at her. "I'm glad you made it."

"Coble."

He gave her a curious glance. "You seem subdued."

Mary glanced toward the back door. "She's pissed and carries a gun. I'd tread lightly, if I was you."

———

A COOL BREEZE kicked up later, more appropriate to October, and several friends sat around the table under the shade.

"Priest, I thought you'd be back to KC by now. How did you get away from Juana?"

"She's not happy, but I'm well enough to come check on you and maybe lend a hand. What happened with the Pianoman? Did you find him and put him back in jail?"

Pianoman. Just the name had enough mystique to grab everyone's attention. Even the twins were quiet.

"Oh, I found him." Coble chuckled. "Or, more accurate, he found me. There's some new blood in Joplin, not the kind of outlaw we're used to. They call themselves Bowlers, and I'd guess they are affiliated with the gangs in the bigger cities. With the city council, the town marshal, and at least one federal judge getting payoffs, there's just not a lot I can do."

Priest gave him a level stare. "Don't sound like you, Coble. There was a time, not too distant, when you would have shot that peckerwood...called him out whether LC liked it or not."

"Yeah, I know. And I did think about it. But that man is dug in like a tick on a hound. Had a few boys backing him with shotguns. LC had already served me with my walking papers as a marshal. If you remember, it was a judge who appointed me, not the US Marshal Service. So, what one judge can do, another can undo. Then, staring at all those shotguns, I had an epiphany."

Fred laughed. "I bet you did."

"Epiphany." Priest rolled his eyes.

He kept a straight face. "Biblical."

Priest sighed. "Alright. I'll bite."

Coble gave his friend a sad look, shaking his head. "I can't kill them all, Priest. There is too much evil, in too many places. The law protects lawbreakers as well as the citizens, sometimes more so. You can't just go marching in laying waste to the evildoers. Not anymore. They're just too organized."

Thinking of the two murderers he'd put away down in the Nation, he almost put a caveat on the statement, but decided to let it go. It was hard to know which hypocrisy to go with.

"So we just give up?" Priest was shaking his head.

"No, we do not. But we have to be a lot smarter than we have been." He paused a moment, looking around the table. "Mary, you've seen me laid out on a table. If I remember right, you even stole my pants. What does my body look like?"

"Whoa, now." Holding up her hands, she cast a worried look at Mattie before answering. "Between cuts, scrapes, and gunshots, you look like ten miles of rocky road. I honestly don't know how you get up in the mornings."

"Sounds about right." Coble nodded. "I'm used up. Tired. Gotta take a rest."

Priest interrupted. "You can't just give up..."

"And what's your body look like, Priest? How many wounds?" He paused a moment, switching his attention. "And you, Pete? You're still recovering from a gunshot, mostly because of me."

"Well," Fred quipped. "You boys are looking kinda long in the tooth. I'm the only healthy one around here."

"So, what now?" Priest asked, ignoring Fred. "Just hang it up?"

"Yeah, maybe. For a while anyway. Maybe I'll spend some time fishing." He gave Mattie a side glance. "I've been catching them hand over fist lately, getting pretty good at it."

Coble continued. "Go home to Juana, Priest. Reopen your church. Preach the Word that tells men to stand on their own two legs, as long as they can, any way they can."

Priest stood, shaking hands with Coble. "I guess you're right. I don't like it, but I'll go back. Send me a message when you're back at the ranch." He looked around at the gathering. "You've got good friends here. I'll leave at first light."

"Don't worry." Coble nodded, giving the man a gentle pat on the shoulder, knowing his friend was thinking this was the last time they'd see each other. "I'll be along sooner or later."

———

TWILIGHT WAS NEAR, and a breeze kicked up a little dust along the side of the building, while bats and swallows worked on the buzzing insects. Sundown was the changing of the guard for them. Swallows used daylight, bats excelled in darkness.

A lone kerosene lamp still sat on the table, bouncing shadows among the trees, serenaded by a lone owl calling for its mate. Some thought the owl hoot was a sign of impending death and would steer away from what they were doing. But it depended on your perspective. If you were a mouse, death was eminent. Anything larger? Not so much.

Thinking he sat alone, Coble was startled by the voice.

"You lied." Mattie's voice was soft. Her face was

briefly illuminated by a twig lighting her cigarillo. "And you're not very good at it."

He sighed. "Sometimes it's best. My friends need to go home to their lives. There's a fair number of people who think I have all the answers, that sometimes the things I do are larger than life. They're wrong. I got a few things done. Got some lucky breaks. That's all. I was never the man they thought I was."

Holding his gaze a moment, she gave an exasperated snort. "You know the trouble with telling a lie, Coble? You always have to tell another to justify the first one."

He gave her a serious look. "Am I going to get a sermon on the meaning of life?"

"Maybe?" She smiled and nodded. "Look. I understand what you're doing. I do. I applaud it. Keeping your friends out of harm's way is a high calling. But not being that man? Please. All I see is a good man trying to do what's right. I may not know you well, but I can see you well enough. That's who you are. I figure you have a plan. It will just take a little time to come about."

"Doctor's orders?" He gave her a small smile.

"Yes. Relax a while. Get bored. Go fishing, take a nap." She pinched off the burning end of the cigarillo, and then put the remainder in her pocket. "Let the evil men stew in their own juices. Things will come to you when needed."

"Sure of that?"

"I am," she said. "One thing, though. I won't be able to help much. I have the twins to think of. I can't risk leaving them as orphans."

"Wouldn't ask it of you."

"I know." She put a hand on his shoulder. "You're a good man, Coble. Sorry about the slap earlier. Been trying to stop smoking these little brown weeds. Adding that to the monthly...well, it takes a toll."

"That all it was?" He knew she was trying to pass off the anger, but she'd seemed more worried than angry at him, which brought up a whole new line of worry. Was he ready for something more?

Her face was in shadow, looking away. "I don't know, Coble. Like we said that first morning you robbed me of sleep. We're trouble magnets. All our days. And you're still robbing me."

She gave him a direct look. "I can't help how I feel."

"Sorry."

"Liar." She hesitated again. "What about Mary?"

Coble gave himself a satisfied smirk. There it was, the question foremost on her mind, trying to sneak it in. "Mary is good people. She's seen her share of trouble, more than her share. The short story is that her husband was killed by the last man I was chasing, the man who controlled Tomlin Harp. It would be her place to tell you any more about it, not mine. We're friendly, have some history, but there's not much there."

"Not much? You need to be sure."

"Life is a conundrum."

Her smile was taunting. "She is definitely built for comfort."

"Don't shoot her."

Mattie's chuckle faded into the darkness, leaving Coble alone with his thoughts and a kerosene lantern casting shadows of spirit dancers against the trees. His hand caressed the walnut grip on his pistol, worn smooth by sweat and use. He didn't know how long he could put it off, but the crazy was coming...sure as God made little green apples.

Chapter Eighteen

COBLE SPENT TIME THE NEXT MORNING GROOMING and working with his horse. The paint was confused at first, not used to the attention. Unfortunately for the horse, it helped Coble think.

Mattie's Café seemed to be the central meeting place for Coble and his friends. Walking in the front door for once, he sat at an empty table.

Mary started out from a back room, saw who it was, and then went back. Mattie came out, wiping her hands on her apron.

"I didn't see you earlier, thought maybe you'd gone somewhere."

He shook his head. "No, just irritating my horse."

"Can I feed you? Coffee?" she asked.

"Maybe some lunch later. Had coffee at Fred's." He rubbed his belly. "It could have been axle grease warmed up over a fire."

Before she could reply, popping sounds came from behind the café. "Dammit, I told those girls to wait."

"What's going on?" By reflex he was already gripping the walnut handle of his pistol.

"Target shooting. Would you like to watch?"

Nodding, he followed her out to the back of the building. They'd set up a target wheel, like he'd seen at carnivals, about fifty feet beyond and up against a mounded hill. The wheel looked like a miniature windmill, or ship's steering wheel, with playing cards attached to each spoke. One of the girls would run and give the wheel a spin, and when she was clear, the other twin would start shooting at the cards.

Coble's jaw dropped. These kids weren't missing much, and their shooting was offhand and relaxed.

"What pistol are you using?"

Mattie pulled a small Smith and Wesson Model One from her pocket. "This is the third edition. Shoots the .22 short. See, it breaks open from the bottom, and the cylinder comes out. You can reload it or put in another that's already loaded. Holds seven shots."

He didn't like that it didn't have a trigger guard but reasoned that if you cocked the pistol, you'd best be shooting it. But if you dropped it, that was a problem. He mentioned that to Mattie.

"Well, the best thing is not to drop it."

The .22 had been around a long time and used to be no more powerful than a BB, but the manufacturer had finally started putting more powder in the casing. He knew a lot of hunters used that caliber for small game.

Both girls had small holsters strapped around their waists. Once the wheel was spun, they would simply draw and fire.

"They're not aiming," he said. "Where did they learn that?"

"The man I worked for in the carnival a lifetime ago taught me. I've taught them. Draw and shoot, just like pointing your finger. It's accurate." She smiled. "Just like you shoot."

The twins had pistols just like hers, and he could see they were well kept and polished. They were reloading, and Riley attached seven new cards to the wheel.

He noticed Rita was very slow and careful, but Riley was the aggressive one.

"What do you think, Mr. Coble? I'm pretty fast," Riley said.

He put his hand on her shoulder. "A pretty famous marshal once said, 'Fast is fine, but accuracy is everything.' You'd be surprised how often someone with what they think is a fast draw puts their first shot into the dirt. They usually don't get a second."

She looked at him with big eyes. "But I don't miss, well not much anyway. Momma never misses."

"Never?" He gave Mattie a long look before turning back to the girl. "Would you do me a favor?"

"Sure thing."

"You're cocking that pistol while it is still in your holster, trying to be fast. You're going to shoot your foot sometime. Try pulling the hammer on the upswing. The motion of your arm will make it more natural. Or better yet, just hold the pistol down by your side. Then cock and fire. Practice slow and sure for a while. Rita has the right idea. Be very deliberate, no mistakes."

Rita laughed at her sister. "See? The tortoise wins the race."

With their pistols unloaded, both girls were practicing.

"How old are these girls?"

Mattie laughed. "They are twelve going on twenty. There's going to be a lot of gray hair on my head in the next few years."

After watching them for a few minutes, amazed at how safely they handled their pistols, he turned to Mattie. "These are fine rabbit and squirrel guns for the girls. But for your protection? Maybe you need something bigger."

"You worried about me, Coble?"

"You're robbing me of sleep, too."

"There is something I learned in nursing school. Well, it was extracurricular. But still useful." She reached out and touched him gently at the crown of his nose. "Soft spot, right there where you're apt to get a broken nose. A .22 caliber bullet is just powerful enough to go in but not powerful enough to punch out the back of your head, so the pellet just bounces around inside. Turns the brain to mush. If someone is hit there, they don't so much as twitch."

He wasn't convinced. "Yeah, but you have to hit that spot."

"We're shooting at fifty feet. Care for a contest? The most cards hit wins a prize." Mattie gave him a smile. "Are you game?"

"What's the prize if I win?"

"You get to take me to the dance next week."

"Well, now. I'll have to see about a suit. These dusty range clothes just won't do. And if I lose?"

"Oh, then you absolutely have to take me to the dance next week. One thing, though. You need to use one of the girl's pistols. If you use that hand-cannon of yours, people will think there's a war going on."

She didn't miss. Seven shots punched the playing card at the top, leaving a little half-moon dimple. And the wheel was spinning. When he tried, he missed three cards.

"Unfamiliar weapon," he groused. "It's too small for my hands."

"Undoubtedly." Mattie tried to suppress a laugh.

"How do you do that? Well, all of you do that?"

"We practice. There's a trick to everything, that's why it's called trick shooting. You don't go chasing the cards, trying to hit them on the fly. Wait until it comes to the top. Each one. Anticipate that and fire. The wheel is just a distraction."

"Right. A distraction."

"It just takes a little concentration and practice." She patted him on the arm. "I'm sure you can do it."

"Sure I can do it? Do you have any idea how many altercations I've been in with a pistol?"

He wasn't used to hearing a grown woman giggle.

"Yes, dear." She stifled another laugh. "I'm sure you'll learn how to do it."

Chapter Nineteen

COBLE WOKE BEFORE DAWN HALF EXPECTING THE twins to be beating on the bars of the jail cell. If he stayed around long, he needed to find a better place to stay than the jail.

Moving out the front door and glancing down the street, he could see a line starting to form at the restaurant. Lights were on inside, and he had to wonder how much sleep Mattie got last night. The line of people started to move forward so he wandered over that way.

The long table outside was filling up, which seemed to be the preferred choice for dining. Remembering the cold winters and ice storms of eastern Kansas, he doubted they'd last much past December.

He smiled, watching the girls bring out heaping plates of food and setting them in front of people. The customers were mostly men from a few scattered independent mines plus farm hands, and there were a few women scattered among the crowd. A few people from New Town, as they called the gambling street, were obvious among the crowd. As long as they caused no trouble, he saw no problem with that.

That line of thinking brought him up short. He was still seeing things like a lawman, and that was Tom Fallon's job here in Hard Times, not his. Old ways die hard, and he supposed it would always be that way.

Hearing the clink of metal, he saw most everyone drop something in a large pot at the end of the table as they left. It was a good system. Eat all you want, pay what you think it's worth.

While he watched, Mary poked her head out the door estimating the numbers. When she saw Coble, she waved and then motioned for him to go around behind the building. But he couldn't go just yet. Not quite.

He'd often told people he looked for a discordant note while investigating. When someone was moving the opposite direction of everyone else, or even doing nothing when others were doing something, they stood out. Would a simple café need a bouncer? As he watched, a scruffy man loitered within reach of the money jar. Seeming to not pay attention, he drifted closer. Coble sighed. Always somebody. His hand closed on the man's shoulder just as he reached for the jar.

He kept his voice mild. "Help you, friend?"

The man tried to shake loose from Coble's grip. "I...uh...no. I was just leaving."

"But you haven't eaten." He noticed Mattie watching, and then she nodded her head toward the table. He shrugged and asked the man, "Are you hungry?"

"I couldn't take free food."

"But you can steal money to pay for it? That

doesn't make any kind of sense. How about you sit down for breakfast? I'll pay." Coble dropped a dollar in the jar. "Seem fair to you?"

"I didn't steal anything."

"Not yet, but you were working yourself up to it." Coble gave the man a hard stare.

Mattie turned up at his side. They had the attention of most of the people there. "Mister, I got a rule here. If you're hungry, you eat. If you can pay, then pay what you can afford. If you can't pay, then catch me next time. No one goes hungry as long as we have the fixings."

"Just be honest about it." She gave him a stern look. "But you don't steal from me."

The man looked around at all the none-too-friendly faces staring at him and then gave her a couple of short, jerky nods. "I understand. And thank you."

"You're welcome." She bustled off through a side door and into the kitchen.

A burly miner made room next to him on the bench and spoke to the man. "Sit. Ain't no crime in being down and out. There's plenty of honest work around here between mining, ranching, or farming. Just got to look for it."

———

"COBLE, what are you doing the rest of the day?" Wiping her hands on a dish towel, Mattie looked to be done working a while.

That was a good question. Other than sit around

and watch the dust devils make their haphazard way down the street, he had nothing to do.

"Figured to take your advice and catch a fish or three. Then I need to look for a place to stay. I'm afraid the girls will sneak in and lock me in the jail some night."

Grinning, she nodded. "I wouldn't put it past them. You could stay here, but Mary is staying with us. I've hired a couple more women to help out in the kitchen, so I'm out of extra room. You'll find something. Anyway, if you are going fishing would you mind taking the girls with you? They're driving me crazy."

A half hour later, the small caravan moved toward one of the many cold-water creeks feeding into Spring River. Rains were few and far between during the summer and beginning of fall, so at best, the creeks were large cold-water pools strung together by rocks and leftover debris from flood times.

A rabbit flushed from the tall grass next to the trail, and Riley mimicked drawing and shooting. "We could take home some rabbits."

"The order was for fish. I'm thinking that's what your mother wants."

Riley pouted. "I don't like fish. Too many bones."

Coble shrugged. "Depends on the fish."

"We don't have fishing poles," Rita said.

The talkative girls made it easy for him today. Rita was wearing pants and a red shirt, for the most part looking like a long-haired boy. Riley was dressed similarly except with a blue-checked shirt. Somewhere Fred had found a couple of small ponies for them to ride that the girls were starting to spoil.

Coble shrugged. "We can cut a couple of poles

from along the banks. Looks like some persimmon saplings are growing here."

He anticipated the next question. "Y'all can round up some grasshoppers for bait, or we can cut up a snake or something...maybe cut a frog and put a hook through him."

"Eeew," both girls responded with disgusted looks.

He just grinned at them.

"There's a lot of people here," Riley, the oldest twin, said.

"I see that." A large number of people, by their looks mostly from the tribes, were camped next to one of the larger pools. Cookfires were going, with drying racks made of saplings, waiting for the morning catch. If they expected to be preserving fish, they'd made a poor start.

Moving next to an older man fishing with a cane pole, he commented. "They biting much?"

The man glanced at him. "You see anybody eating fish? There's too many people stomping around here. It's scaring them off."

Coble gazed at the still waters and then around at the twins waiting expectantly. "What are you using for bait?"

"Rabbit guts. That's usually good for catfish."

"Eeew," the twins chimed in chorus.

Coble glanced around, picking up several sullen looks directed at them. "Folks look hungry."

"That we are." The man gave him a long look. "Haven't had much luck. Hunting's not much better. There are too many people around here trying to live off the land."

Coble nodded. "I can agree with that. How many people are you trying to feed?"

"Must be about thirty of us." The old man glanced at him. "What's it to you? You don't have fish and bread in a basket, do you? Like in the Bible?"

Shrugging, Coble smiled. "Not hardly. I'm just helping a lady out that has a café over in Hard Times. She thought fish would be a change of pace from beef and pork, so she sent me to fetch some."

Coble continued. "She's running a big kitchen over there and will feed folks when they're hungry, whether they can pay or not. Might do to remember that if your luck goes bad. You could at least take the women and kids over sometime."

The man watched his bobber wiggle a moment and then go still. "I'll give that some thought. You got some kind of magic bait that you think will do better than how we're doing?"

Well, now. Desperate times call for desperate measures. "As a matter of fact, I do."

"Mr. Coble?"

He turned to look at the girls. "Yes, Riley?"

"Momma said we could fish, but we don't have poles or anything else. How we gonna fish? Should'a shot that rabbit."

"Well, if it was just us, we'd do it your way, or the way this man is doing. However, there's a lot of people here, and they're hungry. We're going to do something a little different today. It's been my experience that hungry people don't always make good decisions. So, I'm going to help keep the peace by helping these people."

"Can we help?"

Laughing, Coble said, "Not this time. Remember when your mother said there's a trick to everything?"

Coble rummaged around in his saddlebag and brought out a quarter-stick of dynamite with a small roll of fuse. It was a handy thing to have, whether helping someone pull a stubborn stump from a field or convincing some ne'er-do-well not to hole up in a house while running from the law. Fair? Not so much.

While the old timer and the girls watched, he slid a piece of gut over the stick and tied it off to make it waterproof. He knew a foot of fuse burned in thirty seconds, so he cut about three inches and inserted it into the short stick of dynamite.

"Sir," he addressed the old-timer. "If you get some folks to stand at the riffle downstream from here, you might catch some fish."

The man eyed the dynamite. "That don't seem fair."

"Being fair just shows a lack of preparation." Coble glanced at him. "You want fair or fish?"

With wide eyes, the man moved to gather some people. The arguing could be heard from some distance, folks not wanting to stray from what they were doing.

He held out a sulfur match. "Riley, would you light this for me?"

Once she had it going, he held the fuse to the match until it sparked, and then tossed the miniature bomb into the middle of the pool.

The dynamite floated for a moment and then erupted in a muffled thump, showering them in water and debris from the bottom of the pool.

He laughed, seeing the twins wiping moss and mud from their faces.

After a few minutes, people were whooping and hollering at the downstream riffle, grabbing the stunned fish and throwing them on the bank. Some were diving into the deeper water to gather the stunned fish.

A woman walked up to them, handing a rag to the girls. "I don't know how to thank you, mister."

Coble smiled. "If you'd gut a couple of the bigger catfish so I could take them with me, I'd appreciate it."

The old timer moved back to stand next to them. "A couple of those fish must weigh twenty pounds. That will make a lot of fish fry."

"Or stew to feed hungry folks," Coble said.

"Still don't seem fair."

Sighing, Coble replied, "I don't always play fair."

———

RIDING the two miles back to Hard Times was pleasant. The twins chattered constantly about everything they saw. The few times when they asked Coble a question, they never stopped talking long enough to hear the answer. He was good with that. If you don't talk, you can't show your ignorance.

Listening to the twins, he thought Mattie wasn't playing fair either. The girls were growing on him, and he figured they all came as a package.

Arriving in front of the café and holding his two fish wrapped in burlap, he shook his head, watching the girls rush into the café.

"Momma, Mr. Coble blew up a whole river. There was fish everywhere, and snakes, and crawdads..."

Mattie sat reading a dime novel next to a window. Raising an eyebrow, she carefully placed a piece of paper for a bookmark and closed the book. "He what?"

Coble held the wrapped fish in both arms. "You wanted fish for a stew? Here ya go."

She gave him a flat stare. "You used dynamite around my children? They could have been hurt."

He took a step back. "They were thrilled."

"You shouldn't have done that around them. It's too dangerous, Coble."

He guessed in the real world, good moods aren't meant to last. "Dangerous? You have two gun-toting quick-draw artists over there ready to shoot anything that moves. Dangerous?"

"What if something like that goes off early?"

Keeping a straight face, he replied. "Then you'd be calling me stumpy."

Dropping the fish on a table, he turned to leave. "Y'all have a nice day."

"Wait, Coble." Mattie stood, wringing her hands. "We need to talk about something."

"Then you're going to be disappointed."

"What? Why?"

His boot heels echoed on the wooden floor. "Because I ain't here."

Chapter Twenty

THE GROUP OF FRIENDS HAD TAKEN TO EATING together in the evening under the canopy of a huge oak behind the restaurant. Toward sundown, a breeze would generally kick up off the prairie and give relief from the heat of the day.

In lieu of paying for breakfast, someone had brought in a half dozen prairie chickens. The birds were fried along with potatoes, and everyone's mouth was watering.

Mattie generally helped at breakfast, if she wasn't busy at the infirmary next door, but let Mary and the extra help take care of the evening meal. Like most westerners, a noon meal was catch-as-catch-can or not at all.

Mattie and the girls were just settling down at the table, sitting next to Coble. She was on his left and the girls on his right. A slow blush of red began to rise from his collar.

Fred Curry came strolling around the building,

sitting down across from Coble and Mattie. "Hey, Coble. How's the family?"

Coble shook his head, glancing at Mattie. "Very funny."

Riley, the older twin piped up, elbowing her sister. "Momma says she's gonna fatten him up so he can't ride away."

"How long have I known you people again?" Coble asked with mock concern. He still wasn't sure how he felt about all the attention.

Changing the subject, Coble asked. "Fred, have you seen Tom Fallon?"

Fred's demeanor immediately turned serious. "Not since early this afternoon. Said he had a meeting up in the new town."

"A meeting? I thought that part of town was off-limits. You leave them alone, they leave you alone."

"Yeah, well. It don't always work that way. Some-times..." Fred's voice trailed off as he listened.

Gunshots were a common occurrence. People target-practiced. Mattie and the girls were a good example. At night, drunks from New Town might be shooting at the moon, or at anything else that caught their eye. Sometimes it was more deadly. Just like in Joplin, a cart would take away the dead, usually gleaned from behind gambling halls and whorehouses, in the early morning hours.

But gunfire has a certain cadence. In the distance they heard a fusillade of several shots, most sounding like shotguns, and then after a moment's silence, a single gunshot.

Coble glanced at Fred. What they all heard meant one thing. An ambush, followed by one killing shot.

Pushing up from the table, Coble reached for his hat. "Think I'll mosey up that way and see what's going on. That didn't sound right."

Mattie touched his arm. "You be careful, Coble."

"When I can." He met her gaze for a moment. "If I can."

"I'll string along." The old hostler was reaching for his ever-present Winchester rifle. He was rarely seen without it, especially since he helped Tom Fallon walk the streets some nights. Just because there was an agreement with the saloon owners of New Town didn't mean thieves wouldn't trickle down their way.

As they walked up the street, Coble asked. "What was Tom's business this evening? Any idea?"

"There's a new owner at Gold's Emporium. They sent someone down here asking Tom to come to a meeting. Sounded reasonable, so he said okay."

They walked down the center of the street, if you could call it that. Buildings were on either side, with hard-packed prairie between them. When it rained, what passed for a street would become a quagmire of mud and horse droppings. Weeds and prairie grass grew next to the boardwalks where normal travel wouldn't wear them down. Blackbirds dotted the street, feeding on anything they could find. He thought it was early for them to start flocking. That might mean an early winter. Or not.

They passed the deserted opera house, the site of the next dance, on the right and a new two-story rooming house on the left. From this point forward the street was lined with horses tied to hitch rails. The evening was hot, but it seemed the lure of whiskey, gambling, and a soiled dove or two overrode the owner's natural concern for their animals. He could see most didn't even loosen the cinches on the saddles. The front strap wouldn't matter so much, but the back one would be uncomfortable if the animal were fed or watered.

Coble was surprised to see a man moving down the boardwalk lighting the coal oil lanterns hanging outside the buildings. A few other men carried water to the horses and gave them some relief from the saddles.

He nudged Fred and pointed to the men. "How do they get paid or know which horses to take care of?"

"It's a pretty good system when you think about it. They're paid by the businesses. Most everybody on this side of the street is at the bawdy house, so they pay to take care of the customers' horses."

Fred pointed to the left. "There's Gold's, just past the hotel."

"I don't notice as many small buildings as last time."

"Yeah, they come and go. Butcher shop, gunsmith, and a couple of makeshift stables are about all that's left. A few houses like before, but they're mostly shanty-built. There is a café up here. They fix food in the back and send it out on the backs of roaches. Some of them critters are bigger than dogs." He glanced at Coble. "Rumor has it."

"Anyway," Fred continued. "That's why we're seeing more and more people down at Mattie's."

There were several people standing on the street in front of Gold's. Pushing through the crowd, they saw a crumpled form next to a water trough. Fred kneeled by the body to make sure it wasn't his friend Tom, stood, and shook his head.

"What happened here?" Coble asked.

A man with gartered sleeves and a black cloth vest answered. "He accused someone of cheating at cards. They asked him to leave, and he decided to fight it out."

"Really?"

Coble nodded, meeting Fred's gaze. "His pistol is still in his holster. Was he going to throw dirt clods or something?"

When there was no answer, he asked, "Anyone know his name?"

The gambler shrugged, turned and entered the building. Coble followed close behind him through the batwing doors.

The smoke-filled room was crowded with a bar situated on the right that ran the length of the building. The wall behind the bar was filled with mirrors and bottles, with the requisite painting of a nude woman with impossible attributes reclining in repose.

Opposite the bar were gambling tables, men rolling dice on a velvet counter, and one roulette wheel—complete with one marble that you could never win with.

An ever-present piano played in the back. Coble was quick to note the player was not Tomlin Harp, wondering if the man played anymore. Several men with coach guns, short sawed-off shotguns, were scattered around the room to enforce the house rules.

There was a second floor with a railing. A few women leaned over the rail, just in front of their rooms. They hadn't spent much on clothes and had a lot of faith in the carpenter.

In a back corner, Tom Fallon was sitting at a table, and he did not look happy. A saloon girl was leaning on his shoulder, and a man in a bowler hat sat across from him, smiling.

Moving to the table, Coble said, "Tom, we just happened to see you here. How's it going?"

Tom looked startled. "Hey, Coble. I was just leaving."

"Good. We'll keep you company." Tom Fallon was young and inexperienced, with a pretty wife at home waiting for him. He'd proven his bravery on several occasions, but his voice betrayed his anxiety. Coble knew he was out of his depth on this one.

The man in the bowler hat stood abruptly. "I don't believe our business is concluded, Sheriff. We still have things to discuss."

Shrugging, Coble sat next to Tom but away from the table to give easy access to his pistols. He gave the man a hard glance. "So, what exactly is your business, Mr....?"

"My name is JD Fowler," said the man as he sat back down. At a glance from Fowler, the saloon girl wandered off with a shrug. "I know who you are, Mr. Bray, and I'm hard put to see where any of this concerns you."

"Tom is a friend...a good friend. Judging from the little round hat you're wearing, you have to be one of Adair's minions," Coble said, turning to Tom before speaking again. "Some wannabe bad man named Adair seems to be in charge of all the graft and corruption staining the streets of Joplin right now. His men are famous for stupid little hats."

Fowler gave them a feral smile. "We're only ten miles from Joplin. I would think you'd be better informed. For your information, Adair is no longer in charge. There's been a change in management."

He'd expected it, but Coble still felt a little trickle of cold down his spine. "That was fast. Let me guess. Tomlin Harp has killed the boss and taken over his position. Will the big bosses in KC let that stand?"

Looking uncomfortable, Fowler shrugged. "Mr. Adair does seem to have disappeared. But it's no matter. The same rules apply. Which brings us to Hard Times. Each business must pay a fee...New Town or Old Town."

Tom finally found his voice. "I can look aside if you shake down the businesses in New Town. That's just one crook against another. You will not come west to Old Town. That was the original agreement, and it's final."

"That's an unfortunate statement." Fowler shrugged. "You have family, Sheriff? I've heard your wife is young and very good looking. If something were to happen to you, rest assured I'll offer her my condolences...and a job. We can always use new talent."

The sheriff was reaching for his pistol when Coble grabbed his wrist. "Don't, Tom. This is exactly what he wants. Although"—he gave Fowler a hard glance—"your men with shotguns seem to have us in a circular firing squad. If they go after us, they'll shoot all of us including the guards on the other side. Kinda poor planning, don't you think? Of course, I do have a man with a rifle by the door."

"So, Tom," Coble continued. "You want to arrest this peckerwood? If not, I think this conversation has about run its course."

"He's not broken any law that I know of...yet. Stupidity is not against the law."

"Then we'd better skedaddle. I'm pretty sure Marcie is waiting supper on you." As they were leaving, Coble turned back to Fowler. "There's one more thing. Your missing boss, Adair, fixed a small problem for me, which I'm sure you know about. Since I'm not a Deputy US Marshal anymore, I no longer have the constraints of that office. You should remember that if you come to Old Town."

"Thanks for the warning." Fowler smiled, a gesture that did not reach his eyes. "That won't be a problem. We have plenty of men to enforce our rules. We can't play favorites. If you don't pay, bad things will happen."

Coble knew one thing. Even though crooked, Adair was more a businessman and might have been able to be reasoned with. This man was not. He was a killer in a bowler hat, and if the shots were now being called by Tomlin Harp, he had a kindred spirit in Fowler. Things could get bloody in a hurry.

The three men stood in the middle of the street amid the noise of pianos playing, forced laughter from the whores trying to make their customers feel good about themselves, and an occasional shout of anger.

"Tom," Coble asked. "Do you have any people you can get to patrol the streets for you?"

"No one reliable. Most everyone minds their own business. It's just Fred and I."

"That's the way it is," Fred said. "Everyone minds their own business until someone minds it for them. Then it's too late."

Coble shrugged as they moved toward the old part of town. "Just watch your backs. Men like that don't come at you from the front."

Chapter Twenty-One

IT WAS EARLY AFTERNOON, AND LC HAMILTON WAS pouring his second water glass of whiskey when one of his deputies came through the front door of the town marshal's office.

"What are you doing here, Atkins? You're supposed to be patrolling Fourth Street."

The man glanced at the whiskey bottle, then at his boss. "We found another one, LC. That's five girls so far this week."

LC sighed. "All the same?"

The deputy nodded. "Broken necks, one and all. I don't understand how anyone could do something like this, especially to young girls."

"Did you check across the street?"

"I did. According to them, they don't have anyone missing. Maybe they're not whores."

"I'm sure they are, and we don't have any lack of hot-bed joints between Third and Fourth Streets." LC looked at his glass with distaste. He gave a limp-wristed wave. "Go back to work, Atkins. Your job is to collect fees. If you want to be a detective, go be a Pinkerton."

"No, sir." Atkins tossed his badge on the desk. "It don't take much to see what's going on here. I reckon I'll find work somewhere else."

LC picked up the badge, staring at the man before tossing it back on the table. "You're leaving me short-handed."

"Reckon you'll survive." Atkins paused, going out the door. "You need to get this under control, LC. And you won't find the answer in that bottle."

Frowning, LC waved the man away. "I already have the answers. I'm still waiting on solutions. That ain't so easy."

———————

LC PAUSED before opening the gate on the white picket fence. The house in front of him was considered a mansion, but bigger and better ones were already being built by the movers and shakers in the town. Of course, most were being built in Carthage. This particular one used to belong to the head of the bank, next door to his marshal's office and jail. He hadn't seen the banker lately, and the vice president of the bank had already been promoted. Maybe they knew something.

Glancing up, he noticed two men armed with Winchesters watching him closely. Seems the current occupant of the home was well protected. Puffing up his courage and wishing he'd taken one more drink, he moved through the gate and up the stairs to the porch.

"You got business here?"

He looked first at the barrel of the rifle pointing at his gut, then to the guard. "Tell Harp that LC is here to see him."

The guard snorted. "We already know that." The other guard came up behind LC and checked him for weapons, lifting a pistol from his shoulder holster.

"Be careful with that, I haven't shot it in years. Not sure if it even works."

"You'll get it back," the guard said as LC was led through the door.

Tomlin Harp looked impossibly large sitting behind an old, oak desk. Papers were stacked neatly in different piles, each held down by a fist-sized ingot of lead. Another guard sat by a window facing the front, and LC wondered how many were out back.

A young girl lounged on a settee, dressed in lace and feathers and not much else. Looking down the hall, he could see a couple more women moving room-to-room, probably the housekeeper and cook. There were a lot of people to feed.

LC sat in a ladder-back chair across from Harp, a chair not made for comfort.

"What brings you out today, LC?" Harp didn't look up from his papers.

Uncomfortable, feeling like a schoolboy in front of the headmaster, LC answered. "I don't suppose Mr. Adair is available?"

The guard by the window laughed before Harp silenced him with a look. "I'm afraid Adair is no longer with us."

"That's a shame," LC said. "We had a lot of agreements on how we were running the city."

Harp watched him a moment, reminding LC of a

rattlesnake poised to strike. "Any agreements made with Adair are at an end. The new agreement is that you do what I say, when I say, and how I say it. There will be no disagreements."

LC started to speak, when Harp held up his hand. Reaching into a drawer, he withdrew an envelope and tossed it across the desk. "Don't worry, you'll still get paid."

Harp went back to looking at a ledger book, clearly a dismissal, when LC cleared his throat. "There is one more item."

When the other man didn't speak, he continued. "The young girls turning up dead, five in the last few days. That has to stop. People are starting to worry. There's talk that it's unsafe for men to bring their families to town. Less families means people aren't buying in the stores. Hell, even the older whores are afraid."

Harp pinned him with a baleful look. "You think I'm killing these girls? That's dangerous talk."

"There's no proof, but it seems reasonable."

"Get out." Harp sat with his hands flat on the desktop. "What's a few whores to you anyway?"

LC rose to leave. "When the older whores disappear no one notices much. Young and pretty? Everyone notices."

Pointing to the girl on the couch staring at them with a blank expression, LC said, "I'd like to take her with me."

Reaching across the desk, Harp grabbed him by the shirt front, hauling him across the desk. They were nose to nose when Harp spoke.

"You want her? Take her." He released his hold,

and LC staggered back. "I'll have another just like her in an hour. Do you know how many desperate families there are out there in Shanty Town? Walk through there sometime. While the mine owners are getting filthy rich, the miners are starving. They'll sell their kids, their wives, and their souls for their next meal."

The marshal moved next to the couch, taking the girl's hand and pulling her to her feet. As the guard held the door open for them, they were stopped by Harp's voice.

"LC, you're of no use to me. You keep collecting your fees and stay out of my way. If you come around bothering me again, I'll kill you."

Once they were on the street, the girl looked up at LC. "What do I do now? I got nowhere to go, no money, no clothes."

"I'll think of something. One of the churches might take you in."

"I guess I belong to you now," she said. "You should have left me."

"He would have killed you, sooner or later."

"So?" The girl shrugged, tears coursing down her cheek before trudging down the street ahead of him.

————

TOMLIN HARP SAT at his desk, fingers drumming on the smooth surface, watching the receding figures of the girl and LC. Finally he turned to the guard.

"I want him watched. If he complains to the city council or anyone else, we'll have to deal with him."

"Right away, boss."

"And find me another girl. This last one acted like she wanted to die, no spirit at all."

The man hesitated, knowing his boss's violent temper. "That may take a while. It's getting hard to find anyone suitable. The madams are hiding them out, saving them for clientele. How about we bring someone a little more used, at least until we find what you're looking for?"

Harp pushed his anger down and replied in an even voice. "Alright. Fine. In the meantime, check with Fowler over in Hard Times. I hear things are hopping over there."

"Good idea, Boss. I'll send Samuelson today."

As the man stepped out the door and began issuing orders, Harp leaned back and relaxed a moment, before opening a drawer and taking out a bottle of laudanum. He just needed a little, for nerves. He glanced at the piles of paper on the desk. Things were going to change, and the businessmen weren't going to like it. In the past, Adair hadn't bothered the high-rollers much, but that was where the big money was. It was time they shared.

Tomlin Harp smiled. Things were looking up.

Chapter Twenty-Two

"I MISSED YOU AFTER SUPPER LAST NIGHT. I SAVED you some chicken, by the way. Was everything alright in New Town?"

Coble gave Mattie a small smile, avoiding the real question. "You missed me?"

Morning was painting the eastern sky pink as smoke from countless cookfires welcomed the day. He knew Mattie was usually busy in the mornings, so her appearing at his side was a little odd. She seldom did anything without reason.

She held up her hand, her finger and thumb just barely apart. "Just a little. The evening is our time when we can sit and talk. The day is over, and we can relax. The girls enjoy it. So do I."

"I'll admit it's restful. To be honest, you're a good sounding board. I appreciate that. It's good to talk with someone without having an agenda."

"An agenda?" She sat back a little. "Explain that."

Well, that wasn't going to be easy. "With my friends,

it seems they are always trying to push me into doing something...convince me it's the right thing to do. With my late wife, it seemed any discussion always devolved into a control issue—her trying to move me off center —me doing the same with her. I'll admit that with you, that doesn't seem to be the case. We just talk."

"Thank you." She gave him a look. "I think."

She continued. "You might like to know I had a long talk with your friend Priest before he left. He's an interesting man, seems to be educated to a fault. There's hardly a subject he isn't well versed in, you included."

"Since you went to nursing school, that might describe you. I've never seen a nurse or doctor who was stupid. Even midwives or herbal healers seem to have a lot more brains than the rest of us."

"Maybe, although we can sure do stupid things. Care to know Priest's opinion of you right now?"

He looked up at her, wondering where the conversation was going. "No so much. I don't seem to be marching to his drum right now. Is this going to be another control issue?"

"Don't shoot the messenger." She folded her arms across her chest. "He seems to think you're a pendulum. I'm sure you know what that is. On one end of the arc is an abhorrence of violence. He said you're usually the most peaceful man he's ever met. On the other end of the pendulum's swing is bloody hell, like there's a devil in you that you can't control. He has seen that too.

"You're hanging on for dear life to the peaceful side, but he warned me that you're going to slip. He also warned me that you might not be the best bet for my future."

He smiled at her. "Well, that was rude. Unless, of course, you're thinking of a future with me. In that case, it's sound advice."

She shook her head. "I'm nothing like your previous women, and I'm guessing you've had a few. I'm not trying to change you, Coble. Or try to make you do anything you don't want to do. I think my place is to wait and see where the chips fall."

"Again. Sounds reasonable. You and the girls would make someone a fine family."

"Idiot." Mattie then sat across from him at the table. "So, what was the shooting that you and Fred went to see about?"

He took a deep breath, glad for the turn of the conversation. "Just an unfortunate circumstance. It was about some cowhand bucking a stacked deck and probably too drunk to see it. When you gamble in someone else's house, it's a good idea to take what's given to you. Apparently the man thought he was cheated. After voicing that opinion, he was marched outside. Someone mentioned that he pulled a gun, but it was still holstered, with the loop on the hammer. My guess is that they drug him out and gave him lead poisoning."

"Was he cheated?"

"Who knows, it's not like we investigated. But with the circumstances, probably. Half the players at any table are card sharks or shills, just waiting for the next lamb to fleece. Some cow pusher comes in off the range with a wad of cash. They don't realize the saloon girl hanging on their shoulder is most likely passing information to someone. There's no such thing as a friendly game of poker. The more money that's involved, the less friendly the game gets."

Her gaze was intense. "Truth time. If you still had your badge, would you have gone inside and confronted them?"

He thought about that a moment, but he was just stalling an answer he already knew. "I'd have invited the shooter to surrender. If they didn't, I'd have to make a decision."

"If there were several shooters?"

"A complication." He smiled at her. "I'd have to have a strategy meeting with myself. It does no good to go into something blind."

She nodded. "Hence, your decision to leave Joplin."

"Lotta shooters in Joplin. There are games going on there that I have no idea how to play." He gave her a quizzical smile, wondering where this was going.

"So, back to the poker game. Would they surrender?"

Coble shrugged, not liking the questions. "Likely not. It's a matter of power, and a criminal mind, aided by alcohol, always thinks they have all the power."

"I've never thought of it that way. Why didn't the sheriff handle that? I don't know him well enough to judge." Mattie's gaze was locked on his, daring him to look away.

He kept forgetting this woman was scary smart, and it was a good question. "Tom was kinda cornered inside." At her raised eyebrows, he related the rest of the story. "He couldn't say yes to the man, he's too honest. If he says no, he gets shot."

She nodded. "And then you and Fred walked in. That changed things."

"It did set them back a bit. They had him in a pickle."

"You're right about one thing. Before I pay someone protection, I'll just pack up and leave. If they try and run a small town like a big city that's full of graft and corruption, the town will die."

"Well, hopefully all that will stay in New Town."

Her comment was slow in coming. "Do you think it will?"

Coble thought of his conversation with Fowler. Violence seemed inevitable. "Not a chance in hell."

Her gaze had a sadness to it. "So, what then?"

He didn't get a chance to answer, probably couldn't think of one anyway.

Chapter Twenty-Three

FRED CAME HUSTLING AROUND THE CORNER OF THE building, interrupting Mattie's interrogation. "Coble, can you come out front?"

When he followed Fred to the street, Tom Fallon and his wife Marcie were waiting on horseback. A third horse served as a pack animal.

Before he could say anything, Mattie breathed over his shoulder, "Oh, no."

Stepping around them, she said, "Marcie, have y'all had breakfast?"

Marcie shook her head, too tearful to speak.

"We really don't have time," Tom said. "Someone left a bullet on our front porch this morning. We decided it's time to go."

"Make time." Mattie stepped up and helped Marcie from her horse. "A good meal will go a long way in making this a better day."

Watching them walk into the building, Coble turned to Tom. "Are you sure about leaving?"

Tom answered with a sigh and slumped shoulders, "We are."

"Why?" Fred asked. "I thought you had it pretty good here, and we've faced trouble before."

"I learned something yesterday." Tom looked at his friend. "I was scared in that saloon. That's something I don't ever want to feel again. This is different than some drunk cowhand or petty thief. There's just too many of them, and I've got Marcie to think of. All I could think of facing Fowler was what happens to Marcie if I'm killed. I can't chance it."

He glanced at Coble. "And don't you try and talk me out of it."

Shaking his head, Coble said, "Farthest thing from my mind, Tom. You have to think of your family. From everything I've seen and heard, you've done a good job here. It's nothing to be ashamed of to leave."

"Yeah, well." Tom sighed, glancing at Fred. "It doesn't feel that way."

"You can learn something from this, Tom. There is always fear, always a chance you won't come back. Whether it's working as a lawman or chasing cows across the pasture. It's always there."

"So how do you deal with it?"

Coble smiled at him. "You learn from experience. You make the best decisions you can and live with it. You're a responsible young man. You and Marcie will be fine."

Fred grabbed the reins of Tom's horse. "Well, come on. Let's get a meal in you."

———

MATTIE CAME out of the café to stand next to Coble. He glanced at her and grimaced. "I hate to see this happen. They had a good home here."

"There's a good reason, Coble." At his glance, she continued. "She's pregnant. That kind of changes things."

He nodded. "That it does. We're all hostages to something, aren't we?"

She looked up at him. "You're not scared of a little family, are you?"

Chuckling softly, he squeezed her shoulders to him. "The thing I'm most afraid of is letting people down. That includes hypothetical family."

———————

LATER, when Tom and Marcie were mounted, Coble asked, "Any idea where you're going, what you're going to do?"

"Not really," Tom said. "Maybe ride up toward KC, try to find work. There's work around the stockyards for people who can ride."

"If you make it as far as KC, look up my friend August Schuler. It will be the only Lutheran Church there. He's a good man and will help."

"Or if you'd rather..." Coble glanced at Mattie. Seeming to read his mind, she gave a small nod. "I've got a small spread a couple days north of here, just west of Lamar. The house is empty, the place could probably use some looking after. You're welcome to stay there until you decide what you want to do. There's a few head of cattle and horses with the CB brand, maybe some chickens if the coyotes haven't gotten them all."

"That would be..." Tom looked stunned. "I..."

Marcie laughed. "What my husband is trying to say is thank you, from the bottom of our hearts. I know you may think bad of him."

"I don't. None of us do."

"But he never wanted that job in the first place. Neither does Fred."

Watching them ride away, Fred suddenly turned to Coble. "He gave me this."

It was a sheriff's star. Remembering another badge that was thrust upon him, Coble put his hands behind his back. "I'm not taking that, Fred."

Fred stood with his mouth open for a moment. "Why not? I thought surely..."

"There's no reason, Fred. A town marshal needs to be hired by the city, and I haven't been. And I'm not sure I should be, since I don't have much stake here."

There was a gasp behind him, and he turned to watch Mattie walking away. Everyone who'd come out to wish the Fallons farewell was staring at him. Shocked as they were, knowing his reputation, they all would want him to take the job. People want protection from danger, perceived or not. He was also sure none would walk beside him if he took the responsibility of the star. People with good intentions often fade away when the actual work has to be done.

Before he'd always had the righteous weight of the badge. He took assignments because it was the right thing to do. It was a duty to root out bad people, whether he wanted to or not. In his mind, the duty had been worth the risk.

Now there was a choice. Did the duty continue if the badge was taken from him? Or was it an opportunity to pull back and not get involved?

Lately, he leaned toward the latter. He'd put in his time and done his duty. Arguably at the cost of a wife, a few friends, and personal injury.

Most evil will burn in its own fire given time. His job had always been to speed up that process. Hard choices. He glanced around the street. No wonder they named this town Hard Times.

Now there was the added problem of Mattie and the girls. Coble walked slowly toward the café, thinking of how to mend that particular fence. Hopefully he wouldn't get shot doing it.

Chapter Twenty-Four

SALLY WOKE WITH A HEADACHE AND BAD TASTE IN her mouth. Sighing softly, she opened her eyes. Apparently she was not dead. She was disoriented for a moment by the jostling of the wagon she was riding in. The air was cool, and the sky a deep blue of early morning promise of no clouds and a hot day. The rising sun cast a shadow from the side of the wagon. She was lying on bedding, covered with a light blanket, nestled between boxes and bags of supplies. Sitting up, eyes squinting from going from shadow to light, she saw a couple of riding mounts tethered behind the wagon. Saddles were tied to the sideboards, along with camping utensils that rattled and banged with each bump on the trail. She was either with a traveling salesman or a homesteader. It was a mystery she didn't want to deal with.

Rubbing her eyes against the dull ache behind them, she remembered her last drink and toast with the Chinaman. He'd been a gentle lover. She almost smiled. The liar. This was not the expected outcome, and she didn't expect to wake up at all. Looking around, she decided it could be either heaven or hell... depending on the circumstance.

A man's voice startled her. "Good, you're finally awake. Thought you were going to sleep all day."

The wagon stopped, and a man clambered into the back of the wagon, finally sitting on a wooden chest, shading her from the sun.

"Where am I?" She looked from the man to the surrounding landscape showing rolling hills and forest. She couldn't keep the anger from her voice. "How did I get here?"

"All in due time," the man said. "My name is Hiram Lacey. Pleased to make your acquaintance."

She gave him a distrustful look. "Sally."

"How are you feeling, Sally?" He held up a blue bottle and a canteen. "The Chinaman said you might need a sip of this to make you feel better, or I can offer some cool water."

For now, she felt clear-headed. After a long drink of water, she continued, "I'm fine, thank you. Just a mite confused. Why am I in your wagon?"

"Well, you probably won't like this. The short and sweet of it is...I paid for you."

That was the last thing she expected. "You bought me? Like a slave?"

"A slave? No." Hiram chuckled. "Not exactly."

Struggling to control her breathing, Sally asked. "Then what, exactly?"

"Well, it was kind of a finder's fee. I'm heading south to Arkansas, bought some land that's mostly timber. It's going to be hard work and lonely. I was in a bar complaining about it over a shot of whiskey, wishing for a companion, and someone pointed out the Chinaman. When I talked to him, he said there was someone he knew who didn't care if she lived or died, said she'd had a hard time but was a good woman. His idea was that if you didn't care either way that you might as well be put to good use. I couldn't understand that kind of thinking, actually thought he was running some kind of hornswoggle on me. Upshot is, I went to see you."

She watched him closely. "So, you used me like the Chinaman? Got a sample to see if you liked it?"

His face turned red from the neck up. "Nope. I did not. You're easy on the eyes, Sally. Since you don't care what happens to you, I was hoping you'd throw in with me for a while."

"You know what I am, what I've been?"

"I know all about that. You're not a whore anymore."

"I was." She thought for a moment. "There's a bad man who wants me. You've no idea how evil he is."

Hiram shrugged. "I reckon we can bury evil as well as anything else in those Arkansas hills."

"Look," he continued. "The Chinaman assured me you are disease free, and you're not injured in any way. And like I said, he also told me he thought you were a good woman, just caught up in a bad circumstance. Maybe if given a choice at a better life, you might just take it."

Sally sighed, glancing from him to all the things in the wagon. "So, what are you going to do in Arkansas?"

"Well, I'm hoping to harvest some timber to sell. It's late in the year, so the first thing is to build a cabin. Probably just one room for now. I'm a fair hand at that, although we might have to stay in a tent for a spell. It won't be an easy life at first."

"Seems like I don't have much choice," she said. "You bought me along with all the other things you need."

"I'm sorry. I suspect I haven't made myself clear. You do have choices. You're not a slave nor indentured. The money I spent, well...I'd have probably wasted it somehow. I don't expect it back, either way. If you wish, I'll drop you off at the nearest town. Or you can go with me and be my companion, I'll treat you as a wife and with respect. If you don't like it, you can leave anytime."

She smirked at him. "Kind of like a mail-order bride?"

"Nope." He smiled at her. "I got to see you before I spent the money. I've heard some bad, bad stories about mail-order brides."

"Seems to me"—he held up the blue bottle—"your biggest choice is this. The Chinaman said to give you decreasing amounts every day until you don't need it anymore. Or, if you wish, you can drink the whole bottle and go to sleep. You won't wake up from that. I'll find a nice place to bury you. I'd hate it, but I'd do it. It really is your choice."

Hiram sighed, watching her closely. "Sally, I know you've had a hard life, bad enough to make you want to die. The fact that you couldn't take it anymore tells me there is decency in you. All I'm asking is that you give this a chance. I need you."

"Or someone like me."

"Or someone like you, I'll admit that. I'm hoping it's you."

Sally looked him over. He seemed a decent sort, and she'd seen enough men to make a judgment. His eyes were clear, and he seemed clean enough. He wasn't chewing tobacco, which was a big one. As for the wife part, he was just another man. She could deal with that. Standing up, she walked to the back of the wagon and sat next to Hiram. Taking a deep breath of the cool, morning air she realized dying was the easy way out. She'd never done anything easy.

"Alright, Hiram. I'll go with you and be the best companion I can be. I'll try and hold up my end with the work. I can cook and clean. And you can keep your bottle. I don't think I'll be needing it."

The facade of a calm man dropped like a curtain. Hiram looked so excited she thought he might dance a jig. Settling down, he brought her to him in a hug. Releasing her, he held her at arm's length. He was so excited she almost laughed, and she hadn't laughed in a long time.

"I don't suppose we could get to the companion part right away? I ain't had a woman in...actually, I've never been with a woman. There just ain't a lot of them running around out in the hills."

He was suddenly interested in staring at his boots. "I'm sorry. I don't mean to push...I just..."

Sally raised his chin. "Hiram, there's some shade right over there under those trees, and it's kind of private. There's no need to rush, we got all the time in the world."

Chapter Twenty-Five

AFTER WATCHING TOM FALLON AND HIS WIFE RIDE away, and Fred stomping back to his stable in a huff, Coble walked around to the back of the café. There were things to think about.

Before he sat, the back door of the café banged open. Mary came dragging Mattie out by her arm to finally shove her in front of Coble.

"You two hash this out, Coble, or she's going to kill someone. She's armed, there's knives and boiling water in there, and she's pissed off. Experience tells me you're involved. Fix it."

When she left, they stood staring at her retreating form, not meeting each other's gaze.

"I'm not good at this," Coble said.

She folded her arms across her chest. "No doubt."

He took a deep breath. "What I said before, about not having a stake here, was both right and wrong. That's not what I meant to say. I meant that I'm not a marshal anymore, I'm not the town sheriff, nor do I have a business here to worry about. It's just...I've lost purpose, at least for a vocation. I don't know what to do for the first time in my life."

Some of the tension melted from her. "This ranch you speak of, is it paid for?"

"It is until politicians figure out a way to tax me for something I already own." He nodded, giving her a curious look. "Other than that, it is free and clear. Truthfully, I haven't been much of a hand as a rancher."

"So you could raise a few horses, some cattle... nothing big. With a milk cow and a garden, you wouldn't need a whole lot of money coming in. If you had some help, that is."

She continued. "So, there is that option if you decide to walk away from being a lawman."

"I guess you're right."

"Of course, I'm right." She held up two fingers. "Second option. You could be the sheriff of Hard Times. I'm sure they'd like that. It's dangerous, but something you have experience with."

"Whoever is sheriff will have to deal with the New Town."

"That's true," she said. "But it doesn't have to be you."

"Still, it doesn't put me any closer to making a decision. If you had a say in it, what would you suggest?"

"But I don't have a say." She took another step toward him.

He took a deep breath. They were nearly nose to nose. "I love how you smell. Lilac and bread. If you added bacon, you could steal any man's heart."

Catching the slap before it landed, he pulled her to

him. The kiss was long and thorough. Coming up for air, he asked, "Is that answer enough for you?"

"I..."

"What I'm saying is that you do have a say in what I do. I may not take your advice, but I will never discount it."

Her answer was cut off by a thin scream from one of the twins out in front of the café. By the sound, he could tell she was running.

"That's Rita," Mattie yelled from behind him.

Rounding the corner of the building, he was several strides ahead of Mattie. A half block up the street, Riley was fighting with a man while two more stood and watched. Rita was screaming for help as she ran back toward them.

Riley was kicking, screaming in anger, scratching, and punching at the man who held her. Coble had a moment's thought that she might not need help. The man had grabbed a wildcat and now couldn't let go.

Not slowing down, Coble untangled the mess with a hard fist to the face of the man holding Riley's arm. Flinging her back toward Mattie, he turned to face the men.

He wasn't all that surprised. A smiling Fowler was standing a few steps away, beside Samuelson. The man getting up from the ground was a thin, dirty, and bearded man Coble had never seen.

Coble's voice was cold. "I thought I left you in Joplin, Samuelson. And here you are with this skunk Fowler."

Samuelson stepped away from Fowler. "Still trying to earn my hat."

"By accosting little girls? That's a poor choice."

Fowler spoke up. "There seems to be a need in Joplin for young girls. Your friend Harp is going through them pretty fast. We simply offered her a job, and she misunderstood."

"Just a misunderstanding?" Coble gave the man a hard stare. "Lying gets easier with practice, doesn't it?"

"I don't suppose you'd let this go as a bad idea?" There was little emotion in Samuelson's words, and Coble remembered his first impression of the man. Something was off. There was no expression, no feeling. He ignored Fowler and the other man. If there were any rules about dealing with more than one person at a time, it was to always take out the most dangerous first.

Knowing he needed to settle his nerves quickly, Coble took a deep breath. His gun was holstered, and he would need to be calm for this. There was no advantage for either side. "That's not going to be an option for you. You could give yourself up, but a western jury? Trying to kidnap a child and turn her into a whore? You don't get a pass on that."

"No, I guess not." Samuelson's gun was coming up when Coble shot him. The first bullet didn't stop the man, and Coble kept thumbing back the hammer on his pistol and shooting as fast as possible. When the Samuelson's pistol finally dropped from nerveless fingers, the man finally went to his knees and toppled over. A tough man following the wrong path.

Whirling toward the other man, with a brassy taste in his mouth, Coble knew he was too late. He was going to take a hit from the other man's pistol. There was nothing to do, but take it.

There was a sudden scream and popping sound

from behind him, and Coble watched the unknown man wilt to the ground, gun falling from nerveless fingers, like a puppet with its strings cut.

Ears ringing in the silence, he turned to find Mattie clutching Rita to her. Riley stood with her small pistol still pointing at the fallen man. Moving to the man, Coble saw a small hole punched into the bridge of his nose. Surprised to find his first pistol empty, he drew his second and fired one shot into the dead man's face, directly through the smaller wound.

Coble stood reloading his pistols, gazing toward the new part of town, and Fowler jogging away in the distance.

Walking back to the girls, he gently took the pistol from Riley's hand, made sure it was uncocked and slipped it into her holster.

She stood looking at him with tears coursing down her cheeks and then glanced at her mother and sister. "I...he was going to shoot Mr. Coble."

"I know." Coble brought her into a hug. "Thank you. You saved my life."

He was on his knees, holding Riley while looking up at Mattie and Rita. "Listen to me. Don't ever tell anyone that you shot that man. When he's looked at by other people, all they will see is the bullet hole I put in him."

"Why?" Riley asked. "Did I do something wrong?"

"No. You did everything right," Mattie interjected, reaching out to bring her other daughter into her grasp. She nodded to Coble. "What you did was needful, and I'm so proud of you. But some might not understand, and a twelve-year-old girl doesn't need a reputation for killing someone following her around. If anyone ever asks, you just shoot at rabbits and squirrels, rarely hitting them. Right, Coble?"

"Yes." He met Mattie's gaze. "One gunslinger in the family is enough."

People were starting to come out of buildings. Mary came from the café and added herself to the group hug, while Fred came hobbling up holding his Winchester. Coble was surprised to see the sheriff's star on Fred's vest.

"What happened here?"

Mattie answered. "Some men were accosting the girls. When we ran around the building to stop them, they made an issue of it. Coble stopped them."

Fred was looking at the bodies. "Well, they are definitely stopped. This all of them?"

"Just one more. Fowler ran away, back to his saloon."

Fred gazed up the street, and spoke uneasily. "He'll be dug in up there with his men, like a tick on a hound."

"Don't worry about it." Putting a hand on the older man's shoulder, Coble said, "I'll take care of this."

"If you need help..." Fred didn't meet his gaze.

Coble interrupted, looking at Mattie. "No. You take care of things here. This is something I need to do."

Watching Fred walk away, Mattie said, "We could leave. I don't want you to throw your life away. There's no shame in leaving."

Riley said, "Or we can help you."

"I just ran away when my sister needed help." Rita's voice was tremulous. "But I can help too. You know we can shoot. I promise. I won't run away again."

Mattie shook her head a moment, looking at her twin girls. "I may have made a mistake here. I should have taught them to make doughnuts instead of how to shoot."

"No, you didn't make a mistake." Coble chuckled. "They just need a little refinement concerning when and how to use their talents."

"Look, Rita," he continued. "Your sister was in trouble, and you went for help. If not for you, we wouldn't have known Riley was in trouble. You both did everything right."

He continued. "But things may get a little crazy around here, and I want you to promise me you'll take care of your mother. Can you do that for me?"

"We can," both girls replied at once.

After Mattie and the girls went back into the café, Coble borrowed a small wagon from Fred.

"What are you going to do?" Fred asked.

"Well, that new part of town has been a real eyesore. I'm going to take these bodies back and ask Fowler to leave town."

"And then what? You know he won't do that. Maybe I'd better go along, just in case."

Coble smiled at the old man. "I'll be fine. If he refuses, which he will, I'll come on back. Maybe I'll stop at a couple of fancy houses along the way."

"Yeah," Fred said. "I ain't telling Mattie you said that."

Chapter Twenty-Six

It was pushing noon when Coble made his way up the street to the saloon run by Fowler. There were few people on the streets this time of day. If the number of horses was any clue, there weren't many inside either. A good portion of the workers probably weren't awake yet, having worked most of the night.

Stopping the wagon in front of the saloon, he pulled the bodies off to fall onto the street. Standing on the street side of the wagon, with the sideboards for protection should he need it, he called to the guards standing in front of the door.

"Get Fowler out here."

It took a few minutes, but Fowler finally came out. "What do you want, ex-marshal Bray?"

"I brought your trash back. Thought you'd want to bury them."

"They're your meat, you bury them."

Standing by the wagon, the October sun was hotter than usual or seemed that way. He'd admit that some of the sweat running down his back wasn't from the heat. An old red tick hound thumped his tail twice at the spectacle before him and then went back to sleep with a snort. The men on the porch shifted their weight, foot-to-foot, waiting to see what Coble would do. He could hear the nails screech in the loose boards.

"It didn't have to be this way, Fowler. You should have stayed on your side of town. That's all anyone ever asked."

Fowler took off his bowler, wiped the sweatband, and set it back on his head at a jaunty angle. "You have no idea how much your idea upsets me, Bray. The anticipation of hearing what you're going to do about it is killing me. The thing is, you can't do a damned thing about it. We have too many fingers in the pie, between here and Joplin, and then Kansas City and Saint Louis. We're too big for you."

"Maybe." Coble shrugged. "You have one hour to be gone. That will give you time to get your non-combatants out of the way."

"Come on, Coble. I have ten men inside. You couldn't move me if you tried, and I hope you do. That way, after you're dead, I'll come down there and get those pretty little girls, maybe their momma too. How's that sound to you?"

"That's about what I expected from you." Coble climbed into the wagon seat, the barrel of his Winchester pointed at Fowler. "Just remember, one hour."

He stopped at the bawdy house next to the dance hall. Inside, he was met by a portly woman in a plain, blue gingham dress, looking every bit the business woman she was. At one time, she must have been pretty, but now she'd seen too many crooked roads, and looked the part.

"We ain't open yet, mister." Her voice was even, her gaze direct. This was a woman who'd evaluated a pot full of men and found them wanting.

"My name is Coble Bray."

"I know who you are. You're sparking that lady who gives free meals. We all appreciate that. You should tell her. I've also seen you in KC and other places." She gave a half-smile. "A little birdy told me you're not a marshal anymore, so you can't be bringing me that kind of trouble. I suspect you're not hard up for women. What can I do for you?"

"Just stopped by with a warning. There's going to be trouble in about an hour. I'd suggest you load up your ladies and go to Joplin."

She stared at him for a long moment. "I take it you'll be starting that trouble? Like I said, I've seen you before."

"Well, indirectly. But yes, I'm starting it. It would help if you could warn the other folks."

"And who would that be?" she asked.

He was turning to leave the building. "Anyone not associated with Fowler."

———

An hour later he was sitting in front of the table behind the café. He'd already cleaned his Winchester and was working on his pistols.

Mattie came to stand beside him. "You sure this is what you want to do?"

He sighed, setting the pistol down. "No, I'm not sure. But it has to be done, once and for all."

She didn't waste time arguing, he liked that about her. "What can I do to help?"

"Stay here with Fred and the girls. If Mary is here, include her and stay out of sight. Once I start, there's no telling where the roaches are going to run. Protect your kids. That's all I ask."

The twins had come to stand beside her. "How can you take on so many men?" Riley asked. Seemed like it's always Riley. "They'll just overwhelm you with numbers."

Giving her a long glance, he said. "I'll just have to make do."

Riley was holding his saddlebags. "Mr. Coble, why don't you use these?"

Coble felt like a fool, knowing the bags held a few quarter-sticks of dynamite. "You know, Riley. That's a really good idea."

She handed him the bag, and he gently brought out the explosives. Covering them all with waterproof gut, he cut three-inch fuses for each. He had an even half dozen left. While working, a plan had come to focus.

"Rita and Riley, would you go fetch Mr. Fred from his stable?"

Both were gone like a shot.

"What are you up to, Coble?" Mattie was giving him a suspicious glance.

"Your girls figured out how to get those peckerwoods to come out in the open."

When Fred arrived, Coble asked. "How do you fight fires here in town?"

"Well," he said. "We haven't had to. But I reckon I

have a wagon full of water barrels. We use a pump to squirt the water out. Ain't perfect, but it helps."

"Have you noticed anything about the weather from, say, four to four thirty every afternoon?"

Coble had noticed it. This part of the Kansas-Missouri border was dry as day-old bread. Trees and grass were shriveled and withered. But there was rain. Miles to the east, thunderclouds would form and rain would fall. Invariably, when a thunderstorm was building it would suck in air from its surroundings. For Hard Times, it meant the wind would come up from the west and blow straight east.

Fred scratched his head. "It gets windy about that time. If we can't have water, at least the cool breeze helps."

Keeping his attention on his dynamite, Coble said. "Now, if somehow a fire was started here on the west end of the new town, which direction would it go?"

Grinning, Fred replied. "Why, I reckon it'd go straight east and take the new town with it."

"Wouldn't that be a shame?" Coble matched his grin.

"So, to make sure I have this right, we need to start a fire and then try to put it out?"

Coble glanced at him. "No, save the water for here. The wind could change, you know?"

"This isn't right, Coble," Mattie said. "There are innocent people there who'll be hurt."

"Not so much," he replied. "The town is mostly deserted this time of day, and it's late enough that the help will be wide awake getting ready for the evening. No one should be caught surprised."

Coble continued. "Plus, I gave one of the madams

a warning to get everyone out. I think that'll be enough."

Fred was rubbing his head again. "So when does this mysterious lightning strike need to take place? I'm assuming you want me to start the fires in some of the vacant buildings on this side of town?"

"I do. And you might warn folks on this side that something is going to happen. No one needs to do anything but watch the show."

Mattie was patting her foot, with her arms crossed on her chest. "Where will you be?"

"Me?" He smiled at her. "I'm going to take some of these little fish-finders and see if I can't flush Fowler and his men out of their saloon."

"Well, it should work." She didn't look convinced. "And then?"

"I'll invite them to leave town." He hoped it would be that simple. People would be running, some toward the fire, some away. In the chaos, he hoped to isolate Fowler. He didn't have a big interest in killing the man, he just wanted him gone.

Mattie and the girls came and surrounded him. "You be safe, Coble."

He hugged them for a moment. "I can't say this is without risk, but I think I've put the odds in my favor."

"Can I go with you?" Riley asked. "You know I can shoot, and I can throw." She demonstrated by picking up a fist-sized rock and throwing it. "See?"

"That's a good throw, Riley. I appreciate the offer to help. Here's what you're going to do. I'm going to leave a couple of these with your mother. If it looks like bad men are coming this way, she'll hand one to you and you throw it in front of them. Kind of a warning. Think you can do that?"

Riley shook her head. "Mom will never let me do that."

"Well," he replied. "I'm hoping it will never come to that." He gave her a look. "But I'm betting she'd let you if the need arose. Deal?"

He stuck out his hand.

Riley grasped his hand. "Deal."

One more kiss from Mattie, and he shouldered his pack and rifle, moving up the street.

Chapter Twenty-Seven

MOVING PAST THE FIRST OF THE OLD ABANDONED buildings, he saw Fred piling dry brush against the sides. He heard thunder, but it was a long way to the east. He could see lightning dart across the clouds in a near-constant display. Somebody was getting a bad storm.

He paused, feeling the wind off the prairie pick up and get stronger. Turning toward Fred, he gave the older man a thumbs-up signal to start his fires.

It was a chance he felt they had to take. If they did nothing, Fowler and crew would be back with better planning and more men. He realized the fire could get out of hand, the land around was dry. But most of the land past the buildings was dust, with a sparse growth of scrub brush. The brush might burn, but the fire would soon die out for lack of fuel.

He knew that Fowler was determined to rule over his little kingdom and then expand it. Coble felt his job was to make sure there was no kingdom to rule over.

During one flash of lightning, he saw several wagons lined up well out on the prairie. It looked like most people were out of harm's way. Turning, he jogged behind the buildings, moving around piles of old lumber, discarded trash, and garbage.

A few minutes later he was behind the saloon, standing behind a dilapidated outhouse. The smell was overwhelming. Most people could build an outhouse, but were not prepared for disposing of the product. He noticed this one was on wooden skids, so maybe they had an idea.

It was another reason he hated the city. If you're traveling with a group of people, sanitation becomes a problem. With several thousand people? The stench of the outhouses and sewage running down the street was overwhelming. Maybe people got used to it. He couldn't.

Looking west, he could see smoke billowing from the tinder-dry buildings. The hotel and community dance hall would be next, and then the saloon and bawdy houses. He said a short prayer that all the people had heeded the warning.

Denizens of the saloon were getting agitated. Shouts of anger carried against the wind, as doors slammed and people ran up and down the boardwalk. It was time.

Coble picked up his miniature bomb, lit the fuse counting to three, and then tossed it through a window. He'd almost cut it too short, as the explosion was immediate, debris peppering the walls of the outhouse he hid behind. The back wall of the saloon was blown out, along with windows. One of the inner walls was keeping the upper floor from falling. He lit another bomb and tossed it inside against the wall.

Just as he stepped behind the outhouse for cover, the dynamite exploded, and the upper floor came crashing down. He was nearly covered by the dust explosion from the falling upper floor. Satisfied no one would be inside, he walked around the building.

A bucket brigade was being organized, but the only water came from a well and hand pump. There wasn't any way they could keep up. When the wooden buildings began collapsing from the fire, dejected men turned away. Those who found their horses were already riding away toward Joplin.

Fowler stood in the street, surrounded by three men. Armed with a haunted expression, he kept pointing toward the front of his saloon, but the men shook their heads. Maybe he was trying to get them to go inside for something.

Walking into the street, about a hundred feet from the man, Coble spoke above the noise. "Fowler. I gave you fair warning."

The man whirled. "You bastard! Was that you with the dynamite in back? Are you crazy? I've lost everything. It's going to be a pleasure watching you die."

"You and your boys can always leave. There won't be anything to stay for in a few minutes. It doesn't look like any of that rain will come this way. It seems to me you're out of business."

"I'll leave when I have your scalp," Fowler screamed at him. "Take him, men."

One of his men had already lifted his hands and walked away. The other two started to pull their pistols when two shots from Coble's Winchester ended them.

"Looks like just you and me, Fowler," Coble said.

"I'm unarmed." The man's hatred was palpable.

"Not likely," Coble said, watching the man closely. It wasn't like him to give up easily. "Start walking toward Joplin."

In the distance, Coble could hear a mule braying and people shouting. He almost smiled, thinking of waking a mule up and trying to put a harness on it. Dangerous work.

The man stood in the smoky street glaring at him. Finally, with a curse, Fowler pulled out an over-and-under derringer, and started running at Coble. His first shot whipped by Coble's ear, surprisingly close given the firearm.

With a sigh, Coble shot him. He took no satisfaction in it. But he knew the man would never let up and could come after Mattie and the girls. That was unacceptable.

Fowler was on his knees, blood leaking from the hole in his chest. His voice was faint, the wind taking it away. "You can't win. Someone else will come and take my place."

Coble shrugged. "You're probably right. That's why I burned this cesspool down. People like you aren't much on building things. They just take."

But he was talking to the wind, Fowler's eyes were seeing what was on the other side.

Two muffled booms carried on the wind. The girls. As he turned east, running toward the old part of town, rifle fire broke out and then abruptly stopped. The silence was broken by containers popping in the fires and shouts of people behind him. It looked like the exodus had begun.

Running down the street toward the café, he was brought up by the sight of two horses and riders lying in the dust of the cross street. The riders were holding their hands over bleeding wounds. Both horses were lying still, he didn't know if from injury or the concussion of the blasts.

Collecting the men's firearms, he moved on toward the café. He found two more men lying in the street, obviously dead. Glancing around, he saw no other signs of a fight.

"It's Coble," he shouted. "You can come out now."

The door opened, and Mattie came rushing out, hands all over him, immediately checking him out for wounds. The girls came out the doorway, Rita looking scared and Riley with a big grin. He assumed she got her wish about throwing the dynamite.

Fred came last, holding his Winchester.

"What happened?" Coble asked.

"Fred recognized these men right away as working for Fowler," Mattie said. "We shouted at them to go away, but they just laughed at us. They said they'd come for the girls."

"So Riley got her wish?"

"Boy, did she ever." Fred laughed. "We had two of those little bombs thrown before those boys knew what was going on. When the last two rushed the building, I dusted them off. They just don't make smart criminals anymore."

"I reckon you educated them."

"What happened up the street?" Mattie asked. "Is it over?"

"It's over," Coble replied. "Fowler is dead, and his men are either dead or still running."

Mattie was pensive for a moment. "Do you think they'll be back for us?"

Coble shook his head. "Doubt it. There's nothing for them to come back for, the buildings are gone, so all their business will be gone with it. It's only ten or so miles on into Joplin, and the workers will be there by tomorrow. The customers coming to Hard Times for fun and frolic will hardly notice the difference. I expect most will just blend into Joplin, probably work for Tomlin Harp or someone like him."

"What about Harp?" Fred asked.

"Well," Coble said. "That's a lot bigger fish. I'd never get close enough to shoot him, all his men recognize me. I sure as hell am not going to invite him to a wrestling match."

"Still, there has to be some way to cut him out of the herd." He glanced at Mattie. "Sometimes justice is served, other times it serves you up. She's a fickle mistress. But I've got it to do."

"Not today, you don't. Or tonight. You need a good meal and some rest. Tomorrow we'll make a plan."

"I won't argue that."

Chapter Twenty-Eight

TOMLIN HARP SAT BEHIND HIS DESK WATCHING THE disheveled and soot-blackened man before him. "You say Hard Times burned to the ground?"

The man wrung the brim of his hat. "Yessir. Well, just the new part. The old part wasn't touched."

"And why do you think that was?"

"Dunno, sir. We heard some explosions, and the roof of the saloon like to have come down on our heads. When we got outside, we could see the fire in the buildings around us was too far gone...we didn't have much water anyway."

When the man hesitated, Harp motioned for him to keep going. "And then what?"

"We were out in the street with Fowler, and then that Coble Bray feller showed up."

Harp sat up in surprise. "Why was he involved? He's not a marshal anymore."

The man shuffled his feet. "Well, ya see? Fowler and that Samuelson feller tried to pick up some young girls. Right purty too. Anyway, seems Bray is sparking their mother. He'd already told Fowler to get out of town, but we didn't."

"So did you men gun down the ex-marshal?"

"No, sir. There was three of us plus Fowler. Bray had a rifle and gunned down the other two men."

"What did you do?"

"I ain't stupid." The man slumped. "I ran away. I've seen this Bray in action before. Didn't want any part of it."

Harp rubbed his head. He didn't think the man claiming not to be stupid was supported by fact. "Alright, I think I have it. Thanks for the information."

The man's voice was relieved. "I can go now?"

"Sure you can. There are rooms in the back of the house. You can get cleaned up and then tell the cook you need a meal," Harp said.

"Thank you, sir. I was afraid you'd think poorly of me for running away."

"Not a bit." Harp motioned to a man by the door.

"We'll make sure you get everything coming to you," Harp said, his attention drawn back to the papers on his desk, dismissing the man.

When the man was gone, he motioned his guard over. "When that man gets cleaned up, make sure he has a good meal."

"Will that be all, Mr. Harp?"

"No. As soon as he is finished, take the idiot out back and kill him. He had a chance to take down Coble Bray and didn't do it."

"As you wish."

LATER THAT EVENING, after he'd had a steak dinner and bottle of wine at the House of Lords, he was again at his desk pouring over some paperwork. He'd let most of the men go for the evening, not wanting to waste the money. Plus, the peace and quiet would be good. With the town marshal under his thumb, there were no threats around him. It bothered him to have so many men hanging around with nothing to do. Sooner or later they'd get ideas about stealing from him. It was better to find them a job somewhere.

Drawing his attention back to the ledger book, he frowned. When he compared the number of businesses they were collecting from against how much money there was available, there was a glaring discrepancy. Someone was skimming. He needed to find someone good with numbers to find out who and how.

His inside guard came through the door. "Sir, there're some people out here to see you."

Harp was startled. He didn't really know anybody. "Who?"

"It's a man of the cloth, looks like he's pretty frail, and a Mexican woman. I'm guessing she's his nurse."

Harp shook his head. "Send them away. He's probably looking for a handout for his church."

The guard shrugged. "He's pretty insistent, sir."

Harp sighed, placing his hands on the table. "Alright. Send them in. But you stay."

Moments later a dapper man dressed in a black suit escorted a woman through the door. He sported a religious collar, but everything looked too fancy. Especially his hat with its silver hat band and expensive leather boots. The man moved slowly, with the woman holding him by the arm.

Glancing at his guard, Harp asked, "You checked him for weapons?"

"Of course," the guard replied. "He's clean."

The visitor snorted and then replied, "He checked me close enough that I'm thinking he likes boys."

"Enough of that." Harp's voice was gruff. "What can I do for you folks? I'm busy."

The man spoke in a soft voice. "Just to make sure we're in the right place, you are Tomlin Harp?"

Confused, Harp spoke sharply. "I am."

"I am." The man nodded, with a smile. "An interesting choice of words. Biblical even."

"What the hell are you talking about?"

"Unfortunately," the man continued, "You're more of an *I was*."

Harp still had his hands on his desk when a bullet hit him in the forehead. Another shot hit him right on his left shirt pocket. A man of massive strength, Harp slowly fell forward with his face leaking bloody stains on his paperwork.

———

TURNING SWIFTLY, Priest pointed his gun at the guard. "How about you lay that pistol on the table? Gently."

When the guard complied, Priest said. "You have a choice. You can leave, and live. Or you can be stubborn and die. Your boss is dead, so is your paycheck. What say, you?"

The guard's shaking hands were shoulder-high. "How did you get that pistol in here?"

"Not the answer I'm looking for." Priest smiled.

"You forgot to check the lady, and you're wasting time."

"No problem. I'll walk away," the guard said. "It wasn't much of a job anyway."

"Excellent. A wise choice. Are there others in the house who might come looking?"

"There are some young girls, the housekeeper and cook in the back. There are gunshots around here all the time, so I doubt they'll come looking."

Priest hesitated and then glanced at Juana. "Young girls?"

The guard smirked. "Yeah, the boss liked them real young."

"And you helped him with that?" Juana asked. "How could you do that?"

"They're mostly in the whorehouses already." The man was looking at them, apprehension dawning on his face. "Hey, lady. It's just a job. Besides, they're just whores. Who cares how old they are?"

Juana gave him a cold glance. "You should."

———

AFTER LEAVING the building and getting into their rented surrey, Juana asked. "You wrote something on a notepad next to Harp's body."

"I just told whoever was left in the house to split whatever money they could find. They'd earned it." Priest paused to catch his breath.

"For a moment, I thought you wouldn't shoot that guard."

Priest nodded, gently slapping the reins on the horse pulling the surrey. "Someone who procures young girls for the trade is as guilty as the end user. Maybe more so. Don't you think?"

"Agreed. If you hadn't, I would have done it myself." Juana paused a moment. "So, what now?"

"I have heard the House of Lords serves a fine steak for its evening meal. Our train doesn't leave until midnight, so we should have plenty of time."

"We're not going to Hard Times? I thought you'd want to let Coble know that Harp was no longer a threat?"

Priest chuckled. "He'll find out soon enough."

She leaned against him as their horse slow-walked the surrey toward the downtown area of Joplin. "You know I'm with you whatever happens. Why did you decide to eliminate Harp?"

"It was an easy decision. Coble needs to retire. He has a chance of doing that right now. And to be honest? He might have gotten himself killed. We both know he'd have given Harp an even break. Oh, he'll pad his advantage as much as possible, but that's the extent of it. He wouldn't just shoot someone in cold blood. Even if it needs to be done. He's just not built that way."

"It's like the old saying." Priest continued. "Never fight someone on their own terms or give them the advantage. Harp and some of his minions were chess pieces that needed to be taken off the table. I was able to do that."

"That kind of goes against the oath taken to serve the public." Juana's voice was a gentle jibe.

"An oath? Coble took an oath." Priest's smile was small. "I've never made claim to any of that. The only oath I have is to protect my friends."

Juana's gaze searched his face. "Having done this will haunt you."

"It was needful, and my dreams will be nothing but sugar plums and fairies riding over a rainbow into the sunset."

She gave him a nudge. "I'd damn well better be one of those fairies."

Chapter Twenty-Nine

MORNING CAME WITH THE PROMISE OF FALL WITH cool air and fog rising in the low spots. Coble had dug out an old jacket and was sitting at their customary outside table, hat clamped on his head and lost in thought. It was early, and he was the only one of their small group dining.

Mary appeared with a steaming plate, while Riley and Rita carried a coffee pot, cups, and silverware. It was quiet, and everyone seemed subdued, speaking in whispers. He didn't know if it was because of events the day before, or just not wanting to break the peacefulness of the morning.

Looking around and wondering what was going on, Coble shrugged and dug in. There was a rule somewhere about eating a meal while it was hot. He was finished and working on his second cup of coffee when Mattie came out. She sat quietly watching him.

"So, what's the plan?" she asked.

"Well, so far I plan to saddle the paint and go visit

Joplin. If I can find him, I'll round up Harp. Not that I had much luck before. Maybe my luck will change."

"Just that simple?" she asked. "The marshal rides into town, has a showdown with the outlaw, and then rides away? Doesn't sound like much of a plan."

"It's all I have, and I'm not a marshal anymore." He did wish for a better plan but couldn't come up with one. Harp would have guards, and he was sure the man wouldn't have any notion of meeting with him, one one-on-one.

She gave him a hard stare. "I don't like it."

He sighed. "Me neither. But it's all I got, and it needs to be done."

Mattie took a sip of her coffee. "What about the girls and me? Are you coming back?"

"That I can promise. I'm coming back for you and the girls."

"What if you're killed?" Her voice was tremulous.

His hand covered hers, gripping lightly. "Then go on with life without me."

"That won't be easy. I've gotten used to your long-winded answers."

Mary stuck her head out the back door. "Fred says there's a rider coming, and y'all should quit whatever it is you're doing out here and come around front."

"Why do we care about a rider coming into town?" Coble asked.

"He says the rider looks like he's never been on a horse and is making a poor job of it. He thinks it's LC."

By the time the rider came to the front porch of the restaurant, they were all gathered.

"Morning, LC. You're out bright and early." Coble said. "Light and set, we've got coffee on."

"Thanks, but I don't have the time. I've got meetings to go to. The city council is doing some restructuring." He paused a moment, standing in his stirrups and stretching his back. "Looks like you've had a fire?"

Fred stepped forward, making sure LC saw the star on his vest. "It was an unfortunate circumstance. An accident, of course." He grinned. "Although it does solve a lot of problems."

That almost made LC laugh. "I've heard someone warned everyone to leave, except people in the saloon."

"It's a mystery, alright. Sometimes you just can't explain how things work out."

LC shook his head. "Sheriff Curry, your logic astounds me."

He paused a moment before continuing, looking directly at Coble. "Did you do it?"

Coble gave him a puzzled look. "Well, I'll admit I've done many things. You need to be more specific."

"Alright." LC settled back into the saddle. "Tomlin Harp and one of his guards was killed last night. Guards outside his headquarters were knocked out. Looked like a straight-out assassination, one to the head, one to the heart. Harp wasn't holding a gun and neither was his guard."

Coble almost laughed with relief. That was one job he hadn't been looking forward to. "I can't imagine that being of much concern to you, LC. Except you're not under his thumb anymore. He probably got into it with some other criminal element. Are there witnesses?"

LC deflated a little. "No such luck. There was a housekeeper, but she didn't see or hear anything. The safe was open, and all the money was gone."

Coble nodded. "How do you know there was money there?"

If nothing else, LC was a wise old politician. Since there wasn't a good answer to that without putting a foot in his mouth, LC didn't answer.

"So this is out of your jurisdiction." Coble continued. "What are you doing out here on this fine morning?"

LC looked relieved. "Just a courtesy call. I know there was bad blood between you and thought you'd want to know."

"Thanks, LC. You're entirely correct on that point. But to answer your first question, I did not kill Tomlin Harp. Although I was planning to put him back in your jail. I guess someone had other ideas."

"Well," LC said. "We did get a description from one of the outside guards who was knocked out. He said the man was dressed in black and had a priest's collar, but it was a Mexican woman who knocked him down. I discounted it, though. The guard is a known drunk and was probably seeing things."

Priest. What the hell did you do? "Guess I'm off the hook then. Thanks for the heads up."

"Alright." LC gathered his reins. "I'd still appreciate it if you stay out of town."

Coble needled him a little. "Can't promise that, but I'll take it under advisement. Good enough?"

"Guess it'll have to be."

They watched LC ride away toward Joplin, making a poor job of it. Fred was right about that.

He turned to Mattie, relief was lifted like a mantle from his shoulders. "Well that puts a new wrinkle in our plans."

"It does," she said, watching him closely. "It's your turn."

"What do you think about ranch living? Think about it some. You'd probably make more money with the café."

"I signed ownership over to Mary last night. Fred gave his blessing to it."

"Did he now?" Coble gave his friend a sharp glance. Fred grinned back at him.

Coble continued. "What do you think about living as a common-law wife with someone you love?"

Mattie smiled, and the girls smirked at him. At that point, he knew he'd never win another domestic battle. "Fred says there's a preacher comes around every Friday, and that'll give us time to steal back my wagon and horses, then load up supplies." She winked at him. "We'll need to do this right, so we don't starve out on the prairie."

She stood tall before him. "And I'll take that invitation as a proposal."

The girls were standing with them now, and he brought them all into a hug. "I couldn't ask for a better family. It's time to start over."

"The Trading Horse"

A Special Look At
A Western Short Story

There were parts of Kansas City I'd never seen. Between jobs and with time on my hands, I decided riding a cable car down to the bottoms along the Missouri River was the thing to do. I even paid a ticket seller to do it and couldn't understand why he had such a big grin on his face.

My stomach roiled and clenched. I broke out in my first sweat of the day. If a whole passel of Comanche showed up for breakfast, I wouldn't have been more scared. There was no place I could jump out without breaking bones, so I rode it all the way down. I vowed to never make that mistake again—and have a word or two with that ticket seller if I had a chance.

On solid ground, my sightseeing adventure left me gawking around the new Union Depot. It had a clock tower taller than any tree I'd ever seen. A passerby told me it was over a hundred feet tall. He had tickets to sell too, so I didn't believe much he said. That building stood out like a horse in a herd of donkeys—the donkeys being the train tracks, gambling centers, and billiard halls, not to speak of the bordellos. Four square blocks of any adventure you'd ever want to try, given you had the money, in brightly colored buildings painted black with train smoke.

It was a bad decision to stop in an establishment with a hand-painted sign advertising gambling and drinks. Any fool knows those two don't mix. I compounded that poor choice by getting snookered into doing both.

Other men were present at the card table, but the man running the game had a cockeyed look to him and made a show of having clumsy fingers—trying to convince us by dropping a card on occasion with apologies to all. I'd guess he had a theory. If you think someone is a fumbling card player, you don't watch them for cheating.

Dressed in dusty trail clothes, run-down boots, and a hat with a mashed-in crown, I can see where they might have thought I was low-hanging fruit ripe for the picking.

The gambler's first mistake was trying a bottom deal. It was slick, and when that card popped up, he looked at me. There were no words spoken. He knew I'd caught him, and then he decided to shoot me before I could name him a card cheat. It was close. For a skilled man, there is no faster draw than a sleeve gun.

His last mistake was in thinking I hadn't already drawn my pistol. Hidden under the table, it pointed right at him. When he raised his hand like pointing at the ceiling, I knew what was coming. The hand dropped, pointing right at me. When his derringer came into sight, I shot him. Fair? Depends on your viewpoint.

He wasn't good at his chosen vocation. Normally, the town marshal would run men like that out of town with a stern warning accompanied with a few bruises and a dimple in his hat.

I didn't want to shoot him. Given a little time and us being close together, I'd have tried for a shoulder wound. But he was quick with that derringer and gave me no time at all. The gambler was left with a belly wound. If he was lucky, he might be dead by now. A wound like that was a sure ticket to hell, and it takes days to make the passage. I've heard laudanum does no good against the pain.

That little fracas left me with a wound high on my shoulder. Tom Speers was the town marshal and impressed upon me the need to leave the city until things cooled down. Otherwise, he might be inclined to arrest me. The shooting was unavoidable. There were witnesses. But I saw his point and thanked him for his foresight. The card sharp had friends...and I didn't want to put the marshal in a bind.

———

A rough trail lay behind me when I stumbled on the buildings of the Pinder ranch. That gambler must have stored his bullets in an outhouse. By the time my horse stumbled into the ranch yard, I had a high fever and could hardly see straight. My shoulder hurt something fierce.

Dave Pinder introduced himself as he stood by my horse and offered his hand in friendship and hospitality, with a smile on his face and his other hand on his pistol. I remember leaning over to shake his hand. I awoke looking up into the face of an angel holding a wet cloth on my forehead.

I tried twice before my voice worked. "What happened?"

Her smirk wasn't too favorable. "You fell off your horse."

"That's a first. I'll admit to being bucked off a few times, but I've never fallen off anything." I centered my gaze on her eyes or tried to. There were two of her, and both looked good to me.

My smile probably didn't work as well as intended. "Did you catch me?"

She spoke to someone I couldn't see, her sarcasm masked by the twinkle in her eyes. "I think he's getting better."

As she stood to leave, I grabbed her wrist. "What's your name, ma'am?"

Her gaze searched my face a moment before she answered. From her expression I wasn't sure she thought I was worth the effort.

"I am Consuela Pinder. You are on my father's ranch."

Black hair framed lively brown eyes, with a smattering of freckles across porcelain skin. As I watched, her eyes changed color, and her cheeks had a rosy glow. Kings and conquistadors would fight over this woman in far-off lands. I'd read of such and never believed it before. Her arm was warm to the touch and dispelled any idea of her being a dream. I didn't want to let go.

"My name's Jim Murphy. Pleased to meet you, ma'am."

She twisted her wrist in a nifty move to disengage

my hand—an experienced move to ward off unwanted attention and done with a smile.

"Most folks call me Connie."

"Yes, ma'am. I'll remember that."

The Pinder family was kind, asked no questions, and offered a place to rest up until I healed. It was a kindness I appreciated. After they mixed a bitter concoction of leaves with my coffee, and put horse liniment on my wound, I was free of the fever and on my feet in a couple of days. I'd seen yarrow and feverfew growing along the trail, maybe they used those in my coffee.

I do remember hearing a catamount screech when they applied that liniment, and I had a whole new appreciation for a horse that just shivers at the application.

The ranch appeared small and well kept. One of the hands told me I could ride about twenty miles east and find Joplin, Missouri. The hint wasn't subtle. He also told me Indian territory, or the Cherokee lands, were just a few miles south. Since I figured this ranch was in Kansas, he was giving me a lot of directions to be somewhere else if I got the opportunity. I thanked him for the geography lesson.

They were a clannish bunch, but that was normal. The ranch hands didn't know me, and trust is earned not given, as it should be. On my fourth day, I was up at dawn helping with the livestock. Since most cowhands weren't interested in anything they couldn't do from the back of a horse, they watched me with a wary eye, not understanding why I volunteered to milk the two Jerseys or gather eggs. There was a pigpen that was well away from the house, wisely positioned downwind. At least, most days.

Not stooping to domestic or farmer labor, as they called it, didn't stop them from pitching their legs under the table with milk to drink and fried eggs to spice up beef, beans, and potatoes. Adding dried peppers and sourdough bread guaranteed no skinny riders on the place.

The next time Connie spoke to me was during the chicken incident. Part of the barn was a henhouse consisting of crates cobbled together and filled with straw to make cubbyholes for their nests. I carried a small bucket full of eggs when I stopped in front of Big Red. Aside from a rooster, or maybe a turkey buzzard, she was the biggest chicken I'd ever seen. When I'd start to sneak my hand under her to check for eggs, she'd peck me.

One of my failings is not resisting a challenge. I set the bucket down and pulled on leather gloves. Two could play that game. My left hand was reaching for the clucker's neck when Connie came up behind me.

"What on earth are you doing?"

I didn't take my gaze from that chicken. She was damned quick and not above a sneak attack. She had an evil eye no matter which way her head turned.

"Me and Big Red are fixing to come to an understanding."

Her soft laugh didn't do my confidence any good as she put her hand on my bad shoulder. It hurt, but I didn't let on. I'd already shown her how loud I could screech.

"Is that the way you treat unruly females? Grab them by the neck?"

My gaze finally broke away from that chicken. "Well, that depends on how bad she's pecking me."

That answer scored no points as she reached under Big Red with a quick move and came out with two nice-sized eggs. The chicken stared at me while giving a few clucks to Connie.

Handing me the bucket, her voice was soft. "Thanks for your help around here. I mean that. Most men won't do this kind of work. Especially the cowhands."

"Well, I'm not that kind of man."

We stared a little past normal, and then she broke away. "I can see that."

I smiled, hoisting the bucket. "And I like to eat."

She snorted and then laughed. "You and everyone else around here."

The sun highlighted her as she stopped in the doorway. "I'm curious. Do you always wear a gun while doing chores, Mr. Murphy?"

"It's just a tool, ma'am. You never know when you might need one." I looked back at Big Red. "How do you feel about fried chicken?"

The way she laughed, she must have thought I was joking.

I spent a lot of time resting, and Connie spent a lot of time checking on me. I can't say it was distasteful. A couple of times we saddled up to ride around and get the lay of the land. There was nothing to see but rolling hills covered in grass, with a few trees lining the creeks and watersheds. Most folks thought Kansas was flat, but the eastern part was not. It was low hills and plenty of water, perfect for cattle and horses. Gardens did well. It was good country.

Loafing in my favorite rocker, I was surprised when Dave Pinder came to talk to me. I closed the worn catalog I was looking at, my finger holding the place for future reading. The section showed women's finery, and I'll admit to dreaming a bit. He wasn't known for wasting words, so I turned to listen. The chair next to me groaned as it took his weight.

"Jim, I'll be gone a few days moving a herd over to the railhead. They've built loading pens over by Mindenmines and have plenty of stock cars."

"Mindenmines? That's about twenty miles north of here?"

"More like thirty. Pretty close to the Missouri line. We'll ride the KATY cars on up to the stockyards in Kansas City. That railroad sure cuts down on time. Most of the hands are going with me. I've seen you out riding with Connie. I guess you're feeling better?"

"Yes, sir. I'm in pretty good shape and ready to go. I owe you a lot of work and appreciate your kindness. I can set a horse and do know one end of a cow critter from the other."

"No doubt you do." The man looked me over with a critical eye. "I'm thinking you're the Murphy who works for that big cattlemen's association out of Kansas City. You won't remember, but I saw you at the stockyards last year. Still checking brands and looking for rustlers?"

I smiled and nodded. "You have me pegged, but I'm not working now. When the marshal invited me to leave KC, I decided to see some country. Maybe find something to do that I don't get shot at so much."

His look was sharp. "Invited to leave?"

"I caught a man cheating at poker. He called the hand. I had sixes to beat, and he didn't fill."

He pondered me for a moment. "I don't like talking in circles. Save the fancy talk for the ladies."

Fair enough. "A gambler tried a bottom deal. When I caught him, he tried to shoot me. He had one of those sleeve guns on a spring and made a good try. I shot him...didn't have much choice." I goaded him a little. "He'd have made a good farmer. He had the hands for it."

Pinder gave a short laugh and studied me a moment. "Look, I don't blame you for leaving. And your work was a thankless job. I know some of the men you've called on—always mad about something. The people you worked for aren't much better. Most of them aren't above a little iron work to add numbers to their herd."

He paused for a moment and then finally got around to it. "I've got a favor to ask, Jim. I'm taking all the hands that can ride with me. I'll need them to load the cars and at the stockyards in KC. I'm hoping that selling them in the fall will get us a better price. But mixed herds are always a skittish bunch. I'll lose some if I don't take every rider. It'll take a few days."

He gazed toward the house. "I hate to leave the women, but it can't be avoided. Connie rides better than most of my hands and wants to go, but I persuaded her to stay with her mother. And you've seen old Roundy. He can't get around much."

Pinder raked a glance over me. "Roundy won't say it, but I know he appreciates the help around here. So do I." He smiled at that. "Hell, I shouldn't worry, it's settled country around here. But I do worry. Comes with the job, I guess. Will you stick around until I get back? I'd take it as a favor."

I thought about it a moment. Watching Connie wasn't hard work—mighty good scenery. And he was right to worry. This country wasn't settled like most people thought, and it wasn't the Indians you had to worry about.

The good folks were happy doing their jobs and living day to day. The other kind were happy nudging the edges of the law—being as good, or bad, as they wanted or thought they could get away with.

"Alright. I'll stick until you get back." I gave him a serious look. "I haven't worked through your wife's doughnuts yet. Might take a while."

————

"Riders coming."

The soft, low tone of Connie Pinder's voice was noncommittal, and I glanced at her above the old Joplin Herald newspaper in my hands. She might as well have been commenting on the weather. I appreciated her company, although I didn't understand why she wanted to spend time visiting with me. She was the boss's daughter, and that was a line I didn't want to cross. Of course, given a proper invitation I'd leap across it—damn the consequences. But for now, that line was wide and deep.

I guessed her to be about twenty-five, almost a spinster in this day and time, and I was five years older. Was she starved for companionship? More likely bored with ranch life. It was interesting to speculate.

She had a trim figure and raven-black hair gained

from her Spanish heritage. But every day I'd been at the ranch, her temper boiled over at some point. Maybe there was Irish blood thrown in somewhere. It was strange that a woman so beautiful wasn't married. But with that temper, she didn't fit the mold of docile housewife.

Still...it was none of my business. But curiosity gnaws at your mind. Besides, what else did I have to do with my time? Idle speculation can keep you sharp or lead you down a rabbit hole.

Scanning the article in the newspaper, I tried to find my place in the story written by a man named Donnelly, telling of a knife fight in one of the bordellos in Joplin. And it did seem more embellishment than fact. I'd seen a few of those, and they rarely lasted more than a few seconds.

The reporter must have needed something to fill up space in the paper since that occurrence would likely take place at least a dozen times a day in that wide-open miner's town. More if you counted shootings. But he did make it sound exciting, and I admired his writing style.

The paper snapped as I pulled it tight to straighten the wrinkles—being careful because it was over a year old and parts were missing. But it was something to pass the time.

Connie's voice broke my concentration. Again. "What the—Roundy is running toward the house with his rifle."

That brought me out of my chair, wincing in pain at the sudden movement. If that old man was running? He was short and skinny with a hat too big for his head. The newspaper he stuffed inside didn't help much. His bowed legs wouldn't let him move much faster than a snail—unless headed for the dinner table. A horse rolled on him years before, and the Pinders kept him on as kind of a pension.

Lately, we'd formed a partnership in trying to reduce the doughnut population, and his speed did surprise me on occasion.

"Mother is by herself in the house. She'll be afraid."

Connie was moving out the door when I grabbed her. If the riders were unfriendly, running out into the open was the worst thing to do, and I doubted her mother was scared of anything.

"Hang on a minute. We don't know what's wrong. Let's just ease up a bit and see what this is about. Besides, Roundy is with your mother now."

I glanced behind us, uneasy with the situation. In a back corner of the bunkhouse four men played poker for matchsticks. It was a quiet game, and the men were studiously ignoring us—too much so. They'd ridden in a week ago. It appeared they were looking to avoid work and get a free meal. They'd arrived right at the end of the Pinder's roundup, and there was plenty of work to do if you looked for it. These men seemed more interested in cleaning their fancy gun rigs and avoiding sweat.

Except for the Kiowa. I knew he wasn't lazy. He just needed the right motivation to move. Gold usually had the proper result. I'd used the man for tracking a few times looking for rustlers. The first time we'd met was a few miles south of Kansas City. I was sitting on my horse looking at a confluence of tracks all criss-crossing at the same spot. He'd pointed to himself and said. "Me Kiowa—good tracker. You pay gold."

Seemed logical to me. And he did a good job.

When he arrived with the other men, we didn't acknowledge each other. I figured Kiowa knew about KC, and that I wasn't working. So, no source of gold.

Pinder was too kind-hearted toward drifting cowpunchers. My own presence was evidence of that, although I pitched in where I could. The men playing poker may never have chased a cow, but they could have helped with feeding the chickens and pigs or pumping water to the milk stock. Their clothes were too good for all that and the tied-down holsters would have made it awkward. Between jobs? Maybe. It was 1878, and there were plenty of jobs in Kansas for their type.

There was no hesitation in the riders. One pulled up in front of the house and the other four cantered their horses over to the corral attached to the barn. They all had guns out, and it didn't take much to know what they were after.

Roundy came out of the main house with his rifle, and a bullet fired by the man guarding the porch gouged the wood planks at his feet leaving a big splinter sticking in the old man's boot.

"Hold up there, old timer."

The guard didn't shoot him and that told me a lot. I was glad Roundy got smart and laid his rifle down on the porch. At least he hadn't started blasting away at the riders. Maria Pinder was inside the house, and any shooting might hit her. They used milled lumber to build the house and not logs. A forty-four-caliber bullet would go through one-inch pine easily, especially with the new powder they were using.

I watched all that play out while grabbing Connie

by her dress collar and dragging her back toward the door.

"They're after Satan!" She struggled against me as the men roped her prized stallion and put a halter on him. It was easy to do since the horse was a pet. He probably thought he was getting his daily apple.

Connie stomped on my foot and then turned and hit me on my sore shoulder, tearing herself free of my grip. Trying to get her back was like grabbing a wet cat and just as painful.

"Dammit, Jim. Let go of me."

When she whirled to jump off the bunkhouse porch, she stopped with her hand at her throat.

Four men faced us, and they hadn't put away their pistols.

A scruffy looking man with a full beard and a low-crowned dirty hat gigged his horse forward. He had a grin that didn't reach his feral-looking eyes.

"Well, now. We heard there was a thoroughbred racing stud on this place. Didn't know there was a matching filly to go with him. Lady, you're coming with us."

Connie rose to her full height, which wasn't much. "I will not."

The man grinned at her. "That wasn't a request. You'll do as I say, or we'll leave everyone dead and have you anyway."

I stepped out from the shade of the porch so they could see me better.

"Reckon not."

The thief cut a glance at me and laughed. "You're outgunned four to one, mister. Now, you take that pistol out and drop it. We're gonna ride out of here with the stallion and take this woman with us whether you're alive or not. There ain't a damned thing you can do about it."

His men were getting antsy, cutting glances at one another. It seemed obvious this wasn't part of their plan. I stepped more to the side getting Connie out of the line of fire. The move put a porch post in front of me. Not much of an edge, but it was all I had.

The only one pushing this was Scruffy. The others looked unsure—their guns pointed in our general direction, but not centered.

A marshal of a cow town in central Kansas once told me how he dealt with a mob. Make it personal. Pick out the leader, and make them put up or shut up. Most aren't so brave without the men behind them. Cut him out of the herd.

"You need to make up your mind about something. You've started something that won't end well. If you keep going, I will take you down, and maybe a couple more with me."

I glanced at the other men. "You men look smart enough. Think about it. This does not have to end in a shooting. I'm hoping you'll reconsider."

Cold eyes watched me a moment. "You'd draw against all of us? Mister, that's suicide."

I shrugged. He did have a point. "I've been shot at before. But to be honest, it's not my first choice for how this plays out. You might be stealing this horse on a lark, just for fun. Or maybe you need the money that bad, I don't know. But make no mistake about it. You try to take this girl, and there will be a killing."

A chair leg scraped on the floor inside the bunkhouse, and the hair on the back of my neck stood up. I couldn't look and wanted to in the worst way. Were they coming to help? Or still sitting and watching.

Scruffy must have been a mind reader. He looked through the window at the card players and settled the question. "You ain't got any help coming."

All I felt was relief. If those ne'er-do-wells came out, it would be a complication.

"I don't expect any help from them. This is just you and me."

Sighing, I tried to relax. Or at least look like I was. "Look, we're in no hurry here. You've got the advantage. Take a minute and think about it. The last thing in the world we need is a shooting. Your best choice is to take the horse and get out of here."

Connie looked at me, and her burning gaze was hard to ignore. If she had a gun, she'd be shooting—and to hell with the consequences. I admired her spirit.

I tried to get through to the men one last time. "You might make it to someplace and sell the horse. You can get good money for him. Then you can take that money and disappear. I figure that's your plan. On the other hand, if you touch this girl, you'll have to go through me. Then, on the off chance you're still alive after that dust-up and do take her, her father and ranch hands will hunt you down and gut all of you. You have to know that."

"You are trading me a horse for the girl?" The thief gave an uneasy laugh. "Hell, I already have the horse. If we're caught, they'll hang us for horse stealing anyway. Might as well have the whole package and a few comforts along the way. What's that saying? In for a penny...?"

"Alright, have it your way. I've already picked a button on your shirt. I figure at this distance, I can't miss."

This was dragging out way too long, but the man looked unsure. I tried again. "Don't be stupid. You still must shoot across your horse, and he's skittish already. That pistol of yours weighs about four pounds, and you've been holding it a while. Think you can get a straight shot at me? First try?"

I shook my head. "Your first shot will miss. By the time you thumb that hammer back again, you'll be dead."

My glance covered them all. "I'm on steady ground. Even if y'all put lead in me, I'll kill some of you. I'm settled in that. You boys want to chance it?"

The man snorted. "It's worth the risk. That's a fine-looking woman, and I think you're bluffing."

The men behind him backed their horses and turned to go. One of them commented, "C'mon, Jonas. This ain't right, and you know it. We didn't sign up for this."

Jonas sighed, shrugged, and then gathered the reins on his horse. His advantage was backing away and leaving. He stopped for a moment, staring at me. "Who are you?"

I smiled, still watchful. "Nobody you'd know. The only reason I'm here is because the owner told me if I'd hold down one of those chairs on the porch, he'd feed me once a day—my horse too. I tried, but I can't get my horse to leave."

"Funny. You're just a drifter looking for a handout?

I'm not buying that. You're too damned calm about all this, like you're not worried at all."

Guess he couldn't see the trickle of sweat running down my side. I'm not suicidal.

He shook his head. "Everyone's got a name. You got sand, mister. I'll give you that. Since my idiot partner already gave you my name, I'll finish it. I'm Jonas Macrae. Likely you've heard of me. I'd like to know who you are."

I knew the name. He was on most lawmen's wanted list of being rumored, but not proven, to be a rustler and thief. A bad man in the oldest sense. An old wildness was building in me as I watched his gun. If it moved toward me or Connie, I was going to try.

"Jim Murphy."

He stared at me again and then dropped the reins around the saddle horn and rubbed his face, canting his hat back.

"I can't believe I'm doing this. Never heard of you at all. You look like a fighter."

"There's no reason you should know me. I'm a man who likes to sit on the porch and read a good book, maybe talk to a pretty girl occasionally."

It was my turn to smile. "You've got something to hang your hat on when this story is told."

He gave me a curious look as he settled his hat and gathered the reins again. "What's that?"

"You can tell people *nobody* ever backed you up."

"You're trying to be funny again. I don't get it." Giving us a puzzled glance, he shook his head. Still pointing guns at us, the riders moved away. Once past the house and out of pistol range they turned and rode from the ranch with a whoop and a couple of pistol shots in the air, leading the stallion.

I shook my head. Those men must have been three days drunk when they decided on this little excursion. Connie interrupted my sigh of relief when she turned and shoved me.

"You could have stopped them. They were afraid of you."

She wiped tears from her eyes with the back of her hand as I caught my balance. When she tried to shove me again, I caught her arms.

"Will you stop? And, no, ma'am. Those men were not afraid of me. Not one bit."

"But..."

I had to let her go, or someone needed to play a tune. I could go either way, but we had more serious matters to attend to.

"Look. I was trying to avoid a lot of people dying. I gave them choices. They weighed the cost and made the right decision. Those men weren't out to kill anybody, just steal a horse and make some money. I'm glad it went the way it did. No one needed to get shot today."

"You could have told them to leave the horse. They would have done it."

"They weren't leaving empty-handed." Shrugging, I turned away. "Like Macrae said, it was a trade. Everyone gets something in a trade."

Her face was ruddy in anger, jaw clenched tight enough to turn her cheeks white. "I lost my horse. What did you get?"

My gaze took her in, head to toe. "You, although I'm beginning to doubt my sanity."

"We could have fought it out."

"We? You hiding a pistol somewhere I can't see? One man had the drop on Roundy, the others were pointing pistols at us already—and those deadbeats inside are worse than useless, so by now, we'd be dead or shot-up bad. And provided you survived that little dust-up, you and your mother would be on your way to a hard life. After those men finished with you, they'd kill you or sell you to a whorehouse. It's happened before. Is that what you want?"

I shrugged. "And if they didn't kill me, your father would put the boots to me for not protecting you. Can you get that through your head?"

For once, she was speechless as I walked toward the main house. Maria Pinder came out of the door as I stooped and picked up the discarded rifle and handed it to Roundy.

"You doing okay, Roundy?"

"Well..."

My hand went to his shoulder. "You handled that just right. Nobody got hurt."

He looked embarrassed. Maybe he felt shamed in front of the women. "I should have done something."

"No. You shouldn't have. There's a time for fighting, and this wasn't it. We had no advantage. Think about what would have happened to the women if we'd started shooting. Five of them and two of us? We might have lost, Roundy. Probably would have. And if the gunfire didn't kill the women, their fate would have been far worse. You know that."

I didn't point out that he could have dropped his man from inside the house when they rode up, and then we would have had them in a crossfire. That would have changed things considerably and given us a fighting chance. As it was, we had no chance at all.

"Besides," I squeezed his shoulder. "When we meet those boys again, it'll be on our terms, not theirs."

Footfalls and the jingle of fancy spurs announced the bunkhouse layabouts. "Roundy, you keep your rifle on those deadbeats coming up from the bunkhouse. I don't like coincidences."

I turned to Connie's mother. She was a vision of what Connie would look like in twenty years. "Mrs. Pinder? Are you doing alright?"

From the way her dress hung down on one side I guessed she had a pistol stuck in her pocket. Had those men busted in her door, they'd have got a big surprise.

"I'm considerably better now that those men are gone. Thank you for dealing with this, Mr. Murphy. And I agree with your assessment. Except for that one man, the rest of those thieves did not seem disposed to shoot unless we forced them."

She paused, looking in the direction the riders went. "Although, I suspect they'll hang for it anyway. I just wish Dave was here."

I shrugged, rubbing my sore shoulder. "It's not your husband's fault. Those cattle wouldn't deliver themselves. You know that. He'll be back soon enough. Nobody died, and all we lost was a horse. That's the best ending to this we could have."

Her gaze hardened as she looked at something behind him. "Those men weren't any help."

The card players were sauntering toward us. Their leader was a man called Chico—at least, that's the name others called him. He was about as Mexican as an Irish track layer. I hadn't taken the time to learn names for the other two. Mostly, I ignored them all week.

Kiowa was the fourth man, and he was standing in front of the bunkhouse with a rifle across the saddle of his horse. It must have already been saddled. Was he thinking ahead or getting ready to leave before this happened? His gun pointed more toward the three card players, but I wouldn't want to stake my life on the difference.

Taking a chance, I nodded to him and pointed to the trail the horse thieves took. Kiowa hesitated a moment and then leaped on his horse and rode around the barn. Knowing he usually liked his money upfront, it was a tossup whether he would trail the thieves or call it a day and leave. I turned my attention back to the other men.

"You boys volunteering to go after those horse thieves?"

Chico smiled and spread his arms wide. "Perhaps? For a price, we might be willing to find these men."

I didn't like the idea, but it wasn't my call. Before I could speak, Missus Pinder stepped forward. "You had your chance to help and did not. Saddle up and leave. My husband has a soft spot for drifters and bums. I do not."

"Now, you listen here..."

I took a step toward him. Most western men were respectful of women. We seemed to be running into a lot of the other breed lately.

"You be real careful with what comes out of your mouth next, Chico. This family put you up for a week and fed you. You've done nothing in return but lay about playing poker and sleeping. You could have helped stop those horse thieves and chose to sit and watch. Now, you'll ride."

Roundy broke in with a rough voice. "Jim, those men knew about that horse and went straight to him. How'd they know? And they must have known our crew was gone on roundup, or they wouldn't have waltzed in here like they did."

The double-click of a cocking pistol behind me was a surprise, along with the sound of two rifles loading shells. I grinned at Chico.

"Reckon y'all better leave. Right now would be a good time to start. We've been trying to avoid trouble this morning, but you could be the exception. And, boys. You just take what you came with...nothing extra."

A few minutes later, we stood on the veranda of the house watching the men ride away with a flurry of curses and dirt clods. Roundy took off his hat and scratched his balding pate.

"Now, I don't suppose them riding off in the same direction as those thieves was an accident?"

I glanced at him. "Maybe. Maybe not. Joplin's a couple days ride east—just a whole lot of nothing west of here until you hit Wichita. And the horse thieves? I don't think they'll go far. I'm thinking they need money and have a fondness for what it will buy them."

The old man gave him a sidelong glance. "Nine of them now, if they're together."

I watched Connie and her mother move back inside. "Might be eight. The jury is still out on the Kiowa."

"Now." I hesitated a moment. "I'm wondering where they'd go to sell a racehorse?"

Roundy didn't hesitate. "Racetrack over at Galena, little bit southwest of Joplin. They have a race about once a week. Most times on a Sunday."

"Let's think about that a moment. Few people around the track would have the money to buy a horse like that. Most times, the owners aren't there. I'm thinking the serious money is in Joplin, or maybe Carthage. That horse won't sell cheap."

Soft steps marched up next to me, and I turned to see Connie, dressed for the trail. A red ribbon kept her hair swept up behind her, and a flat-crowned hat covered most of it. Her father mentioned she could ride, and she wore a working hat that had seen some sweat and dust. The times we'd ridden together, she didn't wear a hat.

"Going for a ride?"

Her gaze was all black snapping eyes, and her mouth made a grim line across her face. "Those bastards stole my horse. I'm going after them, even if you won't."

Maria came out behind her daughter. "I can't stop her. She's bound and determined."

"You can't go, Connie." I held up my hand to stop her comment. "I promised your father I'd look after y'all until he gets back. That includes your mother. If you leave, I go with you. Do you want to leave your mother here alone?"

"Roundy can stay with her."

The old man scuffed the wooden floor with his boot. "I ain't much help, miss. Proved that already."

"We can't sit around and do nothing." Her voice

weakened as she glanced at her mother and then settled her gaze on me. I knew what she was thinking. She thought me a coward for not stopping the horse thieves.

I glanced at her mother. "How long until Mr. Pinder and the hands are back?"

"It will be a few days. I know you can't wait that long." Maria paused a moment. "Might I offer a suggestion?"

I grinned at her. "Somebody better. We're talking in circles, and your daughter is about to shoot me."

She laughed and nodded. "There's a new settlement called Hard Times between here and Joplin. Well, part of it's new. The people in the old town might wish the new businesses would go away. They're mostly gamblers and bawdy house owners."

"Mother!"

"Oh, come on, Connie. I wasn't born under a rock, and neither were you. You can't keep something from existing by not thinking or talking about it. Anyway, I have a friend who lives outside of the old part of town, Irma Baker. She lost her husband and recently her son. I'd like to visit. Roundy can stay and look after the place while we're gone and let Dave know what's going on when he shows up. After I'm delivered to my friend, you two can try to find the horse. I don't hold much hope in that, but I know you must try. Sound good?"

I tipped my hat to her. "That's why you're the boss, ma'am. Do you have enough money to buy the horse back?"

"What?" Connie whirled on me. "I thought you were a man. Somebody steals my horse while you stand

and watch, and then you want to buy him back? Of all the foppish, limp-wristed—"

I raised my hand, and she stopped with a startled look. I was surprised at that. Surely, she didn't think I could hit her. Not in this lifetime.

"Let's say we find the horse. When you run up against these folks in a crowd, or bring a sheriff once you find them, how can you prove the horse is yours? Last I saw, there was no brand on him. Or are you going to grab your rifle and start blasting away?"

She stared long and hard at me for a moment. Finally, her shoulders slumped. "We didn't brand Satan because I didn't want to hurt him. He's so beautiful. I raised him from a colt. And a brand is just a big burn scar."

I nodded, shrugged. "No doubt. And he's a real pretty horse—makes a fine show strutting around. I'm sure there's not a mark on him. I'd bet he's limp from hoof to hock, scared to death of a mare, but who's gonna tell?"

Her ruddy complexion seemed to pale as she reached out toward me. "Jim, I'm sorry. I didn't think..."

"No, ma'am. You did not."

Her boots left little dust explosions as she stomped off toward the barn. She was mad, but it was sure hard to ignore her walk.

Maria sighed and then continued in a soft voice. "Like I said. Spoiled and headstrong. Dave and I are to blame for that. But she's a good person, Jim. And she likes you. Know that? She just doesn't have much experience in letting you know."

My next words came unbidden. "I'm surprised she isn't married."

"No one has ever come around that piqued her interest."

She gave me a sidelong look. "Until now. And come to think of it, why aren't *you* married? A double harness isn't all that bad."

"Never been caught..." My voice trailed off, the word *yet* obvious, but unspoken. "Looks to me like she hates the ground I walk on."

Maria's laugh was infectious. "If you think that, you don't know much about women."

Roundy smothered a laugh.

"You got something to say?" I tried to look mean, but it wasn't in me.

When he didn't answer other than to grin, I answered her. "You're right about that. At least, not a good woman like her. Although I'm not sure anyone can know her. She seems a mite flighty."

Maria patted him on the shoulder. "You haven't noticed her hanging around you, dressing nice—trying to stop acting like a tomboy? Most of us haven't seen her in a dress for a long time, except for an occasional Sunday meeting."

That made me chuckle. "Oh, I noticed. I'm not blind, and your daughter is a beautiful woman. I'm a little skittish about that...not sure how you and Mr. Pinder feel. And we've just met."

"It's been over two weeks, Jim. My husband knew how the wind was blowing before he left, and you're still here. That should tell you something. Otherwise, he'd have run you off."

My mind turned to the four poker players. They

weren't run off, but that was a different circumstance. Mostly.

Maria turned all business. "Roundy, please bring the buckboard around. If we hurry, we can make it before dark."

Connie had the horses saddled when I stepped into the barn. The Texas saddles were heavy but didn't stand a chance against her anger. I could hear her mumbling as I walked in. More dust explosions danced on sunlight streaming through the hayloft door, giving the interior a golden glow set off by dark shadows. A slight movement brought my gaze to a striped cat licking its paw—unconcerned with the people in its barn.

I paused while Connie pounded her fist on the saddle of her horse. She'd been attentive to me all week, and though I acted unaffected—it was a lie. Anytime I thought of her showing interest in me, her sanity was in doubt.

"Is that some new way to settle down a horse?"

She flinched and then glanced at me. A couple of small mud trails coursed down her cheeks and blended with her freckles. Her voice was soft and rough from the dust she'd stirred up.

"Please, Jim. I regret speaking the way I did. I don't know what's got into me lately. Seems half the time I don't know who I am—other times I don't want to know."

I leaned against the same saddle she was beating, close enough that her faint scent overrode the horse smells wafting through the barn. Gently, I wiped those mud trails away. She gave me a startled glance, it was our first touch, and then she relaxed and leaned into my palm for a moment.

When we confronted the horse thieves, I'd known an unnatural fear. Not for myself. It was the fear that someone I cared for might be hurt. That was a fear steeped in helplessness. I'd read that if you love someone, then you're a hostage to worry. Now, I understood.

My words were not eloquent, though I wished them to be. "It's alright, ma'am. No harm done."

Her gaze was on the strap and buckle of a saddlebag she fiddled with. "Stop calling me ma'am. It makes me feel old."

"Can't."

That got her attention. "And why not?"

I glanced at her as I led my horse outside. "You haven't kissed me yet."

The expected explosion didn't come. When I looked back, she was smiling. That scared me, too. It was a poor way to start a day...being afraid. Twice.

Roundy was outside with the buckboard. When he got Missus Pinder situated, he handed Connie a Winchester for her saddle boot. His eyebrows raised when he looked at my shotgun hanging by a loop.

"Don't you want a rifle? We got an old Henry inside that's a spare."

"No, thanks. Heard a story of a stage driver held up by a would-be bandit. Well, the driver went to shoot the miscreant, and his old Henry rifle jammed. Way he tells it, the only reason he survived is the outlaw had a Henry, and it jammed, too."

My glance caught the women rolling their eyes. "It may not be true, but this old coach gun will work for me. I'm not looking for a long-range war. And it's good for birds and such."

I gave him a serious look. "Speaking of birds, you watch out for that red hen. She'd got an evil look to her."

There was no road leading to Hard Times, at least from the ranch, which made Missus Pinder's choice of taking a wagon for the trip dubious, at best. She seemed spry enough to ride a horse, and I chafed at the slow going.

Connie seemed content to ride alongside her mother, and I let them guide the way. They seemed to know where they were going. I tried to ride far enough back to stay out of the dust, hoping for a crosswind.

Finding her horse would not be easy. Proving it was hers would be impossible. That left few alternatives. If we found the horse, we'd have to take it back by force or steal it. My sense of it was Macrae wouldn't give up without a fight. He seemed a prideful man and dressed himself well enough that turning to thievery seemed unlikely if lack of money was an issue. If he had some other plan working, I couldn't figure it out.

We stopped for a nooning in the shade of a sycamore. A muddy stream made a lazy passage nearby, but I didn't like the looks of it. I soon had water boiling for coffee, and the ladies broke out bread and cheese from a basket.

Maria was taking her cup to the stream when I stopped her. "Ma'am, let's boil this water and add some coffee to it. We'll drink that until something better comes along. That stream water doesn't look good to me."

She cast a baleful eye at the stream and returned to the wagon.

"So, what is your plan, Mr. Murphy?" Connie's voice was mocking. "How shall we get my horse back?"

"When I have a plan, you'll be the first to know."

"I thought you were a detective for some cattlemen's association. This sounds like an easy job for a man of your experience."

My gaze met hers over the top of my tin cup. Two weeks wasn't a long time to get to know someone. I couldn't separate sarcasm from accusation, nor tell if she was digging her spurs in my side just to get a rise out of me.

"You may have an over-embellished view of my last job. If someone complained of losing cattle, or their neighbor selling more cattle than they could possibly raise in a season, the association would send me out to look around. If I found evidence, I'd report it to the local authorities. That's all."

She shared a glance with her mother. "And those you investigated never objected? You never had to use that pistol you wear all the time—the one you're tapping with your fingers right now? Gonna shoot me? You're going to have to replace the grips soon. That walnut is worn smooth from use."

When I didn't rise to the bait, she continued. "My father didn't want me to go into anything without full knowledge, so he pointed out a few things. Like those flashy gun-rigs those deadbeats wore opposed to yours that's functional and worn smooth. You came to us wounded. I assume that wasn't because you dropped your gun, and it went off."

"Connie."

"No, Mother. He's not going to get away with this...this act of a mild-mannered drifter just out to see the world. He's more than that. Even wounded, his gun was never far from his hand. I'm not blind, and I want to know who, or what, he is."

I stepped over to my horse and rummaged around in one of the saddlebags. Pulling out a small book, I leafed through the pages a moment and then showed it to her.

"Have you read this? It's one of Frank Starr's pocket novels. I got it for a nickel before I left Kansas City. This one is numbered one hundred thirty-nine and is all about Kit Carson, called The Fighting Trapper. I figure there's at least a hundred thirty-eight books before this one, and they're all about gun slicks and fast draw artists, mountain men and town-tamers —real, famous men. Each one a hero. Why, it's unbelievable what some of those characters do, or the predicaments they shoot themselves out of. It makes great reading and fine adventure."

My gaze leveled on her. "I'm just a man. No more, no less."

"You...you..." She stomped her boot in the dust and stalked over to her horse. The poor critter was startled when she kneed its belly, driving out its wind so she could tighten the cinch. I vowed to watch that knee in the future.

Mrs. Pinder had put things away during our show and climbed up in the wagon seat. Her shoulders shook, and I couldn't tell if she was laughing or crying. She slapped the reins over the horse's backs and pulled away, Connie rode next to her.

I didn't like being confused, and I was unsure of

my part in this play. Maybe that was by design. By the time I'd kicked dirt over the little fire I'd built, dumped the coffee and cleaned the pot in the murky stream they were out of sight.

It didn't take long to catch up. They'd stopped just around the small hill. We were using a well-traveled trail by now, and the Kiowa sat his horse in the middle of it unperturbed by the business ends of two rifles pointed at him. He'd fooled me. I thought he was long gone.

He nodded when he saw me. "Murphy. You come."

Stopping beside Connie, I gently pushed the barrel of her rifle down. Gently, because her finger was on the trigger, and if I knew anything about her, it was taking up slack with some pressure.

"He's on our side, ladies." As I rode past, Connie started to follow. "Stay with your mother. If it's something you need to see, I'll come get you."

I didn't get a promise from her, but I should have. As we moved toward a cottonwood grove, I could see a tendril of smoke drifting on the breeze from a small campfire. And hear the hoof falls and the creaking of the wagon behind me. Seemed that taking orders wasn't in the women's lineage.

It was an odd feeling. One I didn't like. We'd been taking a noon meal less than a half mile from death. I assumed the Indian tracker had been riding around the hills. And I didn't know it. I couldn't figure out where my head and senses were until I looked around at Connie. Her expressionless gaze looked back at me.

Kiowa didn't need to say anything. Four bodies lay around the dying fire wrapped in blankets, whiskey bottles scattered close to hand. There was a blackened pot sitting to one side of the coals. If they were all drunk, who was drinking coffee?

The first impression to someone coming onto their camp might have been that they were sleeping off a night of revelry, but they'd left the ranch a couple of hours ahead of us. In a sense, they were asleep. Three had ear-to-ear smiles somewhat below their chins. A bullet hole in the chest took care of the fourth man. His blanket lay to the side. A good guess was he heard something—or wasn't as sound asleep as the murderer thought.

I looked at Kiowa, and he shrugged, moving away. My voice stopped him for a moment. "I wouldn't drink any of that coffee and be sure to throw the pot away."

The stream we'd just seen might make you sick enough to die, but it would not be today. If this was a celebration for a successful horse stealing, my guess was the coffee came first to their party and had something added to make the men sleepy. Someone staged the rest—for what purpose, I wasn't sure. Of course, anyone else coming up on this wouldn't know what we did about the men. Did the killer think a passerby would assume they were drunk and asleep and not disturb them?

And why not let them die of poison? Maybe time was a constraint? A sick man can pull a trigger, so someone stayed and assumed friendship to the last drop. And then, made sure.

Riding a slow circle around the camp didn't supply much information. We found their riding mounts hobbled in the grass next to that muddy creek. Judging by the tracks, the horses wouldn't drink it, either.

Conspicuous by their absence was Jonas Macrae and a certain pet stallion.

Kiowa didn't tell me anything I didn't already know. He pointed east. "One rider, one horse."

Dismounting, I walked among the bodies. When I moved the blankets, I found their pockets turned out. They'd piled saddles and tack next to their bedrolls. Their saddlebags and possibles-bags lay empty on the ground. I kicked over that coffee pot.

Turning, I spoke to Kiowa.

"These were thieves and not worth much consideration. I don't care about their guns and horses. But if there are papers showing who they were, I need to turn them over to a marshal so he can notify next of kin. Their relatives should know."

He stared at me a moment. I'd just given him a small fortune, and he knew it. His face was impassive when he shrugged. "No papers."

At my surprised look, he hastened to reply. "Pockets already pulled out. No papers. No money."

Macrae was a thief. He'd take their money or anything else of value. Extra rifles and pistols would be conspicuous. People would ask questions. The same for extra horses. If a marshal identified the bodies, that might lead back to him as people he traveled with, so he'd bury any papers or letters.

According to the ladies, the nearest place east of us was a small spring-up town called Hard Times. It was a reasonable assumption Macrae would head for there before moving on to Joplin. He had money to spend and a horse to sell. His driving hunger was unknown, but I'd bet he would feed it soon.

When I started to dig in my pocket for a gold

piece to pay off Kiowa, he rode close and shook his head.

"No money. Job not done. I stay."

"What about—"

He nodded toward the horses. A couple of men had materialized. Wearing range clothes and slouched on good horses, their braided hair fell from beneath floppy hats. Everything but the bodies would disappear into the Territory a few miles south.

The obvious question went through my mind as my gaze snapped back to Kiowa. His smile was mocking.

"No kill these men." He shrugged. "Could have. Easy."

He was right. And if they wanted us dead, we were easy targets. Those men helping Kiowa were like ghosts. I was beginning to think retirement somewhere peaceful was a good idea. If I ever had a knack for this sort of thing, I was losing it.

"Be sure to tell them to eat or drink nothing from the camp."

Kiowa walked his horse over to the two men, talked a moment and then rode east. Connie spoke up from behind me.

"Aren't you going to bury those men?"

"Nope."

"You can't just—"

"You mean I should give a Christian burial to men who would gladly murder or rape you and your mother? The same men you wanted me to shoot in the first place to save a horse? Those men?"

Her head was shaking as a slow color rose to her cheeks. "We are Christian by what we do, how we act."

"Guess I'm not that good a Christian. With all due respect." I tipped my hat. "Ma'am."

She turned her horse and rode away.

"That's what I thought." It was a weak rejoinder and acknowledged by the look on her mother's face as she turned the wagon around. If Maria was keeping score in whatever game we were in, I wasn't doing well.

Our small cavalcade returned to its journey. One thing was certain. Connie's infatuation with me was at an end. I wasn't proving up to her expectations. If that was a good thing, why didn't I feel better?

I turned in the saddle and looked at the campsite. Why the charade? Who would care? A shadow crossed the ground in front of me. Buzzards. They were patient and would wait for all of us to clear out. Maybe they cared.

———

We pulled into the yard of a ramshackle house an hour before sundown. A slat-thin woman in a shapeless and threadbare dress watched us, shading her eyes with her hand. The three women met in a group hug on the porch.

Connie spoke to me before they went inside. Her expression was neutral—a surprise, considering her temperament.

"We'll stay here tonight. Please let me know if you find my horse."

A dismissal. Abrupt, not waiting for an answer, but expected. Turning my horse, I rode toward Hard Times. All I'd heard of the place was not good. A pop-

up town trying to keep pace with the runaway and
bawdy reputation of Joplin, Missouri. If Joplin were
the whale, Hard Times would be the underbelly—
every decision based on whiskey consumption and
greed.

A perfect place for a thief.

The town had two streets. The new part was
perpendicular to the old, and pointed straight east
toward Joplin. I met Kiowa at one end of a short
street, watching the blades of a windmill turning slow
in the evening breeze. He seemed entranced. Bullet
holes ventilated the blades, and the light from the
dying sun shone through. I'd seen the same kind of
light show at carnivals using colored paper.

He finally acknowledged my presence by nodding
toward the other end of the street. "Horse in corral at
livery."

That was a fine bit of tracking, even for a man used
to doing it. "How did you find that out?"

"Horse has start of split hoof. Needs iron shoes."
He glanced at me. "Thought all Whites put shoe on
horses."

Shaking my head, I tried to explain. "The horse
was Connie's pet."

His look was uncertain.

"Like a favorite dog."

"So, she keeps horse to eat? They have many cattle.
Is strange."

Sometimes, I'm slow on the uptake. Maybe
Momma dropped me on my head when I was a youngster. I did know Kiowa humor wasn't all that funny.

"Do me a favor? You know the house where
Connie and her mother stopped?" When he nodded, I

continued. "Go and keep watch. If Macrae would kill his partners, three women won't slow him down much. Don't be afraid to use your rifle to prevent that."

His accent disappeared. "You're telling me I can kill a white man? I'd be chased clear into Mexico."

"I'm telling you to protect those women. Gather some friends if need be."

He gave me a long look and then rode away.

A man was lighting a lantern hanging from the livery door when I rode up. As I dismounted, another man with a badge on his vest walked over from across the street.

I nodded to them and decided to throw the skunk through the church door. "I'm looking for the horse thief who put the black stallion in your corral."

The hostler glanced at the sheriff. "That kind of talk could get a man shot around here. You got proof of that?"

"Nope. But the man who claims to own him can take it up with me anytime. My name is Jim Murphy. I'll be around a while."

The sheriff stuck out his hand. "I'm Tom Fallon. You from up Kansas City way?"

I nodded as he shook my hand.

"Heard of you." He nodded toward the hostler. "This here's Fred Curry, my occasional deputy."

Recounting the story took a few minutes. By the time I finished telling of the dead men, both were muttering curses under their breath.

Fallon looked at the hostler. "I don't have any jurisdiction outside of town and not much here. So it's either a Deputy US Marshal or the Army's problem, neither of which will be any help right now. We did have a marshal staying here, but he left a month ago."

I described the fake Mexican Chico and his compadres. "Seen these men around?"

They both shook their heads. "They could be in the new part of town, and we'd never know it. Can you prove anything against them, other than being lazy and stupid?"

"Nope. But smart money puts them with Macrae."

"Well, I don't know what you're wanting to do." Fallon pulled his hand down a long face. "We get killings every day in the new part of town. The best I can do is try and keep that from spilling over to the old town. All the original people live on this side. The new part is all saloons and whorehouses. If they want to kill themselves off, I'm all for it. Maybe your friends will take care of that."

He chuckled. "There's one exception to promote gentility. We have a dance at the Pavilion on Saturday nights. Everyone gets all fancied up for that. A truce is in effect. No guns allowed, or range clothes. That's tomorrow night, if you're interested."

A vision of Connie in a gown crossed my mind for a moment. And then I put it away. "You know Dave Pinder and the D-P Connected west of here?"

"Heard of him."

"That horse belongs to him and his daughter. Shoe and feed him, someone will be by to pick him up. I'll pay you for it."

Fred shook his head. "I feel like you're in the right. But far as I can see you both have staked a claim on that horse. There's no brand of ownership and no papers."

"Ownership is not going to be a problem. And Fred? Put a little something extra on those shoes in case he gets away again. I ain't that good a tracker."

A local eatery served a decent supper, and I tried to do it justice. Black coffee and apple pie made me loosen my belt a notch or two...alright, three, but it's a short belt.

The woman filling my coffee cup was a friendly sort until I tried describing Macrae.

"Have you seen anyone looking like that? Calls himself Macrae?"

She gave me a hard look. "Mister, about every other man that walks through that door looks like that. We serve food here. We don't post letters, leave notes for the lovelorn, or sell information. You'll have to find him on your own."

Her voice softened. "On the other hand, you're spreading around that this man is a horse thief. We're honest folks on this side of town and work for a living, so there's no reason for him to be here. They serve food in those fancy houses uptown. Not good food, but most are too drunk to notice. If your man left a horse on this side of town, it's because Fred has a Winchester and hates horse thieves. He won't be back until he wants the horse."

Well, that was straight enough. I thanked her for the education and rode through town at a slow walk looking in windows and scanning the people bustling around the boardwalks. Being in no shape for a fight, it wasn't a real serious attempt.

I'd found the horse, so my job was over. Well, Kiowa found it. Letting a killer get away with murder rankled a bit. But, more than likely, I could get over it if I tried. I didn't know the murdered men nor have any desire for revenge.

Riding toward Irma Baker's house was chancy in the dark, me being unfamiliar with the road. I found a likely spot under a tree, staked the horse on a patch of grass and spread my oilcloth on the ground. Using my saddle for a pillow, I wrapped up in a blanket against the night chill and figured to sleep that apple pie away. The memory of those murdered men prompted me to sleep with gun in hand.

The Baker home didn't look much better in the morning light. There were shingles missing on the roof, and one corner of the porch sagged. It looked as if a groundhog had burrowed around the rocks holding it up. I knew from experience that groundhogs and porches are like beavers and trees. They just can't help themselves.

Kiowa sat on a trimmed deadfall someone made into a bench, eating from a tin plate. He didn't look up when I straddled the bench. I watched him eat for a moment. My pie was long gone, leaving my stomach grumbling.

"You know? A good man like you could sure earn his keep around here. Limber as you are, I bet you could get on that roof and replace those shingles real easy. Kind of pay for your meal. What do you think?"

He stared at me a moment, gravy dripping from his chin. "I'm Indian. Don't know why white men build a house that falls down. Tepee never fall down."

I rolled my eyes. "Kiowa, you speak better English than me. I've heard you."

He just smiled and wiped a sleeve across his mouth.

The swish of a skirt gave me warning. Connie stood next to me holding a plate piled high with eggs and potatoes. Her other hand held a steaming coffee cup. I was starting to like this girl again.

"Can I sit with you?"

"Sure." I glanced toward Kiowa. "Don't forget that roof."

He was up and away like a shot. I doubted if he was looking for a ladder.

"What an odd man." She watched him walk away a moment before her gaze settled on me. "I need to apologize to you for yesterday. Seems that's all I do lately. A lot has happened that I'm not used to seeing, and I didn't react well. I'll admit to being spoiled and am truly sorry."

My spoon made music on that metal plate a bit. Finally, I met her gaze. "It's alright. We haven't known each other long enough to gauge reactions or make judgments."

"Did you find Satan?"

"Well, Kiowa did. Being a detective, I'll take credit for it. He's just a paid employee. Your horse is in a corral at Curry's stable in town."

"Why didn't you bring him with you?"

Her dress was different today, and I hadn't seen her pack a bag. The fresh smell of lilac came gentle on the morning breeze. Her smile was curious, and she didn't seem mad.

"Well, there is a small question of ownership. And

the hostler needs to shoe him this morning. Seems he has the start of a split hoof. Horse could have used some iron on his feet."

Color crept above her collar, and I saw just a hint of temper. Instead, she scared me again. Her smile turned soft and her voice softer.

"How can I help?"

Well, that threw me. "Well, uh...how are you fixed for dresses?"

"What? I had to borrow this one."

"Well, we've found your horse, so...if you want to celebrate, there's a dance tonight in town. Some place called the Pavilion. Seems there's one every Saturday night. I'd like to——"

"You're taking me to a dance?" She stood up straight. "I don't have anything to wear. How can I..."

We were having trouble finishing sentences. "When I rode into town, I noticed a dress shop. With the number of...well, *women* in town, I'm betting they can fix you up quick. And I'd need to buy a suit."

I was talking to her back as she streaked toward the door. Women.

Her voice echoed around the clearing. "Kiowa, saddle my horse!"

The Indian peeked around the corner of the house. I don't know what shocked me worse. That he was holding a hammer and bucket of nails, or that he'd become domesticated. I think we were both embarrassed. I didn't know he could do that, either.

A half hour later saw the women riding toward town, chattering like magpies, two in the wagon and Connie astride her pony. I hung back to talk to Kiowa.

Once again, I tried to hand him a gold piece, and he waved it away. "What's going on with you?"

Gone was the stilted English. "You're a good man, Murphy. These are good people." He eased himself in the saddle a moment. "There is a girl I want to marry. The horses from those dead men will go a long way toward the bride price."

He looked embarrassed again. "The Territory is no place to raise a family. Too much killing. I'd like to work for you at the D-P and bring my wife there. I could build a home. Maybe you could help me with that?"

If pigs were flying, the surprise wouldn't have been greater. "What makes you think I'll be at the D-P?"

A smile split his face. "I said you're a good man, but sometimes not too smart. You're caught. You just don't know it yet."

There were a lot of arguments against that notion, but none that held water. "Alright, let's say that's true. Any ranch can use a man that's good with horses."

An idea was jumping around in my muddled mind. "There's going to be shooting trouble over that black stallion. We know where he is, but there is still the matter of ownership, and a horse thief getting away with stealing it. Something like that blows up and innocents get killed or wounded."

He nodded, watching me with an intent expression.

"I figure if I take the horse, Macrae will try and stop me. I'm sure he has someone watching. Same for me if I hear he's picking up the horse. Now, if that horse disappeared, there'd be nothing to fight over."

His gaze locked on mine as I continued. "Now,

that's a mighty fine horse. I'm thinking it would make your bride price complete, don't you think? Maybe along with a couple of gold pieces?"

Kiowa shook his head. "I'm not stealing from a future boss."

Pulling out a tally book from my saddlebag I started writing on a blank page. "Don't think of it as stealing—well, not right away. That comes later. For now, you're trading horses for your bride."

I let him think on that a moment before I continued. "You're a pretty good horse thief, right?"

He was back to head shaking.

"So, if a month or two down the road, your future father-in-law's prized black stallion goes missing and winds up in the Pinder corral, that would even things out in the end. Wouldn't it?"

"Sort of a horse trade?"

We were matching grins as I handed him a couple of gold pieces from my dwindling supply, along with the paper. "This gives you permission to take the horse back to the Pinder ranch and its rightful owner. It may take a while to deliver it. On the way, the horse gets extra training, and you get a wife. I'd be pleased if it got branded D-P along the way."

"You are a devious man, Mr. Murphy."

He reached across his saddle, and I shook his hand. "We're friends. Call me Jim. I figure around dark tonight will be a good time. Most everyone will be at that dance."

He nodded as I continued. "Don't forget that roof. And that porch could use a rock or two under the corner."

He glanced over his shoulder at the house.

I grinned at him. "You got all day."

Served him right for poking fun at me.

———

There was a different feel to the town this time. They'd decorated the outside of the dance hall with a red, white, and blue paper banner that challenged fickle weather—gambling the heat wouldn't stir up rain and wind right out of the Bible or the wrath of the Baptists.

Tying my horse at Fred's hitch rail, I settled next to him in a wobbly, cane-backed chair. "What's a man do for a bath and haircut around here?"

He pointed toward a building a few doors down. There was no sign, but a line of men stretched to the end of the street. "I ain't seen them throw out any bath water yet, and they been at it a couple of hours. It's share and share alike. And if you're thinking of the horse trough under the windmill, the last one tried that got lead poisoning."

Neither choice appealed to me. "Miss Connie is expecting me to look presentable tonight. Any ideas?"

His glance seemed neutral, but I didn't know him that well. "I got hot water on the stove in back. You can borrow my razor if you want."

The water was hot and after seeing the notches in his blade, I sharpened my own razor on a strop of leather hanging off a stall. I must have done a good job because he borrowed it.

Fred pointed out back toward a jumble of boulders. The spring-fed pool was shoulder deep. Walking in, I swore it had ice floating on it, but that's the way limestone springs are. There was a good flow to the water, and it carried the suds away down a little creek. Some clean clothes from my saddlebag and a curry brush for my hair, and I felt like a new man.

I found him trying to work over his face. "Fred, you going to the dance?"

"You think I'd miss seeing every young galoot around here making fools of themselves? It's better than a carnival and right up there with a revival."

Something was wrong with that, but I wasn't going to dwell on it. Fun is where you find it. "Just so you know, along about sundown the ownership of that black horse is going to be cleared up."

Fred gave me a level stare. I knew he was wanting to be rid of that horse. "So, if I was to leave him tied up...say, outside the fence next to the trees, it might help things?"

Kiowa took pride in moving around unseen and was a master horse thief. It might be an insult if we made stealing the horse too easy.

"That'd be perfect. Now, I need to find me a store-bought suit."

The man settled back into his chair. "Mercantile on the other end of the street. Got all the clothes you need."

It was my kind of store. A man stood outside the door eating a can of peaches with his knife. A good part of it was on his beard. Just inside sat saddles and bridles from workaday to fancy. You could buy a rifle off the rack, pistols and knives from the counter, and shovels and picks to burrow into the ground—and top it off with enough molasses and jawbreakers to tame any sweet tooth. And clothes.

Inside another room were full racks of all manner of clothing.

A portly woman holding a cloth tape measure held court in that room. She had on a bright-flowered bonnet stuck full of pins. I'd heard of pincushions, but it looked as if she made her own rules.

A young man walked out wearing skin-tight pants and polished knee boots. A blue coat with brass buttons completed his Prussian military look. Popular in Mexico, he might get a dubious reception here. If he bent over, he'd split his pants...but he did look dandy. Maybe he could stand in a corner.

The woman raised her eyebrows at me as I walked up to her. I pointed at the man. "No."

Her laugh jiggled her portly frame from head to toe. "Most assuredly not." Her hand gripped mine in greeting. "I'm Sadie."

"Well, Sadie, I have a lady meeting me at the dance tonight. Can you fit me into something not too embarrassing?"

"Of course. Nothing but the finest for the beau of Miss Pinder. I saw her next door with her mother and Missus Baker. I'm sure glad you folks showed up. Missus Baker was about to waste away mourning the loss of her son. Now, she's showing a little life. That's a good thing."

Poked, prodded, and measured for a few minutes, I felt like one of those pet dogs kept for show only. It was an experience. I'm more of a cattle dog myself.

"Now, come back this afternoon, and I'll have a suit ready for you." She handed me a low-crowned, black top hat and walking stick with a silver knob on the end. I figured that knob was fake.

"This will finish your look. You'll be the most elegant man there. And be sure to wear these boots. The soles are soft and perfect for dancing or fighting."

"Fighting?"

"Wouldn't be a dance without it. Besides, you'll have the prettiest chicken there. Lots of weasels in the crowd."

The pushing and pulling had me turned around like a pole-axed steer. "What do I owe for all this?"

"About fifty dollars should do it."

My look must have betrayed me, along with trying to hand the loot back to her.

"Now, look here. We have a dance every week or so. This is an investment. You need all this. Make a good wedding suit, too."

Consulting my money belt and finding the proper fare, I paid the money. There was a chair close, and I sat a moment. I knew the tactic. Want to brand a calf? Run him around in circles to get him confused and tired, then drop him.

She stood by me a moment. "Mr. Murphy, I've seen a good many men."

When I grinned at her, she colored up some.

"You've the look of a gunman—and we've too many of those around here. That concerns me."

Curiosity got the better of me. "How does a gunman look, Sadie?"

Her gaze was steady on mine. "It's the eyes. Most look for the manner and the gun, but no. It's the eyes. But Connie tells me you're a gentle man and hate violence. I'm glad of that. This is a suit for such a man."

Well, now. There's a difference between a gentle

man and gentleman. Deep water and pounding seas seemed to be in my future. I guessed it was the price of living in interesting times.

"I'm well aware of Miss Pinder's opinion of me."

Her hand stopped me as I rose to leave. She searched my eyes a moment. "She's wrong, isn't she?"

When I didn't answer, she laughed. "Oh, this is going to be fun."

Stepping out of the mercantile, the three ladies accosted me.

Connie stepped close. "Jim, I've heard there's a good café just down the street. Let's have a late lunch. There's no food served tonight at the dance, just punch."

"Yes, ma'am."

"Ma'am?"

"Not sure what to call you right now."

She didn't take offense. Instead, she smiled and took me by the arm, leading the way. "You'd better figure something out because we need to talk."

After the meal, we lingered over coffee and pie until almost time to go get dressed, her to the dress shop and me to the mercantile. Both were a short walk to the Pavilion. A few people walked by staring in the window as we looked out. Some of the men stopped before moving on. She was that kind of pretty.

I waited patiently, enjoying her studied indifference while fidgeting on her chair. She finally got around to what she wanted to say.

"Jim, you know there will be a lot more men at the dance than women. Some will have ridden miles to attend."

"This may surprise you, but I have been to a country dance before."

Her gaze was skeptical. "Okay, but there may be some who will challenge you to let me dance with them."

"Really? Most western men are polite about such things. Are you telling me this in case some past or present suitors might show up?"

Holding my hand up to interrupt her denial, I pretended to think it over. "Well, I do believe in dancing with whoever brought you. I've heard that rule bandied about, and it seems like a good one. But then, it always comes down to the lady, doesn't it? Do whatever you think is right."

"I like to dance."

"Me, too. I'm betting there will be ladies I can dance with while you're enjoying yourself with your suitors."

"I don't have any..." Her gaze sharpened. "You'd better not dance with any of those girls from up the street."

My smile seemed to fuel her temper. "How can you tell where the girls are from? Or, for that matter—maybe some of your suitors have danced with those girls. Are they tainted, having touched them?"

Sadie was right. Taken with the correct frame of mind, this was fun.

"I swear, you are the most—"

"It's hard to tell what you're after or what you want my response to be." We were standing by then, and I held her by both arms. "Connie. I don't know what's cooking in that head of yours. It's a dance. Have fun."

"So, you don't care if I dance with other men?"

When you're surrounded, sometimes you must take a chance to break free. I was tiring of the repartee and was never good at innuendo and veiled messages.

"That depends on a lot of things. Let's cut to the chase. We've known each other less than three weeks. You're a beautiful woman, and I've fallen under your spell. Can't help it. Not trying too hard to get away. But I'm looking for a partner in life, not someone I have to worry about what they're doing every minute. How you act and what you do is up to you and what you want to be. This is not a complicated process."

She stared at me, mouth slightly open. When she started to say something, I kissed her. After a quiet moment of staring at each other I linked my arm with hers. I'd discovered a way to make her stop talking. Ever mindful of her knee, I guided her toward the door.

"May I escort you to the dress shop, ma'am?"

Gaining the boardwalk, quick footsteps followed through the doorway. Seemed the two *duennas* were still with us, ever watchful of their ward. If the giggling was any sign, we were quite entertaining.

———

"Sadie, are you sure about this suit?"

Her changing room consisted of a sheet suspended over a wire stretched across a corner of the room. The mirror was polished metal and made me appear fat or thin, depending on my distance. When I walked into the room she smiled and handed me the hat.

"Very handsome. I'm sure all the ladies will agree."

"Not sure about the hat."

Her eyebrows rose. "Trust me."

"I don't know you that well."

Her shrug sent ripples from head to toe. "So? You trust a preacher to speak the Word? A cardsharp to steal your money? A sheriff to keep the peace?"

"Well..."

"Wear the hat."

"These cuffs have ruffles."

With a long-drawn-out sigh of the afflicted, she handed me the silver-headed walking stick and reached up to set the hat on an angle. "Get out of here."

Tom Fallon met me on the walk. "What's with the hat?"

"It's all the rage. You should get one."

The town marshal continued walking as I paused and then stepped inside the dance hall. When you walk into a saloon, you're hit with cigar smoke, clinking bottles on glass, whiskey breath, and merriment from the crowd.

This was a different world. A four-piece string band spread soothing music through the room. Nobody was dancing, but considering the voluminous dresses worn by some of the women, I wasn't sure they could. Tables lined the walls, leaving the floor clear in the center. The floor looked like polished ice.

There was hope for a livelier affair in the two men setting off to the side. With impossibly large *sombreros* and drooping mustaches, they sat holding a trumpet and guitar awaiting their chance.

"You'll need to check your gun."

It took me a moment to recognize the man by

the door. His hair was slicked down and his mustache waxed into points. I'd stepped into a costume show.

"Fred?"

"No guns allowed at the dance."

Holding my coat out so he could see, I tried to keep the laugh from my voice. "Didn't bring one. So, what's with the towel over your arm?"

"Sadie said it was all the style for a doorman." His gaze traveled to my head. "What's with the hat?"

I began to view Sadie as a puppeteer like I'd seen in a circus—pulling strings and having a ball with the outcome.

A pretty girl in a simple dress interrupted us. "Fred, where's Tom? He's supposed to meet me here."

My gaze finally found Connie's mother and Irma Baker holding court. The men talking to them parted as I walked up to the table.

"Where's Connie?"

"She came ahead of us. We thought she was with you."

Pivoting on my heel, I made for the door. She wasn't in the room, or we'd have seen her. Maybe she went back to the dress shop?

"Fred, have you seen—"

A shot sounded from down the street. We both paused a moment. It wasn't an unusual occurrence.

"Nope, she hasn't come in here."

We stepped outside and saw a man running toward us. He stood winded a moment before he spoke to me.

"You that detective?"

"I'm not a detective."

The man nodded. "The marshal's been shot. He

sent me to get you. Said you'd have on a stupid-looking hat."

We found Fallon sitting with his back against a wall, holding a wound on his side. Pulling his shirt out, I was starting to check the wound when he grabbed my arm.

"That Macrae fella, the one you had trouble with? Saw a man looked like him and some other men dragging a woman into that boarding house. There were four men, and it was taking all of them to do it."

He pointed across the street, and I reached for a gun I didn't have.

"Here. Take mine. I sure as hell don't need it."

There was a man behind the counter when I walked in, but I didn't need directions. The scream from upstairs was all I needed. Even through the scream, I recognized her voice, and it was angry.

Connie. Still fighting.

My boot opened the door, and the splintered frame hit a man in the face who stood close.

A frozen moment met my gaze as the man tumbled to the floor and lay still. Connie stood in a corner, on the far side of a bed, holding a water pitcher she'd been swinging at someone. Her dress was torn, one sleeve missing, while rage colored her face. That was the moment I knew. This was the woman to walk beside me. All the times I'd seen her mad? It was nothing like this.

One man stood out of her reach while looking at me. Chico and Macrae stood in the center of the floor, eyes shadowed by the lamp burning above them, back lit by a window with flowered curtains. Curtains? Strange what imprints on your mind in times of stress.

The Schofield I'd borrowed from the sheriff pointed squarely at Macrae. He appeared pale, but with the light, it was hard to tell.

Both men had pistols in their hands but seemed undecided about what to do with them. They'd been surprised when I busted in the door. They were caught between pointing their pistols at me or Connie and knowing if they moved at all, I'd be shooting. Indecision was not a good mantle to wear in times like this. A floorboard creaked as someone shifted their weight.

"Why are you doing this, Macrae? I warned you. Did you think I was fooling?"

"No, I didn't." He shrugged. "Look at her, Murphy. She's the most beautiful thing I've ever seen. Like something just out of reach. You ever do that? See something pretty, and all you can think of is making it your own? She got under my skin, and I'll have her before the day is done."

His smile didn't reach his eyes. "We'll have to break her first."

"We went through this yesterday morning. It's not going to happen. If you leave now, you get a head start. Maybe you can get to the Territory before we catch you. Even if you get away, they will stake you out on an anthill in a week. It's not worth it."

He glanced at Connie, and I almost made my try. But bullets have no conscience and will take anyone in their path. If they started shooting, everyone could get hurt. I needed an edge.

"For a nobody, you sure threaten a lot. And once again, you're outgunned, and all you do is talk. You trying to trade her for something again? I already got the horse, and now I have her."

"You should pay attention, Macrae. This is how a bad day ends. You started with nothing, you'll end with nothing."

"You talk a good fight for someone always trying to avoid trouble. I think you're yellow through and through."

The man at my feet stirred and got a boot for his trouble. With a feral grin, Connie took the opportunity and broke the pitcher over the head of the man in front of her. He stared at her in amazement before crumpling to the floor, his pistol landing on the bed. Those porcelain pitchers used in boarding houses were not dainty in structure.

I shouldn't have glanced at her because when I looked back, Chico was pointing his pistol at Connie.

Macrae laughed. "Why, I think we've won this round. Now, you drop that pistol, or my friend will shoot her. Just to wound her, mind you. This day isn't over. We can stand a little blood to get a piece of that."

Chico was a tin horn. Thinking he had all the advantage, he didn't hammer back his pistol. Guess he thought the threat would be enough.

Macrae grinned as his pistol started coming up.

My first shot took Chico in the head. He crumpled like a puppet with its strings cut. The second took Macrae in the belly. He backed up, dropping his gun. I flinched, half expecting it to go off. Through the powder smoke I was aware of Connie grabbing the pistol from the bed, but I kept my gaze on Macrae.

I shook my head. "Four men killed in their sleep. Good or bad, I don't know. We'll never find out. Two of you dead here, and we'll be hanging two more.

Being around you is like picking at a scab and watching the pus run out."

His eyes were feverish. "I had to have her. Don't you see that? Saw her one day out riding. When we came for the horse, you messed it up. I did it to get her. The men could have the horse." He backed up against the wall, holding his belly and coughing blood. "It would have been...it would..."

A bullet slammed into him, and he slumped to the floor. I was so surprised, I looked down at my gun thinking I'd fired.

Turning, I accepted an armful of weeping Connie and held her while she trembled. It was a chancy deal since we both held pistols and didn't seem disposed to give them up. The acrid smoke in the room watered our eyes. Well, mine anyway.

I caressed her hair as we clung to each other. "You alright?"

She nodded. "I will be."

"If anyone asks, I shot him. Simpler that way. You don't want a reputation as a gunslinger. There'd be no end of people coming against you."

Her hug got tighter. "Whatever you say, Jim."

The two men stirred after a few moments. I stripped their gun belts and handed them to Connie. Both looked sick as they stared at the two dead men. Maybe they were thinking of a trial for kidnapping and attempted rape. Both were bloody and holding their heads.

I got them to their feet. "Now, drop your pants."

One of them spoke. "What? There's a—"

My knife came to my hand, and he almost fainted. His pants dropped when I cut his suspenders.

Connie spoke up. "You were going to rape me, maybe kill me. Now you're bashful?"

I grinned at her. It didn't take her long to recover.

We got to the stairs and the men hesitated, wondering how to navigate down the steps. She solved the problem with a firm push to both.

They tumbled into a heap at the bottom as Fred came in carrying a shotgun.

"What happened to their pants?"

"Didn't have shackles. You ever tried to run with your pants around your ankles?"

Fred snorted. "Just once. Didn't know she was married. Heard the front door slam and decided to dive out the window. I'd a broke my neck if it wasn't on the ground floor."

The marshal was leaning against a wall when we went outside, with the girl from the dance tending to him. He had a hole at the top of his hip. The wound bled a lot and painted her arms red up to the elbow, but she had it under control. Fallon was going to owe her a dress.

He'd be sore awhile, but barring infection, he'd recover. I knew all about infection, but didn't offer my nurse.

Reversing that new Schofield, I tried to hand it to him.

"Keep it. It's a fine gun, and I have more." He laughed at my expression. "This part of town has several killings a week. It's usually my mess to clean up. Another month or so, and I'll have enough hardware to start my own gun store."

The young woman clutched his arm. "You're retiring. Today."

I nodded. "Well, it does have fine balance."

With a word of thanks, I tucked it into my pants. Fred was organizing some men to march the captives to jail, and none too gently. I figured if the locals did not lynch them, the first judge they saw would.

"What about those men upstairs?" The desk clerk had a hand on my sleeve.

"You saw those men drag the girl upstairs?"

He nodded.

"You heard her screaming?"

"Yes, sir."

"Then maybe you better go clean up the mess before I lay you beside them. Bring anything valuable or papers to the marshal. Understand?"

It didn't take him long to leave. I suppose I shouldn't have vented my anger on him. Maybe.

The street filled with horses and the men of the D-P Connected sat facing the boardwalk. One glance at their lathered horses and weary eyes told me they'd ridden straight here from the ranch.

Dave Pinder and Roundy dismounted and walked to me.

"What happened?"

It took a few moments to bring him up to date. He made no sound while I explained, gaze pinned on his wife and daughter.

"I told you to take care of them."

By then, Maria and Connie had him by both arms. Maria spoke first. "It wasn't his fault. He did everything he could, and Connie was snatched on her way to the dance."

"Dad, you should have seen it. He broke into that room and knocked out one man. Then he shot the other two. I broke a pitcher over the head of the last one."

"Sounds like you got there just in time." Pinder's mouth twitched a moment. Maybe he wanted to smile and just couldn't do it yet.

Connie looked at me. "One of those men he shot had his gun pointed at my head." She shook her head. "That seemed chancy."

He looked at me. "Head shot?"

I nodded, watching Connie. "Yes, sir. It was the only shot I had. I couldn't chance anything else. I cut his strings."

"Maybe he was bluffing?"

"I wasn't."

"Good man." Pinder nodded and then wandered off with his family. Roundy stared at me. "What's with the hat?"

Taking it off, I dusted it a little and then put it back on. "I'm beginning to like it."

Glancing at the men, I dug into my money belt for a twenty-dollar gold piece. "The men look tuckered. This'll buy them a few drinks."

He reached in and took the last gold piece I had. "This will do it better."

Roundy handed them to one of the men. "Turn your horses into the stable before you go. And stay out of trouble. When that's used up, charge the rest of your night to the ranch. You've earned it."

I doubt they heard all his advice, heading toward the livery by mid-sentence.

Connie walked up to me, eyes bright with unshed tears as she wound down from the excitement. Sadie had materialized and fixed the torn sleeve.

A small parade of people drifted back toward the dance hall. The show was over, and for this town, a shooting was no more exciting than any other day.

When she came to me, I held her close. She snuffled into my vest for a moment.

"Your pistol is gouging me."

Mindful that she still had a death grip on hers, I didn't give the answer that came first to mind. I took the second. "I still hear music, and you've a beautiful dress to show off."

"How can you—oh, I couldn't. And you? You killed two men, and you want to go dancing?"

"Those men? More like taking out the garbage. I won't mourn their souls."

Shrugging, I tried to explain. "If someone shoots at you and misses, do you go off and die anyway? If a rattler strikes sticks on your boot, do you quit and never walk around the prairie again? You're made of better stuff than that. We keep on going, Connie. What just happened doesn't mean a thing. You deal with it and go on."

She hugged me tight. "I don't know you at all, do I?"

I ignored the smiling people around us. "Nope. Not yet. But I expect you will."

Her smile was sweet—something else I'd learn to watch. "I like the hat."

"It's growing on me."

"Makes you look like someone who can't decide if he's a bull or a heifer."

The hat went flying after the Pinder riders and flew farther than I expected.

We cut quite the figure at the dance. That beautiful green dress she wore flared and twirled at the bottom. The slight bustle bounced and swayed. My soft shoes were kind to my feet. The dance got lively and loud, and I got all her attention. I wasn't sure, but I think the trumpet player put a little something in the punch. The kids were gone by then, and I didn't see any harm in it. Looked like they drank most of it themselves.

Someone carted off Macrae and Chico and closed that room for cleaning. The Pinder ranch took over the rest of the boarding house to sleep it off—those who could drag themselves back from the saloons.

It was after midnight when I gave Connie a chaste kiss on the cheek and surrendered her to her parents. I think Roundy was being fitted for something because I saw him leaving with Sadie. Probably needed a suit.

The next morning, I went early to the mercantile and retrieved my clothes. I folded the suit and packed it away for the next time.

The Pinders broke my solitude at breakfast. They wanted an early start for home.

Connie sat across from me. "Dad checked around some while in Kansas City. Seems you're well known around those parts."

I couldn't tell where this was going, so I kept my mouth shut.

"Sorry." Dave shrugged as he interrupted. "I'm needing a new foreman. The last one broke his leg in a cattle chute. Thought I'd check on you."

"He'll probably be able to work in a few weeks."

"Maybe, but I think he's fallen for his nurse. I doubt we'll see him again." His gaze caught mine.

"That job's open if you want it. Even Roundy approves."

"Well, Roundy did grab my last dollar." Everyone watched me a moment. "But that's a job I believe should be earned. I'm sure you have more experienced men on your payroll."

Roundy tried to hide under his hat as I continued. "Although I am broke and needful of a job."

Pinder laughed. "I have over twenty men, give or take, and they do have a lot of experience. Not much they can't do concerning cow critters. Know where they are now?"

I knew the answer but shook my head.

"You bought them for two gold pieces and now they're hung over. I need judgment, not experience."

He changed directions. "So, have you and my daughter come to an agreement yet?"

My chuckle was short-lived when I saw he was serious. "Well, you might say we've decided to explore the possibility."

"Don't look so scared. Once a woman makes up her mind, ain't nothing you can do but hang on for the ride. That's how it happened to me. And thank God you got rid of that hat."

He drained his coffee cup and headed for the door. "Roundy! We're headed home. If you can peel yourself off that seamstress, see how many of the hands are sober enough to ride. You can catch up later."

The human dynamo named Pinder stormed out the door, and I sat staring at Connie. Her mother patted me on the shoulder as she moved in the wake of her husband.

Connie giggled. "You should see your face."

We walked to the livery where everyone was saddling up and getting the wagon ready. Now I knew why Missus Pinder brought it, since it was piled high with supplies. That woman was always a step ahead. I'd have to remember that.

"Aren't you forgetting something?" Connie stood watching me.

It was a mild question, but storm clouds were brewing.

"Well?" She continued. "Where's my horse? That was the point to this whole exercise."

Pinder was stalking toward me.

"Well, I may have made a trade."

"You what?"

We watched her grab a saddled horse and head out. Pinder's voice was full of wonder. "She sure has a temper. You coming with us?"

"I'll be along, sir. Got a couple of things to do."

He clapped me on the shoulder. "Good idea. Let her cool down."

Fred Curry and Tom Fallon were standing at the marshal's office. I had the new Schofield in my holster and handed him my Colt. "Add this to your collection for when you retire. You wouldn't happen to have another one of these? I like the way it breaks over and loads easy."

After going inside for a few moments, he brought me its mate. Someone shortened the barrel to take away the front sight. It would work well in my belly holster. I don't know why they make them with sights. I never knew anyone who aimed a pistol.

"This is little enough pay for what you did."

I shook both their hands. "Hell, if you hadn't got

shot, I wouldn't have known where to look for Connie. I appreciate it."

Tom rubbed his side a moment. "Don't mention it."

It took a half hour to ride to Irma Baker's place. Kiowa had fixed the roof and porch. That surprised me some, but not as much as Connie sitting on the worn bench, friendly as could be.

Irma stepped off the porch. "Mr. Murphy? I want to thank you for getting my house fixed. That was kind of you."

"I'd like to take credit, but it was Kiowa did it, ma'am. I just nudged him a mite."

"I've noticed that about you, Mr. Murphy. You just stand around all innocent-like, and people do what you ask. You're a good man."

I glanced at a beaming Connie. "Mrs. Baker? Just to keep up my reputation for being meddlesome, I'm betting Fred Curry could use a pie. He seems a handy sort of man."

She snorted as she went back into the house. "I'll keep that in mind. I felt how handy he was last night."

Connie walked to her horse. "So, you ready to go home?"

Home? Was I? We seemed headed toward a certain union. That I wasn't fighting it was surprising. But the day had been full of surprises.

I nodded to her. "I'm glad you waited."

She dusted off her skirt and mounted. "Well, I was almost sure you wanted to come home with me. You're not exactly talkative about those things. But if you did, I didn't want you to get lost."

We were a few miles down the trail when she started.

"I have a couple of questions."

My hat came off in my hands as I examined it. "Do you like this hat? You didn't think much of my last one."

She shook her head, smiling at me. "I'm not going to be sidetracked. We need to have a conversation."

With my fingers tapping the butt of my new pistol, I finally gave in. Her eyebrow raised as she watched my hand.

"Alright. Fire away."

She smirked at me for a moment. "Is your real name Jim Murphy?"

"Actually James Allen, but yes, it is."

"You were born out west somewhere?"

"A little two-by-twice farm west of Springfield, Missouri. I haven't been that way in a long time."

"If things work out, we'll have to visit."

She reached into her saddlebag and pulled out a sheet of paper. "Since you fell off your horse in our barn lot, I seem to have misjudged you at every turn. Or you deceived me. Maybe some of both. That about right?"

Being quiet seemed a good thing to do.

"So, what about my horse? I've looked all around and don't see him."

"Kiowa has him. I figure he'll show up in a month or so with the horse and a new wife."

I went on to explain my thinking on taking the horse away. It didn't work out like expected since Macrae really didn't want the horse, but plans rarely do.

Her voice was mild. "Seems chancy. You trust this man?"

I gave her my best smile. "It is a gamble. He may decide to stay in the Territory with his wife and horse. I think he'll be back, though."

She did not look convinced. "And why would he do that?"

"I still owe him a twenty-dollar gold piece. Maybe I can earn that much before he shows up."

She wore a divided skirt so she could hook a leg around her saddle horn—made it kind of a side-saddle as we rode. Seemed she had a list of questions—even a pencil.

"Now. You told me that dime novel you've been reading was numbered a hundred thirty-nine?"

I gave her a wary look.

Snapping the paper straight, she smoothed it out on her leg. "Well, it just so happens I got a list from the mercantile of all those books. Did you know we can order them? Now, I figure you're on that list somewhere between number one and a hundred thirty-eight. And we are for damned-sure going to find out which story is about you before we get home."

She gave me a sweet smile. "And don't worry, we have all day."

A Look at Osage Dawn:

By Darrel Sparkman

Amid the dust and blood of conflict, there lies a deeper truth.

On the northern Arkansas border of 1804, an Osage warrior and a young trapper pit wits and strength in a deadly battle only one will survive.

When Matt Crane left home to travel the far western lands, he didn't intend to be gone long. Four years later, he returns to find his family dead, his hometown destroyed, and his sweetheart taken captive by Quick Killer, a vicious renegade Osage warrior with a score to settle.

Kidnapping the woman Matt loves is only the beginning of Quick Killer's plan as he seeks revenge upon Matt, the architect of his shame. What he fails to realize, though, is that he faces an adversary far more tenacious than he ever thought possible—one that will push his very limits.

In a showdown that will test their resolve and redefine their fates, Matt Crane and Quick Killer must confront their deepest fears and come to terms with the legacy of their actions—and the ties that bind them.

A fast-paced frontier adventure, Osage Dawn *blends love and raw adventure in the wild frontier, where history was made amid gut-wrenching fights for survival.*

AVAILABLE NOW

About the Author

Darrel Sparkman is an award-winning author of novels, novellas, and short stories. He's been included in three western anthologies, worked as a feature writer for *Saddlebag Dispatches* and blogged a short time for *Sundown Press*.

His ideas come from a diverse past of serving as a combat search and rescue helicopter crewman in Vietnam and volunteer Emergency Medical Technician First Responder. He has worked as a professional photographer, computer repair tech, and was once part-owner of a commercial greenhouse operation and flower shop.

Darrel is enjoying semi-retirement and finally has that job that wakes him up every day—with a smile on his face.